Schooled in Murder

Also available by Victoria Gilbert

The Hunter and Clewe Mysteries

A Killer Clue
A Cryptic Clue

The Book Lover's B&B Mysteries

A Fatal Booking
Reserved for Murder
Booked for Death

The Blue Ridge Library Mysteries

Murder Checks Out
Death in the Margins
Renewed for Murder
A Deadly Edition
Bound for Murder
Past Due for Murder
Shelved Under Murder
A Murder for the Books

The Mirror of Immortality Series

Scepter of Fire
Crown of Ice

Schooled in Murder

A CAMPUS SLEUTH MYSTERY

Victoria Gilbert

CROOKED
LANE

NEW YORK

Copyright © 2025 by Vicki L. Weavil

Published in the United States by Crooked Lane Books, an imprint of The Quick Brown Fox & Company LLC

Crooked Lane Books and its logo are trademarks of The Quick Brown Fox & Company LLC

Library of Congress Catalog-in-Publication data available upon request

ISBN (hardcover): 978-1-63910-923-4
ISBN (ebook): 978-1-63910-924-1

Cover design by Tim Barnes

Printed in the United States

www.crookedlanebooks.com

Crooked Lane Books
34 West 27th St., 10th Floor
New York, NY 10001

First Edition: January 2025

10 9 8 7 6 5 4 3 2 1

Dedicated to the most important
people in the book
community—the readers

Chapter One

I'd stumbled over several things in my thirty-two years of life, including my words and a few relationships, but never a dead body.

I wasn't prepared for that. Not that any previous experience would've prevented me from freezing into an ice sculpture at the sight of a man sprawled over the floor, his arms and legs bent at impossible angles. He was lying face down, the blood pooling around his head adding color to the library's faded gray carpeting.

Thrusting my hand into the tote slung over my shoulder, I fumbled for my cell phone. I wasn't entirely certain that I'd get a good signal from the top floor of the library, an area that housed bound periodicals. Most students and faculty had abandoned print journals for the easier access offered by online resources, so the top floor was often deserted.

I kept my gaze focused on the body as my trembling fingers clutched my phone inside the tote. There hadn't been any movement or sound since I'd discovered the prone figure while searching for an article in a journal whose earlier volumes had yet to be digitized. I'd considered checking for breathing or a pulse, but hesitated, not wanting to disturb the scene. A swift glance up at the mezzanine had revealed a scrap of paper, caught between the filagree work of the iron railing. It fluttered like a white pennant in the air blasting from an overhead vent.

The scrap matched the fan of paper lying just beyond the reach of the man's splayed fingers.

A stack of stapled pages. Probably a student assignment, I thought, noticing that the top sheet looked like a title page. Copious amounts of red ink notes and a large *C minus* scrawled across the paper were almost obliterated by splatters of crimson blood.

A light flared at the far end of the room. The stacks had dim illumination until someone walked into an aisle and tripped the motion sensors. Which meant only one thing.

Someone else was on the floor.

I released my grip on my phone and yanked my hand free from my bag. Clutching the tote to my chest, I backed away from the body, step by step. There were no additional blooms of light from the depths of the metal shelving, but I wasn't taking any chances. I didn't know who was out there, hidden by chunky volumes of bound magazines and journals.

A resounding bang made me spin around and make a dash for the elevator. *Don't panic, whoever it was probably left. There's an emergency exit at that end of the floor*, I reminded myself as I jabbed the elevator button repeatedly.

Leaping into the car as soon as the doors opened, I slammed the button for the second floor and slumped against one of the slick metal walls. The second floor housed the reference department, which, unlike the stack floors, was never deserted. There'd be at least one staff member at the desk and several students using the study carrells and computer workstations.

As soon as the elevator reached the second floor I dashed across the geometric-patterned carpet to reach the reference desk, earning a few stares from students.

The young woman sitting behind the desk looked up from a stack of photocopied materials. With intricately patterned tattoo sleeves covering both arms and indigo dye tipping her tousled chestnut hair, most people would assume she was a student assistant. But Brianna Rowley was an accomplished reference librarian. After she'd helped me with several research requests we'd become friends, or at least the kind of campus acquaintances who could share a lunch in the snack bar or cafeteria.

"Bri, thank goodness it's you. Call campus police." I pressed my palms against the surface of the desk and leaned forward, my chest heaving.

"What?" When Bri leapt off her tall stool, the height of the reference desk hid everything from her shoulders down. "Are you injured, Jenn? Did someone attack you?"

I shook my head. "It's not me. Someone fell from the mezzanine on the top floor. I think they might be"—I sucked in a deep breath—"dead."

At that word, all the students sitting near the reference desk swiveled their task chairs around.

Bri's kohl-rimmed eyes widened. "Alright. I'll call. You take a seat."

As I sank onto the tall chair placed in front of the desk, I could feel several pairs of eyes boring a hole through me. I bent forward, hugging my tote bag like a shield. I knew the students would be texting this news out to entire campus and beyond, but it couldn't be helped.

A campus police officer arrived within minutes. I recognized her as Rebecca Greene, who routinely patrolled the library as well as the writing center. She asked me to follow her to one of the glass-enclosed study rooms that lined the walls of the reference floor.

"It's the top floor," I said as I stood and trailed her. "You need to check the top floor. Someone's fallen. I think from the mezzanine," I added, my voice echoing in my ears. "There's a lot of blood."

"Don't worry, Ms. Dalton," she said, closing the door behind us. "We immediately alerted the town police and emergency services. They should be here any minute. We also sent two of our officers directly to the sixth floor." She slipped a small notebook and pen from the pocket of her starched navy-blue shirt. "Okay, let me make sure I have my facts straight. You're Jennifer Dalton, director of the campus writing center, correct?"

"That's right," I said, slumping in one of the room's hard plastic chairs.

Officer Greene sat down across the small study table from me. "Why were you on that floor of the library?"

"I wanted to check a journal article before I headed home. I'm a writer, you see. Under a pseudonym," I added, as if this woman would recognize me anyway. Although I was ten books into a fairly successful mystery series, my pen name typically didn't ring any bells with the general public. "I was on my afternoon break and wanted to do a little research. I'd just gotten off the elevator when I noticed something fluttering from the railing of the mezzanine. It looked like a scrap of paper. Then I glanced down, and well, there he was." I cleared my throat. "I don't think it's a student, based on the suit jacket and dress pants, but he was lying face down and I didn't want to disturb the scene . . ."

"Thank you for that," Officer Greene said, scribbling in her notebook.

Placing my tote bag on the table, I crossed my arms and hugged my shoulders. I was shivering despite the hot air blasting from the overhead vents. Clarion turned on the boilers in their older buildings following an antiquated schedule that didn't take into consideration the fact that in recent years the weather in early October in northern Virginia could flip from summer to winter within a day. "I suppose I should've checked for a pulse or something, but honestly, I didn't hear the victim make any noise or movements and, well, I didn't think I could do anything to help anyway."

"Yes, best to leave that to the EMTs." Officer Greene's dark eyes narrowed as she looked up at me. "Where were you before you went to the top floor?"

"The basement of this building. I took the elevator directly from the writing center."

"And you saw no one on the elevator, getting off or on?"

"No." I rubbed my lower arms with my hands. "Sorry. Feeling a little chilled."

Officer Greene's gaze softened. "That's understandable. You've had quite a shock. If you want, we can ask the EMTs to check you out as well." She tapped the pen against the table top. "Did you see anyone on the sixth floor? I know you said you'd just stepped off the elevator—"

"I did," I said, cutting her off. "Well, I didn't actually see anyone. But I noticed the lights brighten in one of the farthest rows of shelves, and since it's motion sensor lighting, I thought there must be someone back there. But then I heard a door bang and assumed they must've taken the emergency stairs." I cast Officer Greene an abashed look. "I'm afraid I ran for the elevator at that point. I didn't want to encounter whoever it was."

"Smart move." As Officer Greene intently examined my face it occurred to me that she could be wondering if I was more than a witness.

I could be a suspect.

I straightened in the chair. "I want to assure you that I can account for my movements. Jim Harlow, one of the writing center's student assistants, spoke with me right before I got on the elevator, and then I reached this floor only a few minutes after discovering the body on the top floor. Ms. Rowley at the reference desk and several students can verify that."

Officer Greene tipped her head to one side. "Are you worried about being considered a possible suspect?"

"Well, I was there," I said, thinking about scenarios from my books, a mystery series that featured a retired female detective teaming up with a younger woman to solve crimes in their small town. If I were writing this story, the person who found the body would definitely be a suspect.

Officer Greene's lips twitched in what might have been a brief smile. "We'll ask you to make an additional statement to the town police, and they may take your fingerprints, but as you said, you're probably in the clear, timing-wise if nothing else." She slid a business card across the table before snapping the notebook shut and slipping it back into her pocket. "That's all for now. Just stay in town, okay?"

"Sure thing." I shoved the card into my tote bag with an inward groan. I'd planned to go out of town over the weekend, to visit my mother in Maryland, but now I'd have to alter my plans. Not news I looked forward to sharing with my mom, who hated last-minute changes of any kind.

"Do you want an EMT to check you over?"

I pushed back my chair and stood up. "No, that isn't necessary. I'm a little shaken, but I'm not going to faint or anything."

"Very well." Rising to her feet, Officer Greene looked me up and down. "I never realized how tall you are. I bet you played basketball in high school and college. Am I right?"

I bit the inside of my cheek to prevent a less than cordial response. Officer Greene was simply trying to establish a friendly rapport, but she'd asked *the* question, the one I could never seem to avoid. "I'm afraid not. I may be six feet tall, but unfortunately my height didn't come bundled with athletic ability."

"I see." Officer Greene shuffled her feet. "I used to play. Point guard. Enjoyed it back then, but I don't have time for it now."

"It's hard to keep up with things like that when you're working," I said, slinging the strap of my tote bag over my shoulder.

"Tell me about it. I have three kids too." Officer Greene hitched up her gun belt, which had slid a few inches down over her slender hips.

"I'm impressed," I said. "I can barely work full-time and take care of a cat."

"Oh, you get used to it. Have to stick to schedules, though. Make sure everything is organized." She smiled. "Sometimes that works. Anyway, the town police will be in touch, but you can also always call me. If you remember anything else or whatever." Giving me a nod, she left the study room.

My cell phone buzzed against the side of my tote bag. I pulled it out and stared at the first message, an all-campus emergency announcement stating that all nonessential offices were on lockdown.

The second message was from Andrea Karmen, a professor and one of my friends in the English department. *Have you seen Mia Jackson? Nobody can find her and she's not answering her phone.*

I responded with a simple "no." Mia was one of the students I mentored in a volunteer capacity. She was interested in a career as an author and had come to me to learn more about breaking into the business and other practical matters not covered in her creative writing courses. I stared at my phone screen for a moment, then typed *why?*

Andrea answered immediately. *There's already gossip circulating around campus that it was her assignment. The papers found by the body. Rumor is that was her story.*

Chapter Two

Bri met me halfway as I walked toward the reference desk. "I'm off duty for now. Why don't I come with you to get a cup of coffee or something?"

"I think I'd rather just head back to the writing center," I said. "We have coffee in the break room, and I'd like to get away from any onlookers, if you know what I mean." I inclined my head, indicating the students. Of course, they still had their faces buried in their cell phones. "Or listeners, I guess I should say."

"Sounds good. Let's go." Bri strode off toward the elevator. I followed more slowly, pondering the rumored presence of Mia's story next to a dead body. It concerned me. I didn't like the idea of any connection between my talented mentee and a crime scene.

When we reached the basement, the elevator doors opened onto a windowless hallway. "I just realized I've never ventured down here before. Now what?" Bri stepped into the corridor.

I trailed her out of the elevator. "Go straight to the end of this hall and then make a right."

Bri examined the beige-painted cement block walls. "They didn't give you the fanciest digs, did they?"

"I'm just glad we have anything at all," I said, remembering how thrilled I'd felt when the writing center had been carved out of one corner of the university library's basement. Yes, the floors often felt cold, and there was a limited amount of natural light that spilled in from the narrow windows set high in the walls, but at least it was a dedicated space. Clarion hadn't had any type of writing center until four years ago, when I'd been appointed director.

We turned the corner, halting at the glass-fronted entry to the writing center. Lights blazed in the large central room, which was outfitted with both computer workstations and wired tables used for laptops. Two offices and a few small study rooms lined the perimeter, along with a conference room, staff break room, and a bathroom.

Jim Harlow, one of our student assistants, jogged over to the entry. Recognizing me, he opened the door. "What's going on?" he asked, raking a hand through his shaggy brown hair. "Got a text that we were on lockdown."

I looked up into Jim's boyishly handsome face. Jim, who was six-foot-five and possessed broad shoulders along with a sturdy build, was often mistaken for an athlete. But, like me, he'd never been that proficient at sports. It was something we'd commiserated over during one of our staff potlucks. "There's been an incident on the top floor of the library," I said. "But it's nothing that you have to worry about. It's not going to affect the rest of the building"

"Nobody's here right now anyway," Jim said, closing the door behind us and reengaging the keycard controlled lock.

"Which is good, since Ms. McHenry left early for an appointment." I glanced at my watch as I turned to Jim. "It's already four o'clock. Thanks for covering, but you can leave now. We won't be helping any students this evening, not with a lockdown in place. It may be lifted, but not before we'd close anyway." I flashed him a comforting smile. "Just make sure the doors catch when you go out."

As soon as Jim left, I led Bri into the center's small break room. When the center had been planned, we'd been promised a full kitchenette, but what we got was a little less—a sink, a small fridge, a stretch of counter, and a few cabinets. I'd added a microwave, coffee maker, and toaster oven.

"Could it have been suicide?" Bri asked, sitting in a wooden chair I'd scrounged from the campus surplus property warehouse. "The mezzanine is open to the floor below and it's pretty high up. I know I feel a little uneasy using that spiral staircase."

"Me too. It always felt a little unstable." I filled the coffee maker's water reservoir. "What do you want? We have regular coffee, various flavors, and decaf."

"Whatever's the strongest." Bri studied me as I spun the coffee pod carousel several times. "Something on your mind? Other than finding a body, I mean. You seem distracted."

"It's nothing, really. I just got a text from Andrea Karmen asking about Mia Jackson. She appears to be off the grid for some reason." I popped a pod into the coffee maker and slid a mug under the spout. "Andrea said Mia wasn't even answering her phone," I added, punching the brew button.

Bri pursed her lips. "That's an odd coincidence."

"What do you mean?" I asked, as I set the full mug down in front of her. "You like it black, right?"

"It's the only way," Bri said, with a grin. She knew I didn't drink coffee without at least a splash of cream. "But about Mia, earlier this afternoon I discovered her huddled in a corner of the reference collection. She was extremely upset."

"Did you talk to her?" I started the brew process for my own cup.

"Yeah. I've helped her with some research projects so she recognized me." Bri shook her head. "She'd just come from Doug Barth's class and was equal parts weepy and furious."

Having had a few run-ins with Douglas Barth myself, I made a face. "So what's he done this time?"

"Totally humiliated Mia in front of her entire class. Not to mention he gave her a poor grade on that story you liked so much."

"The one worth 50 percent of her grade?" Cradling my mug, I sat down at the break room's small café table. "No wonder she was devastated. Mia can't afford to get a poor final grade in any of her writing classes, not if she wants to get into that prestigious writing seminar next summer."

"Exactly what she told me. But it seems Barth doesn't care." Bri sniffed. "I've heard he's popular with most students, but Mia said he was always on her case. Apparently, he thinks she's too talented to waste her time writing romance novels."

"That doesn't surprise me—he dislikes any type of genre fiction. He's made his opinion on my books abundantly clear." I grimaced and took a sip of my coffee. "But Mia's story was so beautifully written, its subject matter shouldn't have had any effect on her grade. Not even to Mr. 'only literary fiction matters' Barth."

"Honestly, I thought Mia might try to find you and planned to warn you before she showed up. But then I got called away to help Professor Alexander with a complicated research question and, with him being head of the English department and all . . . ."

I waved this aside. "No, no, don't worry about it. Anyway, she never came to see me. Not before I left the office, and I'm pretty sure she knows my schedule."

"That's odd. She said she wanted to meet before you left for the day. Must've changed her mind." Bri shrugged. "Probably a good thing. She wasn't in any state of mind to discuss the situation rationally."

A series of raps resounded off the glass entry door. Bri and I stood in tandem and walked out of the break room, but once we were in the central space, our responses were scarcely the same. She smiled broadly and trotted toward the door.

I stayed put, my lips curling down. *A bad day made worse*, I thought, as I took my time joining Bri.

The tall man at the door was wearing an ivory fisherman's knit sweater over charcoal gray slacks. He looked like a stereotypical faculty member, although he was nothing of the kind. He motioned for me to open the door.

"We're on lockdown," I said, loud enough to carry through the glass.

"I know, but I was sent here. By the provost," the man said, his light-brown eyes focused on my face.

Just what I need, I thought. *The campus shrink.*

And not just any shrink, but Zachary Flynn, who'd humiliated me once when we'd run into each other at a local bar. He was a psychologist with a private practice in town who also had a contract to work with students referred by the counselors at Clarion's health center. From what I understood, he was only on campus two days a week but was occasionally called in to deal with emergency situations.

I guess Hilda Lange is afraid I might turn into an emergency. I frowned, picturing the imperious provost. Since being appointed over the summer, Lange had made numerous changes in reporting structures and other organizational matters. I'd had a brief confrontation with her after she suggested that my position should report to the head of the English department rather than directly to the dean of the College of Arts and Sciences. My argument—that we assisted students from all schools and departments, not just English majors— had eventually swayed her but not without some rather heated conversation.

"Very well." I unlocked the door, holding it open until Zach had sauntered into the room.

"Good day, Ms. Dalton," he said. "And hello, Bri," he added, acknowledging her with a nod.

"Hi there," Bri said, her eyes sparkling with good humor. I hadn't realized they were friends, but it made sense. I knew Bri was interested in supporting mental health services for students and had volunteered for fundraisers sponsored by the campus clinic.

"You were sent here?" I tapped my rubber-soled loafer against the thin carpet. "Well, sorry to waste your time. I really don't need psychological counseling, so feel free to tell the provost that you met with me and everything is fine."

"I think I'd better be the one to determine that," Zach said. "Besides, that isn't my main purpose."

Zach and I were exactly the same height, which allowed me to look him directly in the eyes. "Oh, then what is it?"

"Hilda thought you should be told in person. Who the victim was, that is. She didn't want you to hear it through the campus grapevine."

"They've ID'd the body?" Bri rose on tiptoe to look up into Zach's face.

"Yes. It wasn't difficult. His wallet was still on him, and I suppose he was pretty well known around campus anyway," Zach said. "It was Professor Douglas Barth."

Chapter Three

I t wasn't just a body; it was someone I'd met. It didn't matter that I wasn't fond of Barth, I knew him. I'd chatted with him at a few parties thrown by the chancellor and served on a committee he'd chaired. Since the building housing the English department was close to the library, I'd also frequently run into him on campus, if only to nod or say hello. He wasn't some stranger—he was someone I knew.

He was dead and I'd seen his body.

I grabbed the back of a task chair. My legs wobbled like overcooked noodles, and dark spots swam like minnows through my field of vision.

A hand gripped my right elbow. I blinked and glanced over at Zach, whose lips were pulled taut with concern. He reached around my back with his other hand and yanked the task chair from my fingers, rolling it behind me just in time for me to collapse onto the seat.

"Delayed reaction," he said. "Not surprising. When one experiences a shock, there's often a period of unnatural calm. It can take a while before the emotional reaction engulfs the brain."

I furiously waved one hand without looking at him. "Don't give me that psychobabble."

"Come on, Jenn, he's only trying to help. And I think he's probably right." Bri bent down to examine my face. "Your eyes are barely focusing and your lips are quivering. Do you need anything?"

"Water," Zach said, taking off in a sprint toward the break room.

Bri straightened but kept her gaze locked on my face. "You should head home. I walked to campus today so I can drive your car if you feel too shaky."

I stared up into her concerned face. "I can't imagine what happened. I suppose it could have been an accident or, like you suggested, self-inflicted."

Bri pursed her lips. "Actually, thinking about it a bit more, I can't picture Barth throwing himself over a railing, so I doubt it was a suicide."

Zach returned, holding out a plastic cup. "Drink this slowly. It may help with the shakes."

Cradling the cup between my hands, I took a long swallow of water. "Thanks," I mumbled, before glancing back at Bri. "Which means either it *was* an accident . . ."

"Or someone deliberately shoved him," Zach said.

Bri lowered her dark lashes over her eyes. "I think that's the option the police are pursuing. Partially because it's odd that he was on the mezzanine. The rumor is that he was undoubtedly meeting someone, especially since it's a good spot for a private conversation."

"Sure, but who'd want to kill him? Or even hit or shove him? He is"—I cleared my throat—"*was* a pompous ass sometimes, but if that was a trigger for murder, a lot more people on campus would be dead."

"Perhaps we should head into your office, or somewhere more private, and talk this out," Zach said. "You seem pretty rattled by this revelation."

I stood, kicking back the rolling chair. "I'm not, it just took me by surprise. I'm fine."

"I doubt it," Zach said, a mulish expression settling on his face. "If I say I'm fine, I'm fine."

"I think I'd better slip out," Bri said, shooting me a wide-eyed look. "Catch you later, Jenn. Text me if you want that ride."

I didn't watch her leave, knowing she'd make sure the main door locked behind her. "I realize you're just doing your job, but I believe it's within my rights to refuse your services," I told Zach.

He used one finger to push his tortoiseshell-framed glasses up to the bridge of his rather hawkish nose. "You're correct. The provost simply wanted you to be informed personally about the identity of the victim, and then given the opportunity to talk to a professional, on the institution's dime. You certainly have the right to reject that"—he shrugged his broad shoulders—"even if, from my clinical perspective, I think it's a bad idea."

I studied him for a moment, noticing a few paler strands gilding his light-brown hair. *A holdover from being out in the sun a lot over the summer*, I thought, figuring Zach was one of those people who'd been blond as a child. Josh, my younger brother, was the same. I, on the other hand, had retained my fair locks, even if they'd faded to a dirty blonde rather than the platinum hair I'd possessed as a young girl.

"I know you want to help, but really, it's not necessary," I said.

Zach's eyes narrowed behind the lenses of his glasses. "Discovering a dead body, especially if it's someone you know, isn't an everyday occurrence. You may feel fine now, but that could simply be your mind's way of coping. Sooner or later—"

"I'll collapse into a puddle of hysterical female panic?" I arched my brows. "Don't worry, it's nothing a strong shot of tequila can't fix."

Zach thrust his hands into the pockets of his corduroy slacks. "That's really not the best coping mechanism."

"So you've told me," I said, remembering the run-in I'd had with him the previous semester, when I'd been drowning my sorrows over my latest breakup at a trendy cocktail bar. On that occasion Zach, recognizing me from a few all-campus meetings, had offered some undoubtedly wise, but totally unsolicited, advice. I'd responded in a less than ladylike fashion, which had made the stylish young woman on his arm gasp and drag Zach away.

"Still holds true," he said without breaking eye contact with me.

"Better than talking about my childhood trauma. Of which I had none, by the way." I tucked a clump of my shoulder-length hair behind one ear. "Sorry to disappoint."

"That's not what . . ." Zach shook his head. "Regardless of what you think, I'm only here to listen if you want to talk. Or we can wait until another time, if you aren't ready to discuss the situation today."

"Still on the institution's dime?" I asked.

"Absolutely. It's a campus issue." Zach studied my face for a moment. "There is something bothering you. Perhaps not Doug Barth's death, but something."

"It's related," I said, giving in to my urgent desire to talk to someone about my concerns. "You see, I mentor Mia Jackson, who's a creative writing major."

"And thus knew Barth."

"Yes, she took several of his courses." I leaned back against the edge of one of the worktables, pressing my palms against the melamine surface to keep my body steady. "Rumor has it that it was her story they found beside Barth's body."

Zach's brow furrowed. "Surely they don't suspect her of murdering her professor."

"I'm afraid they might. That's what's actually bothering me right now. There was bad blood between them, and if he had her story in his hand when he died . . . Also, no one can find her and she isn't answering her phone. Which doesn't look good."

"Mia Jackson?" Zach thrust his hands in the pockets of his pants and rocked back on his heels. "That name sounds familiar, but I don't recall ever meeting her."

"So not one of your patients?" I asked.

Zach shook his head. "I couldn't tell you even if she was."

"Right, right." I stared down at my feet, remembering Bri's comments from before. She'd come across Mia in the library, angry and hurt. *Angry enough to confront Barth, engage in an argument, and shove him?*

"Did Ms. Jackson have a problem with Professor Barth?" Zach asked.

"Understandably." I crossed my arms over my chest. "Her advisor was Andrea Karmen, who's very supportive of Mia's work, but Barth was in charge of the creative writing program, so she had to deal with him frequently. According to the gossip, he thought Mia had talent but treated her badly, humiliating her in front of her peers and downgrading her writing projects."

"Why?" Zach lifted his eyebrows. "Was he jealous of her talent?"

I shook my head. "I don't think that was it. The problem was she didn't write the way he thought she should. Mia wants to write romance, and Doug Barth thinks, well, *thought*, genre fiction wasn't worth much. He pressured Mia to write literary fiction. He said with talent like hers, it was a crime to do anything else."

"I see." Zach's expression grew thoughtful. "Not to speak ill of the dead, but I've heard a few complaints about Doug Barth singling out one or two individuals in his classes for negative attention."

"Which is weird, because he was popular with most students, at least from what I've heard. Most claim he's charming and tells amusing stories and is a great writing coach. But apparently, he can be cruel too. Honestly, I've always thought he was harder on those he believed possessed the most talent. He was into tough love or something."

Zach frowned. "Sounds like he subscribed to the *Whiplash* theory of teaching."

"The what?" I asked.

"It's a term that's come into use fairly recently, based on that movie from about ten years ago."

I nodded. "Ah, okay. That's the one where the teacher relentlessly pushes a student who's got potential, right?"

"Correct. Only I'd call it abusive behavior." Zach slid his hands from his pockets and gestured as he spoke. "You find a lot of that in the arts—teachers and mentors who claim they're only being harsh and demanding to bring out the best in their students. But I think it's simply an excuse to be cruel."

"Agreed. I've mentored plenty of students without torturing them emotionally. Or at least, I hope so," I said, managing to conjure up a wan smile.

Zach didn't crack a smile in return. "I hope so too."

Chapter Four

After ushering Zach out of the center, with a promise to call him if I needed to discuss anything else, I grabbed my purse and a light jacket from my office and headed outside.

I used a back exit to avoid the crowd I was sure had assembled in front of the library. Striding down an alley formed by two adjacent brick buildings, I reached the rear entrance to the student union and slipped inside.

I was following a hunch I wasn't sure would pan out. But after I'd analyzed the situation the way Annabelle, the older of the two sleuths in my books, would, I'd decided to follow her advice to always start looking for someone in the places they frequented the most. Which meant checking the main cafeteria. I'd often spotted Mia there, working on her laptop at a back table, bright pink Bluetooth earbuds pressed into each ear. She told me she enjoyed the activity swirling around her, which baffled me. I needed complete privacy in order to write. But every author had their own method, and as long as it worked for them, I wasn't going to force any of my mentees to change their habits.

Unfortunately, there was no sign of Mia this evening. Perhaps she really had gone into hiding. I frowned and walked over to one of the cafeteria serving stations. "You didn't happen to see Mia Jackson in here earlier, did you?" I asked the older woman slicing pizza on a counter behind a heated serving carousel.

"Nope. Haven't seen head or tail of her all day." The woman kept her back to me, but I could tell, from the steel-gray braids that wrapped around her head and her short, plump figure, that it was Christine Kubiak. She was the manager of this cafeteria and a fixture on campus, having worked at the university for over thirty-five years.

"She usually pops in at some point, doesn't she?" I asked. "I've seen her here a lot."

Christine turned and placed pizza slices on the carousel before meeting my gaze. "Usually. But I guess she must've headed home early today." Her eyes, framed with pale lashes, were blue as Delft china. "She's probably laying low. I guess you've heard how the whole campus is buzzing about her being involved in that incident in the library."

"Are they?" I kept my tone neutral, hoping to hide my interest in this topic.

Christine was not so easily fooled. "I'm sure you know all about it, Ms. Dalton. You were the one who found the body, right?"

"Yes. But I didn't see Mia there, or anywhere nearby."

"Make sure you tell the cops that." Christine whipped off her thin plastic gloves. "I heard they've got some notion Mia was involved, just because someone saw her arguing with Professor Barth and one of her stories was found near the body."

"Has that been verified?" I asked. "I saw papers but couldn't make out who they belonged to."

Christine shrugged. "One of the part-time campus police officers told me it was Mia's story, which is why they're trying to locate her. But her being a killer? That's nonsense."

"It seems you don't believe Mia could have had anything to do with Barth's death."

"Absolutely not. She was a student assistant here at the cafeteria as a freshman and sophomore, before she got that scholarship. Best student worker I ever had." Christine tossed the used gloves in a bin. "Quiet and reliable, and always nice and polite to everyone. I'm sure she has a temper just like everybody else, but I never saw it. No way Mia Jackson would murder anyone."

"I don't think she was responsible for Professor Barth's death either. That's why I was hoping to find her and speak with her. See what really happened." I shrugged. "I mean, if she did talk to Doug Barth in the library today, maybe she saw someone else hanging around before she left the area."

"She may have seen the actual killer?" Christine clutched the strap of the apron she wore over her Clarion University monogrammed white polo shirt.

"It's possible." My shoulders tensed as I recalled all the scenes I'd written where a witness was hunted by the killer.

"Then we need to find her," Christine said, the fan of wrinkles around her eyes deepening as she squinted. "Her roommate is over at that far table. Maybe she knows something."

I turned to follow her gaze. On the other side of the cafeteria, a slight young woman with ebony hair slicked back into a tight bun faced off with a group of girls. Mingled voices made it impossible to understand what was being said, but it was clear it wasn't a friendly conversation.

"I'm going to check that out," I told Christine. Striding across the room, I noticed that the dark-haired young woman was wearing a black leotard under her crimson tracksuit.

One of our dance students, I thought, as I approached the group. *That must be Francesa Silva then. Mia mentioned that her roommate was a contemporary dancer.*

"Sure she had a reason," said a blonde girl wearing a fuchsia sweatshirt and artfully tattered jeans. "After Professor Barth tore apart her story in front of everyone in the class. I'd be out for blood too. But I wouldn't push someone over a railing."

"I'm sure Mia didn't do that, no matter how angry she was," Francesca said, placing her clenched fists on her hips. "It's all speculation, and spreading rumors is cruel."

I tapped my foot against the tile floor to draw their attention. "Is there a problem? We could hear you from across the room."

The cluster of girls facing Francesca drifted apart and silently dispersed like the petals of a windblown flower. They'd obviously recognized me and didn't want to engage in conversation with anyone on the faculty or staff.

"You're Ms. Dalton, right?" Francesa lowered her arms and uncurled her fingers. "Mia's writing teacher."

"More like a mentor," I said. "I don't teach any classes; I just work with Mia in the writing center."

"Yeah, okay. I remember that now." Francesca blinked, fluttering her impossibly thick black lashes. "Before you ask, I don't know where Mia is. Everyone assumes I do, but I haven't seen her since early this morning."

"That's too bad. I was hoping to talk to her—to support her, not cause her any more problems."

Francesca's expression grew troubled. "I don't really know what happened, but there's all this gossip flying around about Mia and Professor Barth. He fell or something, and people are saying Mia was there and somehow involved, which is ridiculous."

"Yes, he fell." I took a deep breath. "Actually, I found his body."

"Oh." Francesa pressed her hand over her mouth.

"But I didn't see Mia anywhere near the scene." I decided not to mention the possibility that someone hiding in the stacks had fled out the emergency exit. No sense adding any fuel to the wildfire of rumors already engulfing the campus.

Francesa lowered her hand. "I'm sure she had nothing to do with it." She reached out and clutched the back of one of the café chairs. "Is he really dead?"

"Professor Barth? Yes, sadly, he is." I studied Francesca's face for a moment. Her deep brown eyes glistened. *With tears?* "Were you acquainted with him?"

"No. I only knew what Mia told me."

"They didn't get along, from what I hear," I said.

"Sort of. I mean, she admired him and said he was a good teacher. They just didn't see eye-to-eye about writing. But she didn't despise him or anything." Francesca rubbed her lower lashes with one finger.

Definitely tears, I thought, wondering if Francesa was telling the truth about not being acquainted with Doug Barth. "I know they disagreed about the trajectory of her writing career. She told me that much. But, as you said, I never got the impression that she hated him."

"You'll tell the investigators that?" Hope brightened Francesca's voice. "I think she's going to need people to back her up."

"Of course. I certainly don't suspect her, no matter what the rumor mill grinds out," I said.

Francesca glanced up at a round wall clock hung on one of the cafeteria's square support pillars. "Sorry, but I've got to run. I've got rehearsal in ten minutes." She grabbed a dance bag from the adjacent table. "It's for Mr. Muir's class. He's only teaching one studio course this semester and I was lucky to get in. Can't be late for this special rehearsal. Don't want him to think I'm a slacker." Francesa hurried away, but paused for a moment to turn back to me. "Hope you find Mia. Tell her to text me if you do," she called out before dashing off.

Wandering back over to the pizza serving station, I waved a hand at Christine. "Francesca hasn't seen Mia all day."

"That's too bad." Christine fixed her brilliant blue gaze on my face. "Let me know if you track her down. And let her know I'd be happy to help any way I can. Like writing up a statement of support or being a character witness."

"Let's hope it doesn't come to that," I replied.

But I was afraid it might.

Chapter Five

I texted Bri and told her not to worry about driving me home, then headed to one of the campus parking lots. It wasn't the closest lot to the library, because that one always seemed to fill up far too early in the morning, and while I had a faculty and staff parking sticker, I hadn't paid the premium to get a reserved spot. I hunted for a spot every day. Sometimes I was close to the library, but often I had quite a hike.

The truth was, I didn't really mind walking across campus. Clarion wasn't as old as heritage universities like Harvard or even the University of Virginia, but it had been established far enough in the past to feature some beautiful brick and stone buildings, an abundance of trees, shrubs, and flower beds, and an assortment of sculptures and courtyards. The more modern buildings sat on the edges of the campus, their steel and glass walls reflecting the verdant greenery they enclosed.

Even in October, when most of the flowers had faded, color blazed in the foliage overhead. As I walked along a pathway shaded by a canopy of trees, a few crimson and gold leaves fluttered through the air, bright as summer butterflies.

I'd almost reached the parking lot and my compact sedan when I heard a shriek rising from behind a tightly trimmed wall of boxwood. Yanking my phone from my pocket, I backed up far enough to find the entry to the enclosed area veiled by the shrubs.

It was one of the spaces carved out behind campus buildings to hide the green metal dumpsters that held trash and blue dumpsters that collected recycling. This one, behind the Chemistry building, had several dumpsters in a row, all overflowing. I looked around, trying to find the source of the sound I'd heard. Finally, close to a tall wooden panel fence that connected with the boxwoods, I saw a petite, dark-haired woman slumped on the ground.

It was Andrea Karmen. Next to her, offering a helping hand was Erin McHenry, the assistant director of the campus writing center. I rushed over to them, waving my phone. "Do you need me to call 911?" I asked as I drew closer.

"No, no. Silly me, I just tripped and fell." Andrea struggled to her feet and met my concerned gaze. "I was taking a shortcut that didn't turn out to save me any time. Luckily Erin was close by." She brushed some dust and bits of gravel from her navy slacks.

As I stepped closer, I noticed a streak of crimson marring Andrea's forearm. "Did you hurt yourself?"

"Just a graze. Nothing serious." As Andrea pulled a tissue from her pocket and dabbed at the blood, a lock of her curly dark hair fell across her forehead

"I heard a noise while I was walking back from my car," Erin said. A woman of average height and build, with pleasant if undistinguished features, Erin projected a reserved demeanor, whatever the situation. She certainly wasn't one to express frustration or anger, even when she might've been entitled to do so. As a matter of fact, I'd been waiting for an explosive expression of Erin's true feelings for four years, ever since I'd been appointed as the director of Clarion University's writing center over her. Not only was she, at thirty-nine, seven years my senior, she also had an MFA in creative writing and taught a graduate course on poetry in Clarion's English department.

My own background in education and my lack of university teaching experience should've given Erin the edge over me, but then again, I'd had several books published while she had none. Genre fiction books, it was true, but my somewhat successful mystery series seemed to have turned the tide in my favor.

Although Erin had never acted as if she were upset with the decision, she did tend to keep an eye on me. Which was why I only conducted research for my books before or after work, or during my lunch hour or scheduled breaks.

Right now, she was studying me carefully. "Is anything wrong?" she asked. "You seem a little rattled."

I clenched my fists, remembering the sight of the body, and the blood. "Haven't you seen the all-campus text? There's been an accident in the library."

"Accident? What accident?" Erin fluttered her lashes. "I haven't checked my phone. I just got back from my appointment and was rushing to get back to work."

"No need," I said. "Everything's on lockdown right now anyway. I closed the writing center before I left." Noticing Andrea pressing another tissue to her arm, I added, "Sure you're alright?" I fished through my tote bag, looking for the packet of Band-Aids I always kept on hand. I'd found them essential to protect my heels when I had to wear fancy shoes for special events, or for times when our student assistants fell victim to vicious paper cuts.

"It's fine, it's fine," Andrea said, even though blood was seeping through the tissue.

"Well, here"—I held out a Band-Aid—"this will keep the blood from staining your blouse, if nothing else."

"So what happened?" Erin asked, tucking a lock of her wavy, ash-blonde hair behind one ear.

While Andrea focused on applying the bandage, I met Erin's inquiring gaze. "Doug Barth fell from the mezzanine on the top floor of the library."

"What?" Erin opened and closed her mouth and her wispy eyebrows arched over her wide gray eyes. "Is he alright?"

"Not exactly." Andrea used her forefingers to sweep what I assumed was some dust from her lower lashes. "He's dead."

Erin pressed her palms against her cheeks. "Seriously? How horrible."

"Worse than that, I witnessed an altercation he had with Mia Jackson not long before it happened," Andrea said, still fiddling with the Band-Aid on her arm.

"Oh no, no." Erin lowered her head with her palms cradling her face. Her eyes were squeezed shut.

"I know it's a shock, especially since you've interacted with him more than I have, being on the faculty of the English department," I said. "Both of you, actually."

Andrea busied herself with brushing more dust from her clothes. "It's a shock, for sure," she said, in a matter-of-fact tone.

Erin dropped her hands and looked up. "I was only part-time, but yes, we were acquainted, through faculty meetings and events and . . ." She blinked rapidly, as if holding back tears. "Oh dear, this is dreadful."

She did look shaken, certainly more so than Andrea who appeared much less affected by the situation. Of course, Andrea had had more time to process the news. I shuffled my feet through the loose gravel. "Yes, it is. And just so you know, because you're bound to hear about it—I found his body."

"You did?" Erin reached out and grabbed my arm. "Poor thing. Did you see him fall? I hope not."

"No, I didn't see anything like that. I had just gotten off the elevator and noticed him lying on the floor. I didn't even know who it was. I was going to call the police, but then I heard a noise and saw a light flare at the far end of the floor. It startled me so much, I fled back to the elevator to reach the second floor and get someone in reference to call." I shrugged. "I suppose it was rather lame of me, running away like that. The amateur detectives in my books would've probably chased whoever it was down the stairs."

Erin's grip on my arm tightened. "I think you did the right thing, Jenn. Heavens, it could've been the killer."

I stared at her, noticing the glassiness of her eyes. Perhaps she was more affected by the news of Doug Barth's death than she wanted to let on. "Well, we don't know that the person in the stacks was a killer. Maybe Doug fell by accident."

"Or maybe it was someone who argued with him but had nothing to do with him falling," Andrea said, looking from me to Erin and back again. "Like I said—and as I had to tell the authorities, I'm afraid—I saw Mia Jackson arguing with Doug not long before Jenn stumbled over his body."

I pursed my lips. Andrea seemed determined to bring up Mia's name in connection with the incident. "Or an unfortunate student who found his body before I did and disappeared because they were as shocked as I was."

"Exactly, exactly." Erin gave my arm a pat after she released her hold. "Poor Jenn. I'm sure it was terribly distressing."

"It wasn't pleasant," I said, as my cell phone vibrated against my palm. I peeked at the screen. It was a text from a police officer from Harburg. Clarion sat on one edge of the town, and except for a few streets filled with eateries and stores catering to college students, there was minimal interaction between the town and the university. Most Clarion students headed to D.C. and its suburbs to experience any sort of nightlife. "Hold on, I need to check this."

The text was a request for me to check in at the police station the next day. Something I didn't mind, although it would cause issues with the writing center schedule.

"Are you available to cover for me tomorrow?" I asked Erin. "Not the entire day, but at least the morning. I know you had a dental appointment off campus this afternoon, and wasn't sure if you were done with everything connected with that . . ."

"Of course. Fortunately, I don't have a class to teach tomorrow morning." Worry lines creased her forehead. "I guess you have to talk to the police again?"

I nodded. "Unfortunately. But I do want to help their investigation any way I can."

"Just be glad you didn't see anyone," Erin said, with a slight shudder.

Andrea's shoulders visibly tensed. "Yes, if you saw anything that could identify the person involved in Doug's fall . . . I'm afraid that could make you a target."

"I suppose you're right. It's probably better for me that I don't really know anything," I said, forcing a smile. "Not good for the investigation, maybe, but more advantageous for me."

Erin gave my arm another pat. "Which is the important thing."

Chapter Six

I was unfamiliar with the area around Clarion when I first moved from North Carolina to take the writing center job. Not wanting a long commute, I had rented an apartment close to campus. But I soon learned this was a mistake—most of the other residents were students, and their raucous get-togethers made it difficult for me to focus on my writing. Saturday and Sunday offered me the best uninterrupted writing time, but of course the weekend was also the prime time for student parties.

Fortunately, I'd chosen a six-month lease and was able to move after Erin shared some information she'd heard in an English department meeting. Emily Moore, who was the university's poet-in-residence, had announced that she was looking for a new tenant for her guest house.

I'd contacted Emily immediately, not concerned that she lived in Taylorsford, a smaller town a twenty-to-thirty-minute drive from Clarion. The idea of having a house to myself, with another writer as my landlady, sounded perfect. Determined to take advantage of this opportunity, I'd rushed over to the building housing the English department as soon as Emily asked me to stop by her office.

Emily Moore only taught a few graduate seminars at the university, but she had one of the nicest spaces in the building. It was a corner office, with windows on two adjacent walls. Tall bookshelves filled the other walls, and a sitting area provided a comfortable place for Emily to meet with guests. The office was even nicer than the one occupied by the department chair, Gary Alexander. *Pretty good achievement for a woman who gained fame as a sixties psychedelic poet and member of Andy Warhol's Factory in New York City*, I'd thought at the time.

Emily had been pleased that I was interested in her rental property and promised a tour of the guest house the following day. As soon as I saw the space—a converted garage that looked more like a city loft than its Craftsman style exterior implied—I was eager to sign a lease.

I found I didn't mind the drive to work. I discovered some alternate routes that avoided most of the traffic and offered picturesque views of the farmland nestled against the Blue Ridge Mountains. The only time I took the four-lane highway between Taylorsford and Harburg was in questionable weather, when the narrow back roads could prove dangerous.

As an added benefit, my famous landlady and I had become friends. Emily Moore was in her seventies but had lost none of the charisma that had brought her fame in her younger years. I was always delighted when she'd occasionally invite me to dinner, knowing I'd hear more amazing stories about New York in the 1960s and '70s.

Tonight, the back door opened as I pulled into my designated parking spot behind Emily's classic brick bungalow. Emily stood in the doorway, waiting until I climbed out of my car before calling out to me, "Jenn, I heard what happened today at Clarion. Please come in and give me all the details."

I slid the strap of my tote bag up onto my shoulder. I would've preferred to relax in my own space but didn't feel I could just brush Emily off. "Alright." I climbed the steps that led to her enclosed back porch and followed her into the house. "As long as there will be wine involved."

"Always," Emily said with a smile. She took off as soon as I was inside, crossing the porch and her homey kitchen at a surprisingly quick pace.

Trailing her into her combination living and dining room, I once again marveled at Emily's vitality and appearance. She certainly didn't match the typical image of an older poet. No long gray hair, flowing scarves, bohemian tiered skirts, or chunky jewelry for her—she wore plain beige slacks and a simple aqua linen tunic. Her hair, dyed a rich brown, was cut in a smooth bob that brushed the strong line of her jaw, and round tortoiseshell glasses framed her piercing dark eyes.

The living room featured an oversized stone fireplace on one wall. Emily gestured toward one of the upholstered armchairs flanking the hearth. "Please have a seat. I'll get those drinks."

After she returned and handed me a full glass of white wine, she sat down in a wooden rocker, turning it around to face my chair.

"I suppose it was something of a shock for you when you heard about Doug Barth." I took a sip of my wine. "Did you also hear that I found his body?"

"I did." Emily's rather stubby fingers encircled her stemless glass. "That *was* a shock. Hearing that someone may have shoved Doug off the mezzanine"—she shrugged—"not really all that surprising."

I scooted to the front edge of my chair. "But he was well-liked, wasn't he? At least, that's the impression I've gotten from most of the students."

"Hmm." Emily took a long swallow of wine. "He knew how to work the students. A good-looking fortysomething man with a great deal of charisma can easily charm impressionable teens or twenty-year-olds. Especially the girls." She tipped her head to one side. "I'm sure you understand that dynamic."

I thought about my own unrequited crush on a young professor when I was in college. "I do, unfortunately."

"I hear the police are convinced it was more than an accident and are focused on a student," Emily said, swirling the wine in her glass.

I cast her an inquisitive look. *How did she know that?* I wondered. *Does she have some inside source?* "Mia Jackson. She and Barth were not on the best of terms. Also, her short story, which he'd given a low grade, was at the scene."

"And she's nowhere to be found," Emily said, studying me intently. "You know the girl, I believe."

"I've been mentoring her. She's interested in a career as an author of genre fiction, so I've been sharing my experiences with agents and publishers and that sort of thing." I took another sip before setting my wineglass on the small mosaic-topped table next to my chair. "She told me they didn't really teach much about those practical matters in your department."

Emily's lips twitched into a brief smile. "That's true enough. Doug Barth felt that students, especially undergrads. shouldn't try to get published. He always claimed there was too much they needed to learn first."

"Right. Mia was frustrated with that, and I can't say I blame her. She's talented and skilled enough to get an agent and publishing deal right now." I slumped back in my chair. "She and Barth were often at odds. I'm afraid that fact isn't going to do much to help clear her as a suspect."

Emily set her own wineglass on a chunky wooden side table. "Perhaps not, but Mia Jackson wasn't the only person who had conflicts with Doug. He may have been popular with a lot of students, but the English department faculty and staff weren't quite so enamored."

"Anyone in particular?" I asked, trying, and failing, to sound nonchalant.

"Well, Andrea Karmen for one. As you know, she teaches courses on genre fiction, and as you probably also know—"

"Doug Barth sneered at everything except literary fiction." I eyed Emily. "And poetry, I suppose. I imagine that was high-class enough for him."

"He did give poetry his stamp of approval. As long as it wasn't—how did he put it? Ah, yes, 'rhyming doggerel only fit for greeting cards.'"

"I know Andrea wasn't his biggest fan, but I can't imagine her getting in a shouting match with anyone." I raised my wineglass back to my lips as the memory of observing Andrea and Doug engaged in a loud argument popped into my head. "Or at least, not a *shoving* match."

Emily drummed her fingers against the wooden arm of her rocker. "I wouldn't rule her out. Doug was involved in a pretty nasty battle with her this semester. I mean, they've never really gotten along, but things really went downhill when Doug decided to lobby the new provost to cut all of Andrea's courses on genre fiction."

"That would drop her down to part-time faculty." My fingers tightened around my glass. "Just when she's trying to get tenure, too."

"Which is as good a motive for an argument leading to violence as I can imagine," Emily said, fixing me with her penetrating stare. "Not to mention her comment in our last departmental meeting."

37

"Which was?"

"Doug said something about adding more specialized courses, including a graphic-novel class, 'over his dead body.'" Emily picked up her glass and took a sip. "Andrea replied, and I quote—'that could be arranged.'"

Chapter Seven

"Are you planning to share that comment with the investigators?" I asked, torn between wanting her to do so to aid Mia and hoping she'd stay silent to protect Andrea.

"If they ask me." Emily gave me a wink. "I learned long ago that it's best to only share required information with the authorities."

Considering her colorful past, that was probably true. I finished off my wine in one gulp and stood up. "I appreciate the information, but I think I should head home now. It's really been an exhausting day."

"Of course, dear. I just wanted to let you know that there are more people who might have a grudge against Doug than just Mia Jackson. In case you're doing a little amateur sleuthing"—Emily flashed a sly smile—"like the characters in your books."

"The thought has occurred to me, but that's fiction, not reality. I'm not sure I'm quite as clever as Annabelle and Olivia."

Emily rose to her feet. "Don't you have to be just as clever to create their stories?"

"Maybe. But I can control the things that happen in my books. I don't have that advantage in real life."

"True enough." Emily looked me up and down. "There is one other thing, in case you do decide to do a little digging. Take a look at Doug Barth's wife, Miranda. Rumor has it their marriage was on the rocks. You know what they say—it's often the spouse or other family members you need to consider in these cases."

"Only if she was on campus, though," I said. "That would need to be verified."

"There you go, already thinking like a sleuth." Emily smiled. "Now, go on. Don't worry about the glasses; just hurry home and relax."

I wished her a good night and left as quickly as I could. She'd provided some useful information, but I didn't want to indulge her desire to help me play amateur sleuth. I wasn't even sure if I wanted to look into the people she'd mentioned. Andrea was a friend, and as for Miranda Barth, well, I doubted I could even get a chance to ask her anything. She was a successful interior designer, with family money backing her. She wasn't someone I was likely to casually encounter. We definitely didn't move in the same circles.

I left through the back door and crossed the gravel parking area behind the main house. My home welcomed me with a motion sensor floodlight that illuminated most of the tidy backyard.

Stepping inside, I was careful to lock the door behind me and engage the security chain. There wasn't a lot of crime in Taylorsford, but that didn't mean I could let down my guard. After living in a few larger cities while finishing my education and starting my career, I'd been trained to secure my house and car, no matter how quaint or quiet the locale.

I flicked on the overhead lights and paused for a moment to appreciate my good fortune in finding this place. The space was wide open in the front, with the living room, dining space, and kitchen all connected. At the back were the master bedroom and bath, as well as a half bath for guests. There was a loft above that could function as a guest room, although it was commonly used as my office. Since my family was scattered all over and my friends and acquaintances from work seemed loathe to drive out to Taylorsford, I rarely hosted any guests.

A loud meow broke the silence. Ash, my fluffy gray cloud of a cat, trotted down the loft steps and padded over to me. She stared up at my face, her amber eyes wide and judgmental.

"I know, I know," I told her as I headed into the kitchen. "I'm twenty minutes late with your dinner. Mea culpa."

Being able to keep Ash was another benefit to living in Emily's guest house. While Emily didn't have any pets, she wasn't opposed to me adopting the tiny kitten I'd found while tossing recycling into the dumpster behind the library. Since Ash was friendly instead of feral, it was apparent that someone had abandoned her. I'd picked her up and kept her hidden in my office until confirming that no one on campus or in the local area had lost a kitten. Or, more accurately, that there wasn't anyone who wanted her back. Once that was established, she'd come home with me.

I scooped out some canned food, barely dumping it all into the bowl before Ash's head bumped my hand out of the way. I gave her back a pat while she gobbled up her food. My parents didn't believe animals should be in the house, so I'd never owned a pet before Ash. Now I couldn't imagine life without her.

"Owned a pet," I said, with a snort. "More like you own me, right, girl?"

Ash lifted her head and cast me a look that said I was correct.

After changing into the loose yoga pants and T-shirt I used as pajamas, I heated up some leftovers for dinner. A little later, I settled on my sofa and turned on the television to watch the most recent episode of the thriller series I was streaming. But I couldn't concentrate on the show. Images of Doug's body kept flashing before my eyes, and Emily's words about other suspects played on repeat in my head.

I couldn't contact Miranda Barth, of course, but I could talk to Andrea again. *Not to interrogate her*, I thought. *Just to chat.*

Andrea answered right before I resigned myself to leaving a voice message.

"Hi, Jenn," she said. "Sorry I didn't contact you after our encounter this afternoon, but I thought you might want to be left alone this evening."

"I'm okay. Naturally it was a shock at first, but I'm calm now." This wasn't the exact truth, but I thought it best to play it cool.

"Goodness, I'd be a wreck." Andrea cleared her throat. "Did you really not notice anyone? In the vicinity, I mean. People have been talking as if the culprit has to be Mia Jackson, but if you didn't see her in the area . . ."

"I didn't. Like I said earlier, I didn't see anyone," I was able to state this confidently as it was, essentially, true. Although I'd heard a mysterious individual flee the stacks, I hadn't actually *seen* them.

Ash leapt up onto the sofa and snuggled up beside me.

"That's probably for the best. I wish I hadn't . . ." There was a short stretch of silence. "I wish I hadn't been in the library today," Andrea finally said. "That argument between Doug and Mia Jackson got pretty volatile."

"Oh?" I couldn't think of anything else to say, except, "You saw them on the top floor?"

"No, on the fifth floor. There weren't a lot of other people around. In fact, I didn't see anyone except Doug and Mia, although there may have been others in the stacks. Anyway, I was going to approach them and try to cool things down, but then Doug said something about continuing the discussion in a more private space. He suggested the mezzanine on the sixth floor and they left." Andrea's nails tapped her phone. "Mia used the stairs and Doug took the elevator. That was the last I saw of them."

So you were the only witness to their argument, I thought as I carefully considered my next words. Emily was right—Andrea had ongoing conflicts with Doug Barth, which made her a possible suspect. I'd actually observed one of their arguments during a recent campus training session, and it was obvious there was no love lost between them. "You didn't see Mia come back down the stairs?"

"I never caught sight of her again anywhere in the library. Of course, I left the fifth floor soon after I saw them, so that doesn't really mean much."

It means you could be telling this story to cast suspicion on Mia because you're actually the guilty party, I thought, absently stroking Ash's silky fur. I shook my head. What was I doing? I was thinking like my fictional amateur sleuths, suspecting everyone.

"I'm sure the actual culprit will be found soon, if there is one," I said. "We can't rule out the possibility of an accident."

"That's right," Andrea replied, with an eagerness that did nothing to calm my suspicions. "I know the police are investigating this as a possible crime, but who's to say Doug didn't slip and fall? It isn't impossible."

"Which is why we should tamp down any rumors about Mia, don't you think?"

"Of course," Andrea said in a more subdued tone. "We certainly shouldn't unjustly cast suspicion on anyone."

After a few more pleasantries, I wished Andrea a good evening and ended the call.

"Ash," I said, scratching behind her ears. "I'm not sure how I feel about Andrea right now. Common sense tells me she has nothing to do with Doug Barth's death, but there's this tiny flame of suspicion still flickering in my brain. What do you think?"

Lifting her head, Ash gazed at me, her golden eyes wide. She opened her mouth in a silent meow, as if indicating her lack of interest in this boring human conundrum.

"That's what I thought."

Chapter Eight

The following day I decided to hand-deliver a signed approval form to Gary Alexander in the English department. A student had requested me as a mentor in the second semester, and I wanted to make sure Alexander received the approval in a timely fashion.

Oh, who are you kidding? I chided myself as I crossed the tree-lined plaza in the center of campus. *There was time to send the form through campus mail. You just want to see if you can glean any additional information about Doug's death from his coworkers.*

The English department was housed in a red brick building with contrasting white casings framing mullioned windows. White columns supported an arched portico over the main entrance. The exterior of the building had a simple elegance completely lacking inside. Years of renovations had created a rabbit warren of offices and classrooms that made navigating the building challenging.

Form in hand, I headed for the faculty lounge. I knew one wall of the lounge featured a wooden structure sectioned into numerous small cubes, creating open mailboxes for the department's faculty and staff. Sliding the approval form into Gary Alexander's cubby would provide an acceptable reason for me to enter the lounge.

Hopefully, once there, I could talk with someone who might have updated news.

Or even gossip, I thought, as I hurried down a hall lined with windows on one side and small offices on the other. There was never a shortage of gossip or rumors on campus. Sometimes they even contained kernels of truth.

One of the office doors sat slightly ajar, yellow crime scene tape dangling from the doorjamb. I stopped to read the plate on the wall that indicated this was, or had been, Douglas Barth's office. The room was dark, but that partially opened door intrigued me. Had the investigators left it like that after searching Doug's office? It seemed unlikely, but perhaps, judging by the broken tape, the room had been cleaned after the police concluded their investigation.

I continued on to the end of the hall and the faculty lounge. A large room with windows on two adjacent walls, it was filled with comfortable but well-worn furniture. I knew from Andrea and Emily that most of the furnishings had been scrounged from surplus, and that the makeshift kitchenette on one wall had been installed by a former professor who'd been a home renovation enthusiast. Unlike the computer or business programs, the English department wasn't given much financial support, at least not in terms of upgrading the appearance of their facilities.

"The campus wants to impress and recruit more students who plan to major in fields that can lead to wealth after graduation," Emily had told me once, when I'd mentioned the run-down appearance of her department. "Who wants more English alumni? They won't be able to donate loads of money, like some business entrepreneur or high-tech guru."

Unfortunately, no one was hanging out in the lounge, so my plan to discover more information on Doug was thwarted. The only movement in the room was a flurry of dust motes dancing in the light spilling through the windows.

I crossed to the mail cubbies and slipped the form into Gary Alexander's box—the largest one, of course. Department chairs were typically changed every six years, but Gary Alexander had apparently secured a lock on the position. "Mainly because he wants it and no one else does," Emily had informed me, with a wink.

Surveying the mail unit, I located Doug Barth's name. His cubby was empty. *Of course, the police would've collected his mail,* I reminded myself. But as my gaze shifted to an unmarked mailbox next to Doug's, I noticed something shoved against the back of the cubby.

Reaching in, I trapped the crumpled piece of paper between two fingers and pulled it out. I assumed it was simply a bit of trash left in the unassigned mailbox when its previous owner had left campus, but before I tossed it into the recycling bin, I carried it over to one of the small café tables set up near the kitchenette.

I smoothed out the paper. It was a ragged-edged scrap that appeared to have been torn off a larger piece of notepaper. The words scribbled across the paper were *Consider this: King Lear, Act 5, Scene 3, Edgar's first lines.* There was nothing indicating who'd written the note, but it was explicitly addressed to "Professor Barth."

"They must've shoved this message into the wrong mailbox," I said, staring at the paper and trying to recall the lines mentioned by the note. I couldn't, of course; the reference was too obscure. I'd have to look it up in my well-worn copy of the *Complete Pelican Shakespeare* when I returned to my office.

Pocketing the note, I left the lounge and headed for the main entry, once again passing by Doug Barth's former office. But this time someone was standing in the hall.

"Officer Greene, is something wrong?" I asked, stopping in front of her.

She cast me a speculative look. "The tape's been broken."

"It was like that when I walked by before," I said. "I thought the cleaning staff might've removed it."

"When was that?" Officer Greene slipped her small notebook and a pen from her shirt pocket.

"Not long ago. Maybe ten minutes?"

"You didn't see anyone in the area?"

"No one." Clearing my throat, I added, "Are you saying someone broke into this office?"

"Possibly. We left the door ajar, because that's the way we found it after Professor Barth's death. But the tape should've remained intact until the investigation was complete. We never authorized housekeeping, or anyone else, to enter." Officer Greene tapped the notepad with her pen. "You still haven't heard anything from Mia Jackson?"

"No, and I suppose you haven't located her yet either, or you wouldn't be asking." I tried to temper the defensive tone creeping into my voice.

She looked up at me, squinting. "You'd tell me if you had, right? I know she was someone you mentored, so I understand if you feel an inclination to protect her, but it's really in her best interests if she's found, sooner rather than later."

"We have a good relationship, but I'm not hiding her, if that's what you're implying," I said, shoving my hand in my pocket. My fingertip brushed the ragged edge of the note. It was undoubtedly something I should share with the police, but . . .

The truth was, I wanted to decipher the clue first. *Besides*, I told myself, *it's probably something that's been sitting in that mail cubby for months, if not years. I'll hand it over later, once I see if it has any relevance or not.*

It wasn't the right thing to do. I knew that. But the suspicion glittering in Officer Greene's dark eyes had triggered my stubborn streak. I didn't like the fact that she wouldn't accept my statements concerning Mia as the truth. I slid my hand from my pocket without removing the note.

"I'm not implying you're involved in anything illegal, Ms. Dalton." Officer Greene looked me up and down, as if trying to read my body language. "I just want to make sure you understand that not providing information could place you in danger. Whoever broke into this office could've still been in there when you were in the hallway earlier. They might've seen you, even if you didn't see them."

I bit the inside of my cheek. Wincing, I met the officer's implacable stare. "I hadn't thought of that."

"Something to keep in mind, if you do discover Ms. Jackson's whereabouts." Officer Greene shoved the notebook and pen back in her pocket. "Now you'd better be on your way. I'm going to call in my partner so we can check the office again to see if we can find any traces the intruder left behind. In the meantime"—she fixed me with a stern stare—"please don't share this incident with anyone. I don't want the news all over campus before we have a chance to thoroughly investigate."

I nodded and mumbled my acquiescence with this request, then strode past her to reach the stairwell that led to an exterior door.

I remained in the stairwell for a few minutes, taking deep breaths to calm my racing heart. It hadn't struck me until Officer Greene mentioned it, but the person who'd broken into Doug Barth's office could've easily seen me when I'd paused outside. Like she said, it's possible they were hiding until I disappeared from view.

Had I made myself a target? I gripped the metal railing with both hands. It wasn't a comfortable thought. *It's a lot different when it's real*, I thought, mentally offering apologies to my characters for the frightening scenarios I'd placed them in over and over again, all for the sake of excitement and forward momentum. But I'd have to think twice about how I'd write Annabelle and Olivia's reactions to scary situations in future books. I may have depicted them being a little too blasé in the past.

Footsteps rattled the metal treads of the steps above me. *Class change*, I thought, rushing down the stairs before herds of students filled the stairwell. I still had to elbow my way past a cluster of young women who were pulling both exterior doors open as I left.

"Did you hear?" one of them said, her voice resonating off the painted concrete blocks of the stairwell. "They think it was Mia Jackson who killed Professor Barth."

"And nobody can find her," one of her companions chimed in. "Which means she's probably on the run."

I paused outside the doors, longing to correct these statements, but walked away instead. There was no way my words could stop the rumors. Only evidence and facts could do that.

And sometimes, I thought, remembering how gossip spread like pollen across campus, *even that doesn't work.*

Chapter Nine

I nstead of circling around to the front of the building, I decided to take a short walk to clear my head. Across a small parking lot was a path that had been beaten down by a multitude of students over the years. Shaded by trees, it ran along the top of a hill that fell away to a small stream. In spring, when rain turned the hill to mud and swelled the stream, some students held competitions to see who could roll down into the water the fastest. This was not a sanctioned university activity, of course, and was always a headache for the health clinic as well as campus police when too many glass bottles—holding the liquor that fueled the competition—got broken in the process.

In October, the hill was covered in a patchwork of weeds and the stream was barely a trickle. I only ran into a few students on the path, most of whom were too buried in their smartphone screens to pay any attention to me. Only one young woman, who we'd assisted in the writing center several times, bobbed her head and offered me a breezy "hi."

The path took a sharp left at the theater arts building, then continued through the alley that separated that building from the limestone-clad music building. Remembering that the music building also housed the dance department, I paused at the end of the path and surveyed the brick-paved area in front of the building. As Mia's roommate was a dancer, there was a possibility I could speak to her again. But I didn't see Francesca—the only dance students outside the music building were clustered around a tall, well-built woman whose sienna-brown hair brushed her broad shoulders.

I recognized her immediately. Karla Tansen only taught contemporary dance at Clarion occasionally, but she was well known to the campus community from her many recital appearances with faculty member and fellow dancer Richard Muir. She and Muir also ran a local dance company that was quickly gaining national attention. I'd been a fan of the company ever since its inception as a summer dance institute and had even contributed a little money to its scholarship drive

I lifted my hand in greeting, but Karla was too involved in her conversation with the students to notice. Someone waved back, though—another person whose workplace was situated on this side of the campus.

"Hello, Jenn," Zach said, striding over to me. "How are you doing today? Over the worst of the shock, I hope."

I looked into his eyes, or rather, the reflective surface of his transition-lensed glasses. "I'm okay, thanks. Although . . ." I couldn't really read Zach's expression, but since he was one of the few people who knew the whole story concerning my discovery of Doug Barth's body, I didn't have to pretend to be perfectly fine.

"Although?" Zach's eyebrows rose above the frames of his glasses.

I looked around and noticed several students strolling toward us. "If you have time, let's head to my office. I have something to tell you that I don't want to share with the entire campus."

"That's fine, I was planning to run by the library anyway." Zach gestured with one hand. "Lead on, Macduff."

"It's actually 'lay on,'" I said, automatically falling into instructor mode. "It's not about a direction, it's about a sword battle. But don't feel bad—it's often misquoted"

His eyes still shadowed by his dark glasses, Zach shot me a sarcastic smile. "Don't worry, I never feel bad when I'm corrected by an expert."

"I'm not really that much of a Shakespeare expert." I took off at a fast walk, matching his strides.

"Really? Well then, I'll guess I can ignore your tutoring on that subject in the future." Zach's voice was sharp as a razor blade.

"I suppose you can ignore anything I say," I snapped. I considered veering off across the plaza and leaving him behind but decided I could put up with him long enough to get his take on the note and the possible intruder in Doug's office.

We didn't speak again until we reached the library elevator.

"I didn't mean to be bite your head off earlier," Zach said, as the doors closed. "I really have to work on my reactions to things that show me up. Pride, you know."

Since my back was to him, I allowed myself to roll my eyes. "It's fine."

"Is it, though?" Zach said. "I know my attitude may have come across as less than congenial."

"Of course," I said, keeping my tone light. "I've heard a lot worse from students, as well as some faculty and administrators."

"I'm sure." Zach reached around me to punch the button for the second floor. "If you don't mind, I think I'll stop by reference first, then head down to the writing center."

After Zach got off on the second floor, I pressed the elevator button for the basement.

Lily Tuan, another one of our student assistants, greeted me as I entered the writing center. "Hello, Ms. Dalton. It's been quiet this morning. No one seems too concerned with their papers or projects today."

"I'm sure they're all still affected by Professor Barth's death," I said. "Did you know him?"

"Only by reputation. And of course I saw him around. But I never had any classes with him." Lily tossed her silky black hair behind her shoulders. "He wasn't too keen on the technical writing course I was taking. I think he believed stuff like that should be taught in the appropriate science programs instead of the English department."

"I'm sure you're right," I told her, glancing at my watch. "Sorry, it seems I'm past time to relieve you. I hope it won't make you late for class."

"No, I have a break in my schedule," Lily said. "And Ms. McHenry was here earlier. But it's been so dead in here, she asked if I was okay alone while she ran an errand, and I said sure. I imagine she'll be back soon."

"Well, you can head out now anyway. I'm here, and if Ms. McHenry was simply running an errand, she'll show up before too long."

I waited until Lily left before I swiped my keycard to enter my office. Once inside I opened the blinds covering the expanse of glass that fronted my office so I could keep watch for anyone entering the writing center.

"But first, the Shakespeare," I said, hurrying over to the shelf to pull out a large volume. I'd had my *Penguin Complete Shakespeare* since my undergraduate years in college, and it definitely showed some wear and tear. But it was still a great reference source.

I placed the book on my desk and opened it to *King Lear*. Paging through the play, I found the notation for act 5, scene 3, and then skimmed through the text to find Edgar's first lines.

It was a quote that made me take a step back from my desk.
Know my name is lost,
By treason's tooth bare-gnawn and canker-bit.
Yet am I noble as the adversary
I come to cope.

"Someone who felt betrayed sent this note to Barth," I mused aloud. "Someone who believed they were his equal, but who he'd dismissed or demeaned."

I frowned. The writer of the note was obviously a person who viewed Doug Barth as an adversary. The quote also described a person who was prepared to act, who was ready to throw down the gauntlet.

It was a description that could easily fit Doug's killer. And the use of the quote indicated someone in the liberal arts, like Andrea Karmen.

And Mia Jackson.

Chapter Ten

"The way you're furrowing your brow, that piece of paper must contain a disturbing message," Zach said as he sauntered into my office.

"It does, as a matter of fact." I met his questioning glance with a frown. "I found this shoved in the box next to Doug Barth's mail cubby, but it was addressed to him. It references some lines from *King Lear*."

"Ah, Shakespeare again." Zach crossed his arms over his broad chest. "Well, I'm sure I won't get the quote from a line reference, so you'd better read it out to me."

I studied his unreadable expression for a moment, then read the passage aloud. "As you see, this could be taken as a threat, or at least a warning," I said when I finished.

"It does seem that way." He stared intently at my hands. "But perhaps you shouldn't have handled that note. You may have contaminated the evidence. Isn't that what they always say in the type of books you write?"

Keeping my gaze fixed on the Shakespeare text, I bit the inside of my cheek to keep from spitting out a few choice words. "They can simply eliminate my fingerprints, you know."

"Your fingerprints are on file somewhere?"

I looked up and noticed the glint in Zach's eyes. "No, but I'll be happy to provide them to the police."

"Along with that note, I hope," he said.

"Of course. I just wanted to check the reference first." I slammed the book shut. "And yes, I know I should've given it to the investigators right away, but my curiosity got the better of me."

"Occupational hazard, I suppose." Zach gestured toward the row of my brightly colored paperbacks on my bookshelves. "From your writing profession, I mean."

"Curiosity is a necessity in an amateur sleuth, or any investigator, for that matter," I said, crossing my arms over my chest. "Not much can be discovered if you're oblivious."

Zach flashed me a grin. "Absolutely true. Which is why curiosity is also pretty valuable in my career. If I didn't care about finding out more about my patients, I wouldn't be much use."

I opened my mouth to make a pithy comment but snapped it shut again as two people appeared in the writing center's central room. "Hi, Bri. Hi, Christine. Can I help you?"

"Actually we hope we can help you." Bri cast an inquiring glance at Zach as he turned to face her. "Sorry, are we interrupting?"

"Not at all," I said, stepping out from behind my desk. "I was just sharing some information connected to Doug Barth with Dr. Flynn."

"Are you also questioning the sudden rush to judgment, Zach? In terms of labeling Mia Jackson a murderer, I mean." Bri bumped Christine's arm with her elbow. "That's honestly why we're here. Rumors and insinuations are flying across campus faster than the speed of light, and we're fed up."

"Truth is, I saw Ms. Rowley in the cafeteria and knew you were friendly, Ms. Dalton," Christine said. "I asked her to direct me to your office, and she said she'd come with me, since we both agreed something needs to be done. Poor Mia, I expect she's hiding somewhere, afraid to show her face 'cause of all the gossip and flat-out lies."

"What do you think you can do?" Zach asked, glancing from Christine to Bri. "I understand wanting to help the girl, but the best thing would be for her to turn herself in and tell the truth to the authorities. If she's innocent, she can clear her name fairly quickly."

Christine snorted. "Really? I guess you've always lived on the right side of the tracks, Dr. Flynn, so you wouldn't know how people can be railroaded into confessions and that sort of thing."

"I know that can happen, but I don't believe it would in this case," Zach said.

"Why not?" I walked around him to join Christine and Bri in the outer room. "Sentiment on campus is already against her, and she was seen arguing with Barth not long before he died."

Zach squared his shoulders as he gazed at the three of us. "Because Mia Jackson is a young woman with an exemplary academic record, not a hardened criminal. I can't imagine the police not taking that into account."

"Sure, if you think logically, it doesn't make much sense. But I'm not certain logic will prevail in this scenario." Bri tossed her azure-tipped hair. "Which is why I'd like to help uncover a few more suspects or at least some mitigating facts. I'm not saying the police won't conduct a thorough investigation and reveal the truth, but in the meantime, I'd hate to see Mia, or any student, put through the campus rumor wringer. It could have some harmful psychological effects, right?"

"It's possible," Zach admitted, his expression turning thoughtful. "But again, what can you do? I think it would be best to leave the investigation to the professionals."

Christine's blue eyes widened. "Even if they get it wrong? And as for what we can do, well, I have a couple of ideas about other suspects . . ."

"Hold that thought," Bri said, lifting her hand, palm out. "I don't think you want to share that at the moment."

I spun around at the squeal of the entrance doors. A cluster of students pushed their way into the room, their chatter filling the air like birds at a feeder. They plopped down at the computer stations, dropping their bookbags on the floor.

The lines bracketing Christine's thin lips deepened. "I guess this ain't the time and place."

"Not to share that kind of information, anyway," Bri said. "Look, why don't we all meet up at my house after work today? It's within walking distance of campus, so you don't even have to move your cars if you don't want to."

"I don't think that's a good idea," Zach said.

Bri reached over and tapped his forearm. "Oh, come on. We can talk there without worrying about being overheard by anyone. Besides, we could use your psychological insights, right, Jenn?"

"Well . . ." I said.

"Go ahead, have fun with your amateur detective society, but count me out." Zach slipped past us and headed for the main doors.

Bri watched Zach leave with a frown. "What a stick-in-the-mud. Should've expected it, though. He's a decent guy, but a bit too unbending, if you know what I mean." She turned to Christine. "I'm not taking no for an answer from you. Before you leave campus, make sure I have your number so I can text you my address. Will seven o'clock work?"

Christine nodded. "Fine by me."

Bri smiled. "Good. What about you, Jenn?"

"We'll see. I'm not really sure what my schedule looks like this evening," I said, knowing full well that I had no plans. "But for now, I need to check with the students who just came in and see what help they might need."

"Sure thing. You know where I live, so just show up around seven if you can. Okay, let's head out," Bri said, tapping Christine on the shoulder.

I waited until the doors closed behind them, then rushed over to the computer stations to assist the students. As I approached, I heard them talking about Mia being missing and speculating if she'd already fled the country.

"Maybe she'll become an international fugitive," one girl said, her tone conveying a sense of excitement over this idea.

I hadn't been certain that I'd show up at Bri's house after work, but now I was convinced I should. It might not do any good, in terms of discovering the real culprit, but perhaps Bri and Christine and I could at least come up with a few ways to counteract the rumors about Mia.

"I think everyone needs to remember that people should be considered innocent until they're *proven* guilty," I said, keeping my tone as neutral as possible.

The side-eye I earned from the group was epic.

Chapter Eleven

I didn't bother to leave campus after work, choosing to eat the frozen meal I'd stored in the kitchenette's refrigerator for this purpose.

"One of the reasons I have a cat and not a dog," I told Erin. "I don't have to worry about walking Ash, and I always leave some dry kibble out in case I'm late."

"Cats are more convenient, but you know me, I'm still a dog person," Erin said, pouring a mug of coffee.

"But you don't have one," I pointed out.

"Not at the moment. But I'm thinking about it." Erin leaned against the edge of the counter and swirled a packet of fake sugar into her mug. "It's a big commitment. I've had so much on my plate lately, I simply can't imagine adding anything else."

I eyed her, convinced she'd never actually adopt a pet. "How many cups is that?" I asked.

"It's the none-of-your-business cup." Erin's spoon clanked against the inside of her mug as she continued to stir.

"I just wonder how you get any sleep at night, drinking full-octane caffeine all day long."

"You know I'm a night owl, which is why I prefer working here from eleven to seven while you cover eight to five. Evenings are my most productive time."

"I do recall that," I replied mildly. When we'd opened the writing center, I'd asked Erin if she'd prefer a few earlier shifts, so she could have more of a social life, but she'd told me it wasn't necessary, especially if I agreed to cover for her when she taught her poetry class. The schedule worked for both of us, with our shifts overlapping to provide time for planning and discussion, as well as to allow us to alternate assisting students in the center and presenting in-class training sessions.

"Do you know what they plan to do about Barth's classes?" I asked before finishing up my macaroni and cheese.

"The rest of the department is filling in. Except for me, of course. I volunteered to teach one of his morning classes, but Gary said it wasn't necessary." Erin took a long swallow of her coffee. "He said he didn't want to affect the writing center schedule."

I laid down my fork. "It wouldn't, though. Not if the class was over by eleven."

"Which I explained in words even a toddler could understand." Erin sniffed. "I think he just doesn't want to give me any more leverage in the department. If I teach additional courses I could have more of a voice."

I stood and carried my dish and utensils to the sink. "I don't see where that would be an issue. You're as qualified as most of the faculty in that department."

"That's the problem, I guess." Erin's voice was edged with bitterness. "Gary knows I'm more progressive and would support Andrea Karmen and others who want to introduce new courses that actually reflect the current state of reading and writing. Like Doug, our department head has always quashed any movement toward new directions."

I turned my head to study her profile. She appeared disgruntled, which wasn't unusual when this subject came up. I knew Erin would've preferred a full-time teaching post, with the possibility of tenure, over working in the writing center. But in the four years since the center had been established, no faculty positions had opened up in the English department.

Until now. As I squirted a little dish soap on a sponge, I thought better than to mention the possibility of Erin applying for Doug Barth's position. It seemed a little ghoulish, given when, and how, he'd died.

After cleaning up from my impromptu meal, I retreated to my office to do some research for the next novel in my mystery series. I was off the clock and didn't mind Erin knowing what I was doing. I even shared some information when she poked her head around my office door to inform me that it was past six-thirty.

"Thanks for reminding me, but did you know," I said, twirling a pen between my fingers, "that if you spike someone's coffee with tetrahydrozoline, which can be found in almost all eyedrops, you can kill that person in a relatively short period of time?"

"Really?" Erin looked me over, her eyebrows raised. "Honestly, Jenn, I'm surprised the FBI hasn't raided us long before this, given your search history."

"What can I do? I'm ten books into the series. I've used all the normal methods. I have to come up with a few new ways to dispatch people."

Erin offered an exaggerated shudder in response. "All this talk of murder and death. Can we please give it a rest?"

"Sure, sure." I stood and turned off my computer. "I'm heading out now, unless you need me to stay to help close everything down. I just realized you'll be on your own, since none of our student assistants are here this evening."

"It's fine. There's less than thirty minutes left, and I can keep watch while finishing up some grading." Erin turned away and headed for the open door of her office.

Grabbing my jacket and tote bag off the coat tree near my desk, I rushed out of the writing center. Bri's house was only two streets away from the edge of the campus, but it was still a ten-minute walk.

Bri's neighborhood was popular with the lower-paid lecturers and university staff, and its eclectic style reflected their wide-ranging tastes. Most of the homes were bungalows, their brick or wooden siding contrasted by vibrant trim. In keeping with environmental awareness, many of the front yards were filled with shrubs and flowers instead of grass.

Bri's white-painted brick home, one of the smaller houses on her tree-lined street, boasted a three-color trim pattern—violet framing the windows, sky-blue scalloped siding on the dormers, and a front door as blazing yellow as a daffodil. I climbed the concrete steps to her front porch and rang the doorbell. Its melodic sound was echoed by the numerous wind chimes Bri had hung along the edge of the porch roof.

"Welcome," Bri said, opening the door and ushering me inside. "Now that we're all assembled, we can get down to business."

The interior of Bri's home was as colorful as the exterior, with a decidedly bohemian vibe. Colorful Indian-print cotton throws enlivened the wicker and rattan furniture, and the bookshelves were filled with interesting objects as well as books.

Christine, who was standing near one of the floor-to-ceiling white bookcases, picked up an embroidered fabric elephant. "You have quite a collection of stuff from other countries. Do you travel a lot?"

Bri tossed a few quilted pillows on the floor and flopped down on one end of the worn beige sofa. "Not me. My job doesn't allow that much free time. But my partner, Rachel, works for a nonprofit that helps craftspeople in developing countries sell their works around the globe. She's always collecting pieces from her travels."

"Is she off somewhere again?" I asked, as I draped my jacket over the back of an upholstered swivel chair and sat down.

"Unfortunately." Bri pursed her lips. "I applaud what she does, of course, but often feel like a widow. Glad we at least have video calls, or I might forget what she looks like."

Christine crossed the room and sat on the other end of the sofa. Rummaging through her voluminous leather purse, she pulled out a small spiral notebook. "Speaking of widows, that's one of the people I think the police need to check out."

"Miranda Barth?" Bri asked, with a quirk of her lips. "That seems unlikely."

"Not if you hear all the talk I do." Christine poured herself a glass of water from the plastic pitcher Bri had placed on the coffee table. "That's one thing about running the cafeteria: you can't help but pick up on a lot of conversations. Seems like people forget anyone's working behind the counter when they're choosing their food."

"They ignore the fact that you and the other workers are there, I guess," I said, mentally questioning how often I'd done the same thing.

Christine shrugged. "Being invisible has its perks."

"So what did you hear?" Bri asked, adjusting her position to face Christine.

"That things weren't going so well in the Barths' marriage."

I slid forward to the edge of my chair. "I heard rumors to that effect too. Were they actually talking divorce?"

"According to gossip, yes." Christine opened her notebook. "Also lots of whispering that Professor Barth was cheating on his wife."

"But if that's true, wouldn't his wife have the upper hand in a divorce?" Bri poured a glass of water.

"You'd think so, but it doesn't always work that way," Christine said. "And the thing is, Miranda Barth had the most to lose if they split."

I drummed my fingers against the padded arm of my chair. "Why?"

"Because there was no prenup, or so I've heard." Christine set her glass back on the coffee table.

Sensing Bri's interest, I added, "Miranda Barth comes from a wealthy family and has her own successful interior decorating business."

Bri flashed a wry smile. "Yeah, I guess a professor's salary couldn't compare to that."

"Not hardly," I said dryly. "She would've lost a lot to Doug if they had to split assets fifty-fifty."

"Couldn't using the rumored adultery help her? I mean, that is one of the few reasons you can file for a divorce claiming fault in Virginia." Bri shrugged when both Christine and I looked at her. "Had to research that for someone recently."

"If she could prove it." Christine's grim tone made me wonder if she'd dealt with a similar issue in the past. "That takes a lot of evidence, and even then, the judge might not grant any special considerations."

"If Doug wanted the divorce, and Miranda knew she'd stand to lose a small fortune . . ." Bri absently ran her finger around the rim of her glass.

I raised my eyebrows. "She may have decided that killing him was financially advantageous? But if she was the culprit, someone should've seen her in the library that day."

"Why would they notice? She'd be just another patron. Unless someone on staff or a student knew her personally, they wouldn't pay any attention." Bri took a sip of water. "Our library is open to outside patrons as well as the campus population, at least in terms of using our resources on site. We get a lot of local people wandering in and out. Miranda Barth could've come and gone with no one the wiser."

"Okay, she should go on the suspect list," I said.

Christine scribbled in her notebook. "Maybe add the mistress too? If Professor Barth was one of those guys who promise to leave their wives but never actually do it, she could've gotten angry enough to snap."

"Do we know who that is?" Bri asked. "I mean, according to rumors."

Scribbling again, Christine nodded. "Somebody called Paige Irving. Former student, they say. I don't remember her, but not all students eat at my cafeteria."

"Really? She sells real estate now. Haven't you seen those bus advertisements with her face plastered all over them?" Bri asked.

Christine shook her head. "I never take the bus. Live too far out for that."

"Paige Irving is a very attractive blonde in her late twenties. Nice enough, if a bit plastic." Bri held up her hands. "She showed us some houses before Rachel and I found this one. They were all too pricey, so I think she usually works with wealthier clientele."

"Interesting. I wonder what her major was when she was at Clarion," I said.

Bri gave me a wink. "English literature and creative writing."

"Aha!" Christine slipped the pen into the spiral binding and snapped shut the notebook. "Maybe this was a long-running affair?

If Professor Barth was stringing her along for years, she really could've snapped."

"Anyway, we've identified two more suspects," I said. "Which should help take the focus off of Mia."

"If the police listen to us." Christine's tone was glum.

Bri jumped up off the sofa. "They have an anonymous tip line. I can call in this info and urge them to investigate Miranda and Paige."

"They'll probably investigate Doug's wife anyway, but it wouldn't hurt to add fuel to that fire," Christine said. "Of course it's all based on gossip and circumstantial stuff."

"But so is the evidence against Mia at this point," I said.

"That's right." Bri hurried over to a console table and grabbed her cell phone. "Here we go, step one in our plan."

"Hopefully, it won't require too many more," I said.

Chapter Twelve

It was already dark when I left Bri's house. Gripping my keys in my fist with one key poking out, I was grateful for the presence of a few students once I left the more brightly lit neighborhood streets behind.

But as I headed away from the library, the number of students wandering the campus dwindled. I increased my pace as I reached the far end of campus, near the darkened science buildings. The lights of the parking lot beckoned, their bright orange-white glow promising more illumination than the decorative lampposts lining the campus walkways.

I'd just stepped onto the blacktop of the lot when a hand landed on my shoulder. Spinning around, I swung my tote bag, ready to slam it in an assailant's face.

"Whoa, no need to attack," Zach said, dropping his hand and stepping back.

"What are you doing, coming up behind someone at night like that?" I said, inwardly cursing the tremor in my voice.

"What are you doing, walking alone in the evening, with a possible murderer on campus?" Zach countered.

"It isn't that late." I shifted my tote bag strap to my other shoulder. "And I don't believe the person who murdered Doug Barth is some sort of serial killer, wandering around Clarion and indiscriminately striking down victims."

Zach looked me over with an expression that appeared, in the garish glow of the parking lot lights, rather sardonic. "This is based on your expansive knowledge of such killers, I suppose?"

"I do write murder mysteries," I said, straightening my spine to emphasize my full height. "Besides, I'm not the most likely victim. Being tall and rather big-boned has its advantages in some ways."

"Nonsense." Zach's expression hardened. "None of that matters if your assailant has a knife or a gun."

"Well, I've almost reached my car without any incident. Besides, there are still students roaming about."

Zach tapped one foot against the blacktop. "That didn't stop Doug Barth's assailant from shoving him off that mezzanine, now, did it? Walking by yourself at night is not smart, Jenn. Surely you know there are volunteers who work with campus police as escorts. You just have to call them when you leave your office at night."

"I didn't come from my office. I was at Brianna Rowley's house, off campus. It's close enough that I didn't bother to move my car." I turned and walked away from him. "Which is right over here, if you feel the need to play escort. Personally, I just want to get home."

"Don't tell me you were actually meeting up with Bri to create some sort of Scooby gang," Zach said, as he followed right behind me. "I know you're both determined to prove Mia Jackson wasn't involved in Doug Barth's death."

Reaching my car, I turned to face him. "Actually, Christine Kubiak was there too." Seeing his confusion, I jangled my keys. "Remember, she was with Bri today in the writing center."

"Yes, and I was trying to place her. Isn't she's one of the cafeteria managers? I was wondering why she wanted to get involved," Zach said.

"That's easy to explain—Mia was a student worker at Christine's cafeteria in her freshman and sophomore years."

"Which means what? That Mia was such a competent worker that she couldn't possibly be a killer?" Zach's eyes glinted behind the lenses of his glasses. "I'm not saying Ms. Jackson murdered Barth, but you need more than character witnesses to vouch for her innocence."

I leaned back against the cool metal of my car door. "We know that. But I, and the others, feel like the police are zeroing in on Mia without considering all the other possibilities. That was what we discussed—other people who could be suspects."

"I'm sure the police will consider the same individuals," Zach said. "They always look at a spouse, for example."

"Yes, but maybe they won't realize that the Barths were close to a divorce, or that Doug had a girlfriend. Or even if they do, they might not pursue those possibilities until *after* they've traumatized Mia."

Zach zipped up his ski-style jacket. "I still think you should leave such things to the police, but it's getting cold, so I won't bother to offer any more of my obviously unwanted opinions tonight. Get in your car and drive home. I'll wait until I see you drive away."

"Wow, you really like to play white knight, don't you?" I turned and unlocked my car door. "Anyway, if you actually want to help, maybe you could join me on a little fact-finding mission."

As I climbed into the driver's seat, Zach grabbed the top edge of my door. "Such as what?"

"Such as accompanying me to Miranda Barth's interior design showroom and playing the role of a homeowner seeking to renovate their house. I could tag along, saying we're friends." I looked up and met Zach's amused gaze. "I think if we could talk to her off the record, we might find out a lot more than the police will be able to discover."

"Are you asking me out on a date, Ms. Dalton?" Zach leaned over until his face was at the same level as mine.

"No," I said, with a frown. "I just want your help. I could go by myself, but I want to have another witness to whatever Miranda Barth might say."

Zach straightened and stepped away from the door. "Wouldn't I become part of your merry band of amateur detectives, then? What would I gain from this favor?"

"My undying gratitude," I said, in a tone that didn't support such words.

Zach shoved up his drooping glasses with one finger. "Hmm, not sure that's enough of a carrot."

"A free dinner at a restaurant of your choice?" I asked, shooting him a glance.

"That might be more of an inducement. I'll think about it and let you know." Zach grabbed my door handle. "Drive safe," he added, slamming the door shut.

I kept my eyes focused on the windshield before starting my engine and driving away.

Chapter Thirteen

The next day I received a text from Zach that simply said *M.B. visit, when?* I replied that I'd check to see when Miranda Barth would be back at her interior design company and received a terse *OK* in response.

The rest of the day provided no surprises until close to five, when I was preparing to leave. I'd already thrown on my fleece jacket and stuffed my small purse and a compact umbrella into my tote bag when Erin ushered a student into my office.

"Sorry, Jenn, but this young lady says she only wants to speak to you," Erin said, her lips curving down into a frown. I wondered if she was displeased with this request. Although she'd never said anything, it was possible she didn't like the idea that students might prefer me to her.

"It's fine," I said, meeting Francesca Silva's pleading gaze with a little bob of my head. "Just shut the door, would you?"

Erin mumbled something but complied.

"Sorry, but I need to tell you something in confidence," Francesca was dressed all in black, in a long, cardigan-style hooded jacket over a leotard, dance skirt, and tights.

I set my tote bag back on my desk. "Does this concern your roommate?"

"Yeah." Francesca stared down at her feet, one of which was pointed in an unconscious dancer's pose.

"You know where she is?"

"She wants to talk to you, but only you. I can take you to her, as long as you promise not to alert the police or anyone else," Francesca said, keeping her voice low.

I pressed my hand to my heart. "I promise."

Francesca looked me up and down. "Okay. But I'd like to leave first and have you follow me in about five minutes or so. I don't really want anyone to see us together." She tossed her dark hair, now free from its customary tight bun.

"Where should I meet you?" I asked, slinging the strap of my tote bag over one shoulder.

"You know that alley between the theater and music buildings? Let's meet there, then we can enter the music building through the back entrance." Francesa squared her slender shoulders. "I smuggled Mia into one of the dance studios that's never used this late in the day."

"Alright, you head out now. I can talk to Ms. McHenry about tomorrow's schedule to use up some time before I leave." I followed Francesca to the door. Pausing with my hand on the doorknob, I stared down into her deep brown eyes. They were still wary. "Don't worry. I won't tell anyone where Mia is."

Francesca tightened her lips and gave me a brisk nod. I opened the door and wished her a good day as she headed for the exit.

Erin, who was fiddling with the cords of one of our desktop computers, strolled over to me. "What was that all about? I've never seen that girl in here before, and she seemed unusually distressed."

"Nothing, really. Just the usual panic before a major project's looming due date."

Erin frowned. "I could've helped with that. You didn't have to stay late."

"It was only a few minutes," I said with a shrug. "Anyway, I wanted to ask you about tomorrow's schedule. Do we have enough student assistants signed up? You know how busy Fridays can be."

Once Erin retrieved the schedule from her office, I made a big show of examining it before I surreptitiously checked my watch. Five minutes had definitely passed. I offered Erin a quick "Good evening" and headed out of the writing center.

I reached the alley a short time later. Francesca, leaning against the brick wall of the theater building, stared at her cell phone screen in a perfect imitation of typical student behavior. But as I approached her, she straightened and waved me forward.

"Follow me," she said under her breath.

We circled around to the back of the music building and climbed the concrete steps of the loading dock in silence. Francesca tapped her student ID card on the keyless entry box.

"They allow students to use the building after hours for extra rehearsal time," she said. "Up until midnight, anyway."

"Won't there be too many people here right now, then?" I asked as I followed her inside.

Francesca flashed me a smile. "Not that many dancers take advantage of the late hours. We do our workouts and practice early, and at this time in the semester most of us are rehearsing some production or other in the theater spaces upstairs."

"Ah, I see." I quickly assessed the dim corridors lined with closed doors. Signs on the doors indicated a mix of studio space and offices.

One of the office doors opened, causing me to stop in my tracks. A handsome man in his forties stepped out into the corridor. I recognized him immediately—Richard Muir, the frequent dance partner of, and co-company director with, Karla Tansen.

"Mr. Muir, why are you here so late? We didn't have a rehearsal this evening, and I thought you only taught that one studio in the morning." Francesca batted her black lashes as she stared up at his face.

Richard Muir's neutral expression told me that he was accustomed to and unmoved by the flattering attention of young dancers. Only his clear gray eyes, framed by lashes as dark and thick as Francesca's, expressed a touch of amusement.

"Paperwork. Always the bane of my existence," he said, with a glance at me. "Are you here to rehearse, Francesca?"

I breathed a sigh of relief. He probably assumed I was some accompanist Francesca had hired so she could work on pieces for her graduate recital.

"No. I just left a book in the studio earlier and thought I'd stop by and pick it up." Francesca gestured toward me. "This is Ms. Dalton from the writing center. Once I grab that book, I'm going to buy her a coffee as a thank you for helping me with a project for my dance history class."

"Hello." Richard Muir's smile was definitely charming. I could see why so many dance students had crushes on him. But I also knew, from those same students' despairing comments in the writing center, that he was devoted to his wife, one of the codirectors of the public library in Taylorsford. "I don't believe we've met, Ms. Dalton."

"No, but I understand that you aren't on campus that much these days," I said, shaking his proffered hand. "I'm a fan of your new dance troupe, which I imagine takes up most of your time."

"That and choreography projects," he replied. Turning to Francesca, he added. "Let me know if you need any coaching for your

recital. I'd be happy to sit in on one of your rehearsals at some point."
He glanced back at me. "She's quite talented. I hope she might audition for our troupe once she graduates."

"Might? Of course I will," Francesca said, with a fervor that brought another smile to Richard Muir's face.

"Good. Well, I'd better get going. I promised my wife I'd pick up some dinner on the way home tonight, and I can't be too late or my ravenous twins will pester her to death." Richard Muir tapped his forehead in a little salute. "Nice to meet you, Ms. Dalton. Always happy to greet a fan of the company."

"Nice to meet you as well," I told him before he turned and strode away.

"Too bad he's married," Francesca said, after Muir exited through the back doors.

I looked down at her, my lips twitching. "He's a good bit too old for you."

Francesca sighed. "Makes it more romantic."

"That's only in books and movies. That sort of age gap usually doesn't work out too well in real life."

"Anyway"—Francesca rolled her shoulders as if tossing off my words—"here we are. Mia's inside. I'll let you in and then leave you two alone to talk. Oh, and she asked that you drop your cell phone on the table just inside the door." She tapped her ID card against the scanner and pulled open the door to a dimly lit studio. "I think she's hiding out behind the piano in the corner."

I thanked Francesca, who waved this off and walked away once I grabbed the door and held it ajar. Slipping inside, I closed the door behind me, then pulled out my phone and laid it on the table. I made my way across the bare wooden floor toward the piano Francesca had mentioned, which was an old black upright, turned so I couldn't see the keyboard.

I waited until I was closer to call out Mia's name. "It's Jenn Dalton. Your roommate says you want to talk to me."

"You didn't tell anyone? And no one followed you?" Mia's voice sounded ragged, as if she'd been crying too much for too long.

"I'm all alone," I said, lifting my hands.

Stepping out from behind the piano, Mia stared at me for a moment. "So am I," she said, before bursting into tears.

Chapter Fourteen

I rushed to her and gave her a hug. "I'm so glad to see you."

"Happy you're here." Mia returned my hug, then stepped back. She yanked a tissue from her pocket and wiped her eyes and nose. "It feels like everyone else is against me. Not counting Francesca, who's been great."

"There's been much too much of a rush to judgment," I said. "It seems like everyone's convinced you killed Doug Barth because of your argument and the story found near his body, but I simply don't believe that."

"I knew you'd be on my side." As Mia squared her shoulders, her oversized cotton sweater slipped down her arm, exposing one shoulder. I felt a flicker of concern that she was running around without a coat until I noticed a heavy black cardigan draped over the top of the piano. "I was going to come forward sooner, but I was afraid no one would believe me."

"You did argue with Professor Barth the day he was killed, though?" I asked.

Mia tugged her black sweater back over her shoulder. "Yeah, but when I stormed off, he was still alive, I swear."

"I believe you but must warn you—at least one person witnessed your fight." I examined Mia. She appeared to have lost weight, something she couldn't afford to do. She was nearly as tall as me, yet I suspected she weighed at least twenty pounds less than I did. "Are you eating properly and getting enough sleep? You look worn down."

Mia made a face. "Yes, *Mom*, don't worry."

"Appearances to the contrary, I'm not old enough to be your mother," I said dryly. We'd had this discussion before, when Mia had complained that I was nagging her as much as her mother did. But I knew Mia wasn't really upset by my concern for her. I'd mentored her ever since she first came to the writing center to interview me for the student newspaper. While we spoke about the center, Mia became intrigued by my second career as an author. As she'd told me at the time, she wanted to write romance novels, including historicals and rom-coms, and was intrigued by my success in genre fiction.

"I know." Mia shuffled her feet. "I should've stayed on the scene when I found him, but I was so shocked—"

"Wait, you saw Doug Barth *after* he fell?"

Mia bit her lower lip. "I came back to get my story. We'd argued about the grade he gave me. I was sure it was simply because he disapproved of me writing genre fiction, not the story itself. He told me it was the writing as well, but I knew that both you and Ms. McHenry had loved that story, so I told him he was lying and threw my story at him. I dashed off then, but once I was in the stairwell, all the way down at the first floor, actually, I thought better of abandoning my manuscript because I needed that copy, dripping with Professor Barth's very biased comments, to plead my case with Dr. Alexander."

"So you went back and found his body," I said, eyeing her with sympathy.

"He was on the floor, all crumpled and bleeding . . ." Mia buried her face in her hands.

"You're sure he was already dead?" I asked.

Mia looked up at me, tears glistening in her dark brown eyes. "I checked to see if he was breathing, but it didn't seem like he was, so I . . . I panicked. I'd never seen a dead body before, and we'd just been talking, and . . ." She raked her fingers through her tight black curls. "I know I should've immediately called 911, but it was like my mind went blank."

"You didn't see anyone else in the area?" I asked. "I mean, the murder had to have occurred soon after you left the first time."

"That's the worst part, I did, I did." Mia leaned against the side of the piano, gripping the edge of the top as if needing a support to remain on her feet. "I heard a noise above me and looked up and saw a figure standing on the mezzanine. They were wearing dark clothes and were all bundled up. Like in a hoodie, with a scarf wrapped around their nose, mouth, and chin, and the edge of the hood pulled down to shadow the rest of their face. From my angle, I couldn't tell much about their build or height or anything like that. Not even if it was a man or a woman."

"But they saw you?" I asked, a frisson of fear running down my spine.

Mia audibly swallowed. "They had to have seen me pretty clearly."

"What happened then?"

"They spoke—in some fake, growly tone. They warned me if I said anything, I was next." Mia wrapped her arms over her chest, hugging her own shoulders.

I inhaled a deep breath. "They threatened you?"

"Yeah, so I ran. Into the stacks at first. But when you showed up, I decided to escape. I just couldn't face anyone, or anything, right then. I dashed down the stairs and out into the main floor lobby and then ran outside. After that, I don't really remember. I know I ended up at my dorm room, and Francesca was there."

I laid a hand on Mia's shoulder. "Is that the other reason you're hiding out now? Because you believe the killer saw you?"

Mia gnawed on her lower lip and bobbed her head.

I dropped my hand and examined her tear-streaked face. Her story sounded plausible, and I could certainly understand how fear could have driven her into hiding. *But,* I reminded myself, *the mysterious stranger on the mezzanine could simply be a fabrication.*

The truth was, no one else had mentioned this person, and they'd certainly have had difficulty fleeing the library before I arrived on the scene. Although, to play devil's advocate, the culprit could've removed the hoodie and scarf easily enough, dashed to another floor, and blended in with other library patrons.

I held out my hands. "I understand why you'd feel too frightened to come forward, but I think you have to. You need to tell your side of the story and clarify the facts. Otherwise the police will continue to keep you as their number one suspect."

"I wish I could do that, but I'm sure the real killer is watching me. If I go to the police, they'll find a way to murder me too." Mia gripped my hands.

"The police can protect you," I said.

"Really?" Mia dropped my hands and took a step back. "Francesca has kept me up to date on all the rumors. Everyone believes I killed Professor Barth, even the campus and town police. What makes you think they'll bother to protect me when they're convinced I'm the murderer?"

"Not everyone. You know I don't believe that you're to blame, and neither do Christine Kubiak or Brianna Rowley. In fact, we've formed a sort of amateur detective team to try to uncover other suspects and information that can clear your name."

"Ms. Kubiak is doing that? And that reference librarian I've worked with once or twice?" Mia dabbed at her eyes with the tissue. "That's . . . really sweet. But I still don't feel safe enough to come forward. Maybe if you discover some real evidence that'll exonerate me, I'll reconsider." Mia backed into the shadows. "Tell Francesca if you do. She'll know how to find me."

Before I could protest this arrangement, Mia grabbed her sweater off of the piano and slipped out the studio's back door. Caught off guard, I stood motionless for a moment, then ran after her.

But when I exited the studio the same way, the corridor was empty. At the far end of the hall, a heavy door closed with a bang, alerting me that Mia had fled the building.

I decided not to chase after her. From my research, I knew I was on shaky ground already. If, by some fluke, Mia had killed Doug, even accidentally, what I was doing could be considered "aiding and abetting."

No, I wouldn't run after Mia. I'd leave the building through the front doors and head for my car and drive home instead. I still wanted to help her, but I had to be sensible about how I went about it.

The protagonists in my novels could take wild chances, but they always had me to get them out of a jam—or jail. But since I didn't live in a book, I didn't have that luxury.

Chapter Fifteen

The sun had slipped behind the frieze of trees that lined the northern edge of the campus when I descended the stone steps of the music building. Violet ribbons streaked the charcoal sky as the light swiftly faded. I reached the main brick pathway that separated one side of a stretch of lawn from classrooms and other buildings just as the solar-powered lamplights flickered on.

I tightened my grip on my tote bag and lengthened my stride as I headed for the parking lot. That morning I'd been able to park closer to the library, which hadn't turned out to be an advantage, since it was farther from the music building. I also had to cross over to the other side of the central lawn, which included a few small groves of trees.

The campus appeared strangely quiet for early evening. I glanced around me, unnerved by the lack of activity. I supposed it was because it was dinnertime, and most of the students were in one of the dining halls or had already left campus for the night. I wasn't usually around at this time of day, except when attending performances or special functions, and hadn't realized how deserted the academic portion of campus could feel in the evening.

A rustle of leaves was followed by the fall of footsteps. I stopped short and turned in a circle, looking for the source of the sound, but saw no one.

I took off again. The path that crossed the lawn led down through a depression encircled by trees and filled with rhododendrons and azaleas. The lamplights were spaced farther apart, casting pools of light amid growing shadows. I reached into my tote bag to grab my cell phone, planning to use its built-in light like a flashlight.

My fingers scrabbled over my wallet, comb, several pens, and other objects without landing on the smooth surface of my phone. It was then that I realized I'd left it on the table in the dance studio.

Swearing under my breath, I slid the bag strap back up on my shoulder and took off at a jog, my hard-soled loafers thudding against the packed-dirt path. But the sound seemed strangely syncopated. *That's not just me*, I realized. My footfalls were being echoed by other steps behind me.

As I spun around, a dark figure disappeared behind the intertwined branches of two tall shrubs. It wasn't my imagination, then—I was being followed.

Silently cursing my lack of a cell phone, I glanced wildly around, hoping to find a large branch or some other object that could function as a weapon. I could try to run, of course, but I wasn't the fastest and had no idea how swiftly the person tracking me could move. If they overtook me, I wanted something I could use to beat them off. But spying nothing I could grab quickly enough, I simply took off at jog again.

Hands slammed into my shoulder blades, shoving me forward. I stumbled and fell, my tote bag flying off my shoulder as my hands flailed against the air. Hitting the path with my knees first, I retained enough sense to catch myself so my forehead didn't bang against the hard ground.

The edge of a long black garment fell across my body and an obviously disguised voice whispered in my ear, "Stop now or you won't live to regret it."

I rolled to my side, attempting to catch a glimpse of my attacker, but at that moment a thunder of footfalls overtook the sound of anyone slipping away.

"Oh, man, are you alright?" A husky young man in a fluorescent orange tracksuit knelt down in front of me.

I struggled to a sitting position. "I'm fine."

"Not really," said a girl who was also wearing running gear. "Your hands are trashed, and your knees don't look too good either."

I glanced down at my pants. One knee was caked in dirt and the other sported a gaping rip stained with blood seeping from a jagged gash. A quick examination of my palms also revealed scraped skin and smears of blood.

"I am a mess, aren't I?" I said, trying to sound nonchalant. "That's what happens when you don't pay attention to where you're going. Anyway, could you help me up?"

The students each took hold of one of my elbows and lifted me to my feet. "What happened?" the young man asked. "Did you trip over a rock or something? It's kind of dark in this area, which is why we're always extra careful when we run this route."

I considered mentioning the stranger who'd pushed me but thought better of it. My attacker had obviously been following me. Since I was their target, I was pretty sure they wouldn't bother these students, and I really didn't want to say something that could morph into another campus rumor.

And there was that black garment. So similar to the sweater Mia grabbed when she left the studio . . .

"You're right, I was just careless," I said, shaking that thought from my head. "Thanks for your help, but please go on with your run. Like I said, I'm fine. I'll probably have to toss these pants, but other than a few scrapes, there's no real harm done."

The young woman eyed me dubiously. "I don't know. That knee is awfully banged up. Why don't we walk you to health services? They always have someone there for emergencies."

"Really, that's not necessary," I said, as the young man leaned down to pick up my tote bag. "I'd hate to interrupt your exercise."

"It's okay, we can just run another circuit after we drop you off." The young man slung the tote bag strap over his shoulder. "And that way I can carry this for you."

With the initial shock fading, pain was blooming throughout my body. I didn't look forward to hauling the tote bag to my car, and the dampness of my right knee and lower leg told me that blood was still flowing from that wound. "Alright. I appreciate it. By the way, what are your names?"

"Max," the young man said. "And this is Laura."

I thanked them again before hobbling back to the brick path, Max on one side of me and Laura on the other. We reached the student health center right at the moment the pain in my knee forced me to collapse onto one of the chairs in the small waiting room.

An older woman popped out of an office with a plate glass window and blinds opened to allow its occupant to keep an eye on anyone entering the building. "Oh my, what happened?" the woman asked. The name tag pinned to her lilac scrubs identified her as Caroline Bell, RN.

"She fell on that path that runs across the middle of campus," Laura said. "Good thing we were out running and saw her."

"That was fortunate." Caroline Bell offered the students a warm smile. "That gash on your knee might need stitches," she added, shifting her gaze to me. "Unfortunately, I can't do much since you aren't a student. We have restrictions about treating faculty and staff, unless it is an absolute emergency."

"Didn't realize that," Max said, shooting me a sheepish smile. "I guess we should've called 911 or something."

"It's hardly that serious." I shifted in the chair so I could face the nurse. "Maybe just give me an extra-large Band-Aid? If there's a public restroom, I can wash up and bandage the worst spot myself, then be on my way."

"What's this?" Zach stepped out of one of the doors that apparently led to a private area of the clinic. He strode over to my chair. "How did you get injured, Jenn?"

"I fell on a path. Luckily these two students were taking an early evening run and helped me out."

"That's good." Zach's gaze swept over Max and Laura before landing on Ms. Bell. "Can't you do anything, Caroline?"

She crossed her arms over her chest. "You know the rules, Dr. Flynn. Our insurance doesn't cover faculty and staff."

"Right, right." Zach knelt down in front of me and examined my blood-soaked knee. "That's a nasty cut. I think it would be best to see someone at an urgent care facility."

I waved my hand in his face. "No, no. If I clean it up and slap on a bandage, it'll be fine."

Zach's glasses had slipped down his nose. He shoved them up as he fixed me with an imperious stare. "When was the last time you had a tetanus shot?"

"Um, well . . ." I cleared my throat. "I guess I don't remember."

"Oh, you need to check on that, what with getting a cut on a dirty path and all," Caroline Bell said.

"See." Zach stood up. "The medical professional has spoken. Come on, Jenn. I can drive you to the closest urgent care. It isn't far."

I slid back in the chair. "It's too much trouble."

"Hey, I'd do it," Laura said, concern clouding her eyes. "We just learned about tetanus in my health sciences class and it's nothing to mess with."

Max vigorously nodded in agreement. "Better go with the doctor. And since you're in good hands now, we'll be off."

I thanked the students again. Waiting until they'd left the clinic, I rose to my feet. Or tried to, anyway. I hadn't counted on how wobbly my legs would feel. Wavering slightly, I clutched the top rail of an adjacent ladderback chair.

Zach grabbed my other arm. "Sure, you'll simply slap on a Band-Aid and do what? Stagger to your car? Good way to develop a bad reputation."

I shot him a fierce glance from under my lowered lashes. Those words reminded me of his impromptu lecture that night in the bar. "I may need to rest for a few more minutes, but I can manage."

Caroline Bell tsked and shook her head. "You should accept Dr. Flynn's offer. He's right about that knee wound needing proper care. And a tetanus shot wouldn't go amiss, not if you don't remember when you had one last."

"Oh, very well." I reached for my tote bag, which Max had set on the chair beside me.

Zach loosened his grip on my other arm. "Are you feeling steady enough now for me to let go? I just need to grab my jacket and briefcase from the office and we can head out. My car's in the lot nearby, so you won't have that much of a walk."

"I'm fine," I said.

When Zach disappeared through the door that obviously led to exam rooms and offices, Caroline Bell looked at me with a critical gaze. "If you're sure you're okay, I'm going to head back to my own office. I have a ton of paperwork to tackle, as always."

Gritting my teeth as a flash of pain stabbed my knee, I waved her aside. "Thanks, I'm good."

"I'll leave you in Dr. Flynn's capable hands, then. Sorry I couldn't be more help, but we have to be careful of lawsuits. I'm sure you understand."

I mumbled something about red tape as she returned to the office.

Zach paused as he entered through the other door. He fiddled with the doorknob, obviously making sure the door had locked behind him. "Sorry, but I didn't want to leave my things here, especially since I won't be back until next week."

"You really don't need to do this," I said.

He studied me as he slipped on his jacket and slid the strap of his briefcase over one shoulder. "Please stop complaining about me helping you. It's part of my responsibility as a doctor."

"You're not that kind of doctor," I said.

Zach tucked one hand through the bend in my arm, adjusting his hold to provide me with extra support on the side with the injured knee. "Mind and body, body and mind, it's all intertwined, don't you think?" he said while guiding me out of the clinic.

I grimaced when we stepped onto the rough brick walkway. "The only thing I'm thinking about right now is putting one foot in front of the other."

Zach cast me a sardonic smile. "Maybe you should've been thinking about that before you fell."

Chapter Sixteen

We didn't speak as Zach drove me to the urgent care facility, until he parked and ordered me to stay seated until he could help me out of the car. I didn't protest, happy to lean on him to traverse the parking lot and enter the building. Not unexpectedly, the urgent care facility was crowded. I squirmed on the hard plastic seat of the chair the receptionist had pulled from one of the back rooms. With all the cushioned clinic chairs full, Zach was forced to stand, leaning against one of the walls.

"Really, you don't need to wait here with me," I told him. "I can get a ride to my car easily enough."

He looked down at me with a frown. "That's not necessary. I don't have any particular place to be this evening, so I'll just wait and give you a lift home. Not sure you should be driving."

I winced as I adjusted my leg. "And how would I get to work tomorrow if my car is left on campus? Besides, I live in Taylorsford. That's probably going to be out of your way."

"That's actually what makes it so convenient," Zach said. "I live in Taylorsford too."

"What? I've never seen you around town," I said, shooting him a surprised glance.

"Between working at my practice in Harburg and at Clarion, I'm not around much. At least, not where I'd run into a lot of the locals." Zach straightened until his back was away from the wall.

"You own a home there?" I asked.

"I do. A small cottage on the lane behind the library."

"What made you buy there when your work is here?"

"Why do you live there?" Zach countered, his frown replaced by a faint smile.

I shrugged. "Got a good deal on rent, and I really like the town. It's quieter. A good place for writing."

Zach slipped off his glasses and wiped them with the lens cloth he'd pulled from his pocket. "Oh, right, I forgot about your second career."

I opened my mouth to protest that my writing wasn't exactly second to my work on campus, then closed my lips. If Zach had forgotten about it, he was obviously not one of my fans. "You must prefer living in Taylorsford as well, then."

"I do, but it's more about self-preservation." He put his glasses back on. "In my profession it's preferable to live at some distance from work. At least far enough that you aren't continually running into patients on your morning jog."

"I hadn't thought of that," I said, admitting to myself that it was a smart move.

"Jenn, what happened to you?" asked the slender, dark-haired woman striding out from hall that led to exam rooms. She had one hand on the shoulder of a boy who was nearly her height but looked to be no more than twelve. One of his sweatshirt sleeves was pushed up to his elbow and a gauze bandage wrapped his forearm.

"Just a minor fall," I said. "But what brings you here, Laney?"

"This guy." As Laney patted the boy's shoulder he rolled his eyes. "My son, Elliot, is a regular. Today it was stitches after falling off his mountain bike."

"Mom," Elliot said, drawing the word out.

"This is Jenn Dalton. She runs the writing center at Clarion," Laney told her son. She looked at Zach, her forehead wrinkling. "I know you from Clarion too. Doctor something?"

"Flynn," Zach said. "I work in the health clinic part-time. Psychologist," he added, "so not as much help with illness or injuries."

"That's right—You presented a lecture to my department once." Laney thrust out her free hand. "I'm Laney Lee, a lecturer in the English department." After a quick shake of Zach's hand, Laney turned her attention back on me. "Sorry to hear you hurt yourself, Jenn, especially after everything you've been through recently."

"I guess everyone knows all about that," I said glumly.

"Well, I heard it from a direct source, not just the rumor mill," Laney said. "Andrea Karmen, whose office is next to mine, told me what happened. She just barely missed finding the body herself, you know. She witnessed a fight between Professor Barth and that student. If she'd followed them to the sixth floor—"

"Yes, she told me," I said, eager to wave aside this speculation. "Anyway, this injury is no big deal." I let out a squawk as I shifted my legs, belying my words.

"That's a nasty cut. Injury on top of emotional trauma, so unfair." Laney glanced at Zach. "I guess you also know that Jenn stumbled over poor Professor Barth's body in the library. It must've been such a shock."

"It wasn't the best day I've ever had," I admitted.

"You found the dead guy?" Elliot's deep-brown eyes widened.

"Unfortunately." The boy's obvious interest in this subject reminded me why I'd never wanted to work with preteens. I knew their innate fascination with all things ghoulish or gross was a normal aspect of growing up, but I'd never wanted to deal with it as a teacher.

"I've thought of that," Laney said, with an exaggerated shudder. "I don't think I'd have handled it as well as you have, Jenn. I'd probably need to make an appointment to see you, Dr. Flynn."

"Zach," he corrected.

Laney nodded. "Got it. I suspect you're distancing yourself from your profession because of strangers asking for psychological advice? I know the drill. My dad was a cardiologist and people were always pestering him outside the office."

"It is an occupational hazard," Zach said, with a smile.

Elliot banged Laney's arm with his elbow. "Come on, Mom. I wanna go home."

"Okay, okay." Laney shot him an exasperated look. "Nice to meet you, Dr. Flynn. And you take care, Jenn. I hope they can deal with your cut without stitches."

"Hopefully," I said, gazing down at my knee with a frown. "But it will heal, in any case." I wished her and Elliot a good evening.

"So Andrea Karmen was there too?" Zach asked after Laney and her son left the clinic. "I mean, in the library when you found Barth's body."

"Apparently. She says she saw Doug Barth and Mia Jackson arguing a little while before his fall, but then they both went up to the top floor." I glanced over at the message board that indicated who was in line for treatment. Thankfully, my name was next.

"I assume no one has confirmed that information?"

I looked up at him, registering his thoughtful expression. "Not as far as I know. And yes, I've wondered if she was somehow involved. I hate to think that way, but—"

"You can't help but be suspicious?" Zach shot me an inquiring glance. "It would be convenient to say you saw two people arguing before one of them was killed. If you were the murderer, that is. It immediately throws suspicion on the other person, the one you claimed was part of the original confrontation."

I narrowed my eyes as I continued to stare at him. "Now who's playing amateur detective? Andrea Karmen is a friend of mine. Not a close friend, but—"

"Friend or not, if you're determined to investigate, you have to consider all the angles."

"I know," I said with a sigh. "She did have opportunity and also apparently had a motive."

"Still, it would be a shame if a friend turned out to be a murderer." Zach's expression turned stern as he crossed his arms. "This is what you're playing with, Jenn. People's lives."

Before I could respond, my name was called by a nurse holding a clipboard. Grimacing, I rose to my feet. Zach reached for my arm, but I waved him aside. "I can manage, thanks. And I really can get myself home, so you can take off now."

Zach sat down in my vacated chair. "I'll wait."

Chapter Seventeen

Fortunately, once my knee wound was thoroughly cleaned, the doctor said all I needed was antibiotic cream and a proper bandage. She also prescribed some painkillers along with topical and oral antibiotics.

"The thing is, you shouldn't drive for a couple of days," she said, as she cleaned the scrapes on my hands. "You're going to be stiff and sore, and unfortunately, it's your right leg. It'll be tough to grip the steering wheel properly too. Can you manage without a car?"

"Not if I want to get to work," I said, gritting my teeth while she rubbed cream into my palms.

"Might need to get a ride to and from, then," the doctor said, rolling back her stool and stripping off her surgical gloves.

I thanked her and left the exam room, muttering about the inconvenience of the situation as I crossed to Zach's chair.

"All done?" he asked, standing to face me.

"Yes, although I need to stop by the drugstore to pick up the prescriptions the doctor called in," I said. "Which is going to put you out even more, I'm afraid."

"Don't worry about it. Consider it contributing to my good karma." Zach picked up my tote bag off the floor.

96

I didn't respond to this, simply hobbled out of the urgent care facility with him following close behind me. "Too bad we had to park so far out," I said as we slowly made our way down the sidewalk.

"Why don't you wait here. I can bring the car around," Zach said, stretching out his arm to prevent me from stepping onto the blacktop of the lot.

"That's really not necessary," I said as he dashed off, my tote bag banging against his hip.

With my right knee throbbing and the rest of my body aching, I relinquished any attempt to follow him or to retain my pride. *It doesn't matter*, I told myself. *This is one of those situations where you have to take any help that's available.*

His midnight-blue compact sedan pulled up in front of me, parking lights flashing. Zach got out and crossed around to the passenger side to open the door and help me gingerly climb inside.

Zach took the same back roads that I usually did, which was another mark of intelligence in my book. We didn't speak for the first several miles. Finally, Zach asked for directions to my house.

"Do you know where Emily Moore lives? She's something of a celebrity in Taylorsford so I thought you might know her house."

Zach side-eyed me. "You live with Emily Moore?"

"No, I rent her guesthouse."

"Ah, okay. It's on Main Street, about a block from the library, right?"

"Correct," I replied, then whimpered as Zach's car hit a pothole.

"Sorry. This road needs to be repaved, but they never seem to get around to it." Zach glanced over at me. "I assume you'll stay home from work tomorrow?"

"I will, but just the one day," I said. "I'll have to figure out something after that."

Zach lifted one hand off the steering wheel. "Well, I travel to Harburg every day, either to my practice or to the campus. I could easily drop you off, even on my non-campus days."

"That's very generous, but—"

"You don't want to owe me any favors?" The lilt in Zach's voice clearly betrayed his amusement.

I leaned my right arm against the doorframe. "That's part of it. Also, our schedules might not match."

"My schedule is pretty flexible. Appointments can be shifted around if necessary." Zach gripped the wheel again, his eyes fixed on the windshield.

"I don't want you to have to do that. Anyway, about that favor thing—I did want to ask for one, and I'm afraid you acting as my chauffeur might be pressing my luck."

"What's that? Are you planning to take me up on that free hour of therapy?"

"Hardly. No, it's the visit to Miranda Barth's design studio. There's no rush, since I found out she won't be at work for a week or so, but I'd still like to do that," I said.

"Right, the visit where you want me to pretend I'm redecorating and you're along as a friend, or some such thing." Zach cast me a sly grin. "I suppose I could pull that off, even if I think it's a fool's errand."

"All the same, if you agree to that, I don't want to impose on you for anything else."

"It's not an imposition," Zach said, as we turned off a back road onto the main road leading into Taylorsford. "Your place isn't that far from mine. I can easily swing by and pick you up in the morning and drop you off in the evening."

"Just on Friday," I said. "I should be fine after the weekend."

"We'll see. Now, I assume your prescriptions were called in to our one and only drugstore?"

"Exactly. The one in the strip mall coming up on your left."

Fortunately, even though it was the sole drugstore for miles, it had a drive-up window. I was glad I wouldn't have to get out of the car. But my hands shook so hard when I tried to pass my ID to Zach to hand to the clerk, my driver's license fell into his lap.

He picked it up, glancing at my decidedly unattractive photo before handing it off. "Must've been another rough day," he said.

I wrinkled my nose. "Everyone has bad license pictures."

"A generalization, but relatively accurate." Zach turned to me, his eyes hidden by the semi-darkened lenses of his glasses. "But that photo really doesn't look like you. For which you should be eternally grateful."

I hmphed and slid back in the car seat. The clerk handed over three brown bags, each labeled with the medicine's name and an instruction sheet.

Zach passed the bags to me. "You might want to stuff these in that tote bag of yours. It'll make them easier to carry."

"I think I could've figured that out," I said under my breath.

I expected my words to be swallowed by the rev of the engine as Zach pulled away from the drugstore, but Zach's wicked grin told me otherwise. Deciding that silence was my best response, I stared straight ahead once we were back on the road.

Zach slowed down as we reached the center of town, where there was more pedestrian activity. "Have you been to the library here?" he asked as we passed by the vintage stone building. "It's small, but the staff is very helpful. They've gotten me several interlibrary loans faster than the Clarion library ever has."

"No, I honestly haven't," I said. "Since I work in the university library, I never thought I needed anything from the public library."

Zach cast me a questioning glance. "Really? It's a great space, even if you aren't looking for resources. One of the original Carnegie libraries. They also house the town archives, which I imagine could provide interesting materials for a local writer."

"I'm not really a local. I grew up elsewhere and only came here for work." I tapped his arm. "It's the next house on the right—the brick bungalow."

"I know," Zach said, as he turned into the driveway. "I assume your rental is around back?"

"Right here," I said as he pulled up in front of the guest house. "It's a converted garage."

"Very nice." Zach got out of the car.

"Just open the door for me," I said. "I can walk from here."

Emily appeared on the back porch. "Who are you?" she called out to Zach.

He paused, his hand on the door handle. "Hello, Ms. Moore. You probably don't know me, but I work at Clarion too. At the health clinic. I'm Dr. Zachary Flynn." He opened my door and helped me out. "Ms. Dalton had an unfortunate accident on campus today and isn't supposed to drive, so I escorted her home."

"He lives in Taylorsford, you see," I said, as Emily hurried out the back door and down the steps.

"Oh dear, what happened?" she asked, crossing to us.

"Just a fall on a dirt path. Nothing too dire," I replied.

Emily examined me, her gaze resting on my bandaged knee for a moment before she looked up into my face. "Goodness. You really took a tumble. Are you sure you'll be okay on your own tonight? I have a spare room you can use if necessary."

"I'll be fine. Truly." The thought struck me that this was an extraordinary gesture on the part of a woman who liked to protect her privacy. I offered her a warm smile. "But thanks so much."

There was a glint of calculation in Emily's eyes as she shifted her gaze from me to Zach and back again. "Of course, if Dr. Flynn is staying with you . . ."

"No!" Zach and I said in unison.

Emily chuckled. "No offense meant. Not that you can't have men over, Jenn. You know I don't care about such things. I just draw the line at raucous parties." She winked. "Even if I was a participant in quite a few when I was a good bit younger."

I fished my keys out of my tote bag and hobbled over to my front door while Zach exchanged a few more pleasantries with Emily. But before I could sneak inside, he ran over and slipped a business card into the pocket of my jacket.

"Let me know about picking you up on Friday," he called out as he walked back to his car. He offered Emily a warm goodbye, then took off.

Emily followed me into the guesthouse. "Are you certain you want to be alone tonight?"

"Yes, please. I appreciate the offer of help, but I just want to collapse into my bed. Besides," I added, as a plaintive meow filled the air, "I'm not totally alone."

Emily made me promise to call her if I had any problems. Pausing in the doorway, she wished me a restful night, then added, "You say Dr. Flynn lives in Taylorsford? That's convenient, isn't it?"

She didn't wait for my reply before closing the door.

Chapter Eighteen

I spent the following day on the sofa, binge-watching a British mystery series on TV, with Ash curled up next to me. My body felt like I'd been rolled around in a giant rock tumbler, complete with the rocks. But later in the evening I still called Zach on the landline Emily had installed in the guest house and asked him to pick me up the next morning.

We didn't talk much on the ride in on Friday. I blamed my lack of concentration on my pain pills, but the truth was I was just too tired to try to spar with Zach. For his part, he appeared content to remain silent, except for an occasional query about how I was doing.

Zach dropped me off near the back door to the library so I didn't have too far to walk. I slipped inside and reached the elevator as quickly as possible, but my shuffling gait and scraped hands still drew unwanted attention as I entered the library. Several students and staff asked me what had happened. I simply repeated, "Fell on a walking path. Nothing serious," which seemed to satisfy their curiosity.

Erin, who I'd contacted the day before to explain my absence, wanted more details.

"It was simply me being clumsy and falling over my own feet," I said. "Fortunately, some students were out jogging and they took me to the clinic." I decided not to bring Zach's name into the situation, just to make the story less confusing.

I also didn't tell her I'd been pursued and pushed. That was a piece of information I hadn't even told Zach, due to my concern that it might further implicate Mia. She'd been wearing all-black when I met her in the studio, and her cardigan had a hood she could've pulled up to hide her hair and face. I didn't want to believe that Mia had waited outside the music building and stalked me, but I couldn't rule it out.

Of course, Francesca had been wearing black too. Not wanting anyone to jump to conclusions about either girl before I had a chance to do a little more digging, I didn't mention the attack.

I called Bri around lunchtime to fill her in on my "accident" and to ask her if she'd run to the dance studio and see if my cell phone was still there.

"Sure thing. I'll bring it to you if I find it," Bri said. "But what were you doing in a dance studio?"

"Practicing my pliés," I said dryly. "Sorry," I added, with a quick glance out my office window. Erin was puttering around in the main room of the writing center. Although I didn't think she'd deliberately eavesdrop, I felt it was best to share sensitive information with Bri in person. "I'll tell you if you come to my office, phone or no phone."

"Alright then. It's almost time for my lunch break, so I'll see you shortly," Bri replied.

I'd just finished my simple lunch of hummus and carrot sticks when Bri sailed into my office, holding my phone aloft. "Amazingly, it was still sitting on the table." She lowered the phone and examined it for a moment. "Of course, it's not like this is the latest model, or even the next-latest, so I guess the kids weren't too tempted."

I rolled my chair back from my desk. "Okay, okay, I get it. You know I'm not a tech devotee like you. As long as the thing makes and receives phone calls, I don't need one with all the bells and whistles."

Trotting around the desk, Bri handed the phone to me. "You're welcome."

"Oh, right—thank you," I said, with an apologetic smile.

"De nada. Happy to help." Bri perched on the edge of my desk, swinging her feet. "Now how about you give me the full scoop on Wednesday's events?"

I leaned back in my chair and recited the sequence of events, starting with the message from Francesca through my fall and subsequent visit to the health clinic and urgent care facility. To avoid any unfounded speculation, I omitted Zach's participation, although I did mention someone giving me a ride home.

When I finished speaking, Bri jumped down from the desk and started pacing. "Wow, that really changes things, don't you think? That person in black who followed you and knocked you to the ground easily could have been Mia, or Francesca working on Mia's behalf."

"I had the same thought," I said morosely. "But I really didn't get a look at their face, and anyone can wear a black outfit if they want to stalk someone, so we can't positively conclude that it was one of the girls."

Bri paused and turned to look at me, her eyes shining with excitement. "True. The fact is, if someone else—I mean, like the actual killer—was keeping tabs on Mia, they might've caught wind of your meeting and decided to attack you. Maybe they planned to question you about what Mia confessed, but then those runners showed up so they didn't get the chance."

"Perhaps." I gently rubbed my palms, which were beginning to itch, against my pants. "I think the main takeaway is that, if we rule out either Mia or Francesca as my attacker, there must be someone else involved in Barth's death."

"Exactly. Although I don't think we can eliminate Mia as a suspect."

"Maybe not, but even if she's innocent, she could also be in danger." I closed my eyes for a second as the full import of my statement hit me.

Bri let out a low whistle. "Because the real killer might attempt to harm her like they tried to hurt you? Honestly, Jenn, this is getting scary."

"I know," I said, opening my eyes to meet her concerned gaze. "Maybe we should back off, like Zach said."

"Oh, Zach." Bri audibly sniffed. "He's just too worried about getting in trouble. Whereas *trouble* is my middle name."

"You don't say." I cast her a wry smile. "So you think we should proceed, just perhaps a bit more cautiously?"

"Of course. You got some good intel from Mia, and now we know there might be someone else desperately looking to cover their tracks." Bri pressed her forefinger to her chin. "Which brings us to my suggestion for the next step in our inquiries."

I leaned forward, resting my arms on my desk. "Which is?"

"Having a candid conversation with real estate agent Paige Irving." As Bri tossed her hair, the blue tips flashed like sparks. "Just in case, I reached out to her and set up a meeting tomorrow. I phrased the request as me introducing you to her because you're thinking about buying a house. I figured that if you didn't want to pursue that angle, I'd just meet her for lunch, no harm done. But if you want to join us . . ."

I snapped my fingers. "You and I could work out a script ahead of time—a clever way to lead into a discussion of her relationship with Barth?"

"Exactly. Great minds, huh?" Bri grinned.

"That sounds like an excellent idea. But I'm afraid you'll have to drive to Taylorsford to pick me up. I don't have my car yet." I made a face. "It's still parked in the library lot."

"That's no problem. In fact, if you feel like you can drive by then, I can pick you up and then take you to your car when we're done. Kill two birds with one stone, so to speak."

"That would be great." I smiled, pleased at the possibility of solving that problem without involving Zach.

"It's a date, then." Bri wrinkled her nose at me. "Just don't tell Rachel. I think she's already a little suspicious of our friendship."

I rolled my eyes. "Ha-ha. As if. Not only are you not my type, but also, Rachel is ten times more beautiful than I am."

"Yeah, she is." Anticipating my response, Bri made a dash for the exit. But she paused in the open doorway and turned to add, "I'm curious—who is your type? I don't think I've ever heard you say."

I waved her off. "No, and you won't hear it now either."

Chapter Nineteen

On Saturday I was able to catch an early ride to Clarion with Emily, who wanted to go into her office to prepare for a lecture the following week. Having exchanged my thicker bandage for something more flexible, I texted Zach and told him I wouldn't need him to pick me up or take me home anymore as I was driving my car back to Taylorsford. I received a terse *ok* in reply. I also let Bri know I had access to my car again.

But despite this, Bri insisted on driving to our meeting with Paige Irving.

"I kept it casual," Bri said, as we reached the outskirts of Harburg. "Told her you were really in the preliminary stages of buying a home, and not to expect you'd want to look at anything for several months."

"Good, because I'm perfectly happy where I am for now."

Bri cast me quick smile. "I know. It just felt like we should have some reason to meet, other than trying to ferret info out of her."

"It's funny—I'm always having Annabelle and Olivia pull these kind of stunts, but I don't think I ever realized how uncomfortable they should be. Lying to a suspect while trying to uncover clues doesn't feel great."

"See, this is useful for your writing as well as our sleuthing operation." Bri pulled into the small parking lot beside a modest brick building downtown. In the front yard, an oversized sign, complete with a full-color photo of a beautiful blonde woman, declared this to be the office of Paige Irving, Realtor.

As we approached the front door, I tugged down the hem of my well-worn Clarion sweatshirt and brushed cat hair off my jeans. "I should've dressed up a little more, I guess. I probably don't look like someone who could buy any sort of house around here."

Bri waved this aside. "Don't worry about that. Paige looks at your bank accounts, not your clothes."

"I might be in trouble there too," I said ruefully.

Entering the office, I was struck by the traditional design of the interior. It looked like every bank or insurance office I'd ever visited. Reproduction colonial-style furniture filled the space, and framed prints of local scenery covered the walls. An older woman seated behind a wooden desk looked up from her brightly colored paperback as we approached.

"Hello, are you Paige's two o'clock?" she asked.

I studied her carefully tinted blonde hair and attractive features. *Must be her mom or aunt or something*, I thought. *The resemblance to the photo on the sign is uncanny.*

"Yeah, we're a little early," Bri said.

The woman stood and crossed to a door near the desk. "Just let me check. I think Paige is free. No need for you to wait if she can see you now." She pushed the door ajar. "Your two o'clock is here. May they come in?"

A pleasant "Yes, of course," floated out from the inner office.

The receptionist gestured toward the door. "Please, go ahead. Paige doesn't like to be too rigid about appointment times."

I followed Bri into Paige's office, not surprised to see the interior design concept repeated in this smaller room. *A traditional sort of girl*, I thought, while noticing the award plaques from various realty associations perched on the bookshelves.

Paige stood and circled around her desk to greet us. She was prettier in real life, the slightly plastic look of her official photo replaced with a genuine welcoming expression. Her periwinkle suit was tailored to perfectly fit her petite but curvaceous figure, and her makeup was flawlessly applied.

"So good to see you again, Brianna," she said, clasping Bri's hand before turning to me. "And this must be Jennifer Dalton."

"Please, call me Jenn," I said. "Everyone does."

"Very well. Have a seat, Jenn. And Bri, of course." The gems in her rings flashed as she waved one hand to indicate a pair of wingback chairs. She pulled the task chair from behind her desk and rolled it over to face us. "So, Jenn, you're interested in purchasing a place in Harburg?" she added, when we'd all taken our seats.

"Possibly. I rent a guesthouse in Taylorsford right now," I said, glad I could truthfully mention something.

"That is a bit of a drive to the university." Paige's sparkling blue eyes examined me with interest. "What about the area around Harburg? Would you like to look at something outside of town but still closer than Taylorsford?"

I tucked a lock of my hair behind my ear, fiddling with it for a moment to hide my nervous fingers. "I'm really not sure. Everything's on the table right now, I guess. But to be fair, I want to let you know this conversation is very preliminary."

"I realize that. Brianna made it clear that you are in the beginning stages of contemplating a move." Paige straightened until her back wasn't touching the chair. "We can talk in generalities if you wish."

"That would be great," I said, settling back into the buttery leather of my own chair.

Paige launched into a spiel she'd obviously given many times, discussing the types of housing available in the area, as well as information on credit scores, down payments, financing, and other matters. As she took a long breath, Bri scooted to the edge of her chair and leaned forward, her hands gripping her knees.

"Sorry to interrupt, but I realized I hadn't expressed my condolences," Bri said.

Paige blinked rapidly. "What do you mean?"

"About Doug Barth, I mean. A terrible loss for everyone, but I've heard you two were close . . ." Bri allowed her words to trail off in the suddenly charged atmosphere.

Paige crossed and uncrossed her ankles. "I wouldn't say that. I mean, we were friends. He was my faculty advisor back in college, and I helped Doug and Miranda buy their new home, so I knew him fairly well, but . . ."

"Paige, Paige, Paige," Bri said, shaking her head. "I know there was more to it than that. Rachel and I saw you two at that fancy restaurant when we were celebrating our anniversary, remember? It seemed like you were celebrating something too, what with the flowers Doug brought and your cozy togetherness."

Roses bloomed in Paige's cheeks. "Okay, so you caught us. Anyway, I guess it doesn't matter now. Yes, we were more than friends, although I'm not sure why that matters to you."

"I realize it's none of my business." Bri's tone was infused with sympathy. "It's just that Jenn and I are trying to help a young woman who's been targeted by the police in connection with Doug's murder. A current Clarion student."

"Mia Jackson," Paige said flatly.

I nodded. "That's right. She was the last person seen with Doug, and they weren't on the best of terms, so of course the authorities have her at the top of their suspect list."

Paige audibly sniffed. "As they should."

"Perhaps, but Bri and I thought there might be other people with more reasons to kill Doug, and maybe you'd know something about that." I studied the mulish expression on Paige's face. "As close as you two were, we wondered if he'd mentioned anything about enemies or receiving any threats."

Paige ran her fingers through her perfectly coiffed hair, freeing a strand that fell over her forehead. "You mean, besides Miranda?"

"Who was planning to divorce Doug?" Bri shot me a glance before turning her gaze back on Paige. "That rumor has been running rampant at Clarion for some time."

"That's wrong. He was the one who wanted the divorce, not Miranda." Paige lifted her chin and fixed us both with an imperious stare. "Doug wanted to marry *me*."

"Ah, okay. I guess his wife would be rather upset about that," I said.

"That woman. I wouldn't put it past her to murder Doug, not if it meant she wouldn't have to give him what was rightfully his in the divorce." Paige clasped her hands together in her lap.

I tapped my shoe against the thick red and gold patterned rug under my feet. "Miranda had the most to lose, I understand, as she had a significant inheritance and her business, while Doug was on a professor's salary."

"Doug did alright. It wasn't like he didn't contribute to their lifestyle." The knuckles of Paige's clenched fingers whitened. "Besides, he was the one about to come into some real money. Something he'd unfortunately have to split with Miranda in the divorce, but still, it was a decent amount. He and I had written a book together, you see."

I sat up straight. "What kind of book?"

"A novel. A grand, sweeping, epic." Pride rippled through Paige's words. "We had an agent and a great deal with one of the biggest publishing houses in the country. We were set to receive a significant advance." Sorrow replaced the happiness flashing in her eyes. "Now everything's been upended."

"If you have a deal, the book can still come out," Bri said.

"I'm not sure." Paige's shoulders slumped. "Doug was handling all the business stuff, like the contract. Doug told me we had the deal, but I don't know that anything was finalized. I never signed anything, which I'd have to do, right?" She sighed deeply. "I guess I have to get in touch with our agent. Just haven't felt like it."

"That's understandable." I studied Paige, who appeared to have crumpled into herself. She looked like a sad child. *She may be a high-powered businesswoman in her field, but it's obvious she knows nothing about how publishing works*, I thought, without any trace of disdain. Few people outside the book business understood it. "I'm sure there's time for that, though. If you haven't signed the contract yet, the publisher can rework it to benefit Doug's heirs and you, and then move forward from there."

"So Miranda still gets a cut?" Paige made a face. "I wouldn't be surprised to hear she killed him just over that, the greedy cow."

Bri and I exchanged looks. "I'm afraid I went too far over the line. I apologize, and since Jenn has a good sense of the real estate market in this area now, I think perhaps we should leave."

"Yes, we shouldn't take up any more of your time." I rose to my feet. "I know how to contact you. When I'm ready to look at houses, I'll definitely give you a call."

Paige bobbed her head. "That's fine. But please"—she turned her gaze on Bri—"don't say anything about the book to anyone. We were trying to keep it a secret until all the papers were signed."

"No problem," Bri said, standing and stretching out her right hand. "Thanks so much, Paige, for the very valuable information." As Paige clasped her fingers, she added, "But tell me, what's the title of your book? You know I'm a curious librarian. I want to keep an eye out for any announcements about it in the future."

"It's called *A Time for Eternity*," Paige said. "The publisher might eventually change that title, but that's how it was pitched."

"Interesting. I'll be sure to look for that." Bri dropped Paige's hand and turned to me. "Shall we?"

I thanked Paige for her time, and offered my own condolences concerning Doug, then followed Bri out of the office. "She really didn't seem too broken up over Barth, did she?" I said, when Bri and I reached her car.

Leaning against the driver's side door, Bri looked at me over the roof of the compact sedan. "No, she didn't. And I might know why. Get in, I'll tell you once we're on the road."

"What are you being so secretive about?" I asked as I fastened my seatbelt.

Bri drummed her fingers against the steering wheel. "We should add Paige Irving to the top of our suspect list, and that book is the reason why."

Chapter Twenty

I raised my eyebrows. "The book Paige says she wrote with Doug? Why would she want to murder him over that? They were collaborators."

Bri kept her gaze focused on the traffic before pulling out onto the street. "That was why I asked about the title of the book. As a librarian, I have access to a lot of information on upcoming publications. Online catalogs from publishers and things like that. I remember recently seeing a forthcoming title written by a Douglas Barth. I thought that was simply a coincidence—no way would our Doug Barth have a book coming out that the entire campus didn't know about."

"But it was the title that Paige mentioned?" I turned my head to stare at Bri's stoic profile.

"The very same." Bri cast me a wry smile. "Written by, as I said, Douglas Barth."

"Wait"—my shoulders jerked—"with no mention of Paige Irving?"

"Nope." Bri lifted one hand from the steering wheel. "Apparently our illustrious professor conducted a little business behind her back." She swept the hand through the air. "Cast her aside like trash."

"Whoa. Do you think, despite all her disclaimers, Paige could've known about Barth's treachery?"

"I think it's possible. Like you said, Paige didn't seem too distraught over his death. Maybe because she killed him?"

"If she knew he'd stolen all the credit for a joint project, that would be a solid motive. Especially since she can now go back to the agent and publisher and assert her rights before the book is released."

"Exactly."

I tapped my chin with my index finger. "But can you picture Paige shoving someone over a railing? She's a fairly small woman."

"It wouldn't require that much strength if you took someone by surprise. If Barth was leaning back against the railing and someone flew at him and hit his shoulders with both palms, there could be a sort of fulcrum effect." Bri shrugged. "Maybe. I'm no expert, but I don't think we should rule her out simply because of her size."

"Okay, she stays on the list," I rubbed my temple, trying to stave off a headache. "Will you share the book info with the police, or should I?"

"I'll tell them. I was the one who noticed the book publication news, so I can start with that, and then mention something about talking to Paige and hearing that she was his collaborator." Bri flashed a smile. "I'll keep things a little obtuse. No sense in letting them know we're basically interviewing people."

"Good idea. Once they start pulling that thread, the investigators will undoubtedly find out about Paige and Barth's relationship, among other things." I settled back against the fabric cushions of the passenger seat. "Now we need to talk to Miranda Barth."

"You told me that you and Zach were going to visit her showroom or something." Bri turned onto the main road between Harburg and Taylorsford. "Is that still on?"

"I guess. We agreed to wait until next week, though. I had my doubts about her even being at work until then. She just lost her husband, after all."

"True. She'd probably stay away, if only for appearances' sake." Bri glanced in the rearview mirror and swore at a driver who was riding her bumper.

"This is why I take the back roads," I said.

"Well, I don't, because despite the bad drivers, I prefer roads with more lanes and less sharp curves and deer."

I couldn't argue with her about the deer. They did tend to spring out of the trees and underbrush lining the back mountain roads. "Honestly, since you made the effort to transport me to and from this meeting, I'm not going to quibble about the route."

"You're also going to buy me dinner, right?" Bri asked, casting me a sidelong look.

"Was that part of the deal?" I grinned. "Sure. As long as I choose the menu. You'll have to hang out at my place for a couple of hours, though. My favorite restaurant doesn't open until five."

Bri pressed the back of one hand to her forehead. "I think I can endure it. Especially since I get to play with Ash."

"If she lets you. She's a cat with a mind of her own."

Bri wrinkled her nose. "Isn't that all cats?"

* * *

I spent Sunday taking care of chores. Although I wasn't fanatic about housework, I also didn't like to live in a messy or dirty environment, so forced myself to clean at least every other weekend. Besides, as my mother often said, it wasn't like I had a social life to distract me.

That was one of the problems with being an author—when I wasn't working at Clarion, I had to spend so much time writing that I couldn't really get involved in community events, sports, or hobbies. I'd tried to join a choral group when I'd first moved to Taylorsford, but inevitably my book deadlines conflicted with their rehearsals and concerts. I also had to carve out time to do promotion for my books, which meant traveling to conferences and conventions across the country.

"My time is not really my own," I told Ash, who stared at me with a baleful expression, still irritated that I'd deployed that evil monster called the vacuum cleaner.

After finishing the housecleaning, I worked on outlining my next book while running a load of laundry. Unfortunately, the outline was not coming along too well. I kept deleting half of it and rewriting everything. Like I'd told Erin, it was difficult to create new and unique plots after writing so many books in a series. It would come to me, though. It always did.

As I sat staring at my computer screen, my cell phone rang. When I saw the name of the caller, I almost let it go to voicemail, then changed my mind.

"Hello, Zach," I said. "What's up? Like I told you, I do have my car now, if you're calling to see if I need a ride tomorrow."

"My memory isn't that bad," he replied. "No, I wanted to ask if you're still up for visiting Miranda Barth's design studio sometime this week. I asked a friend who knows her and they said Miranda was planning to be back at work starting tomorrow."

I gazed blankly at my phone screen for a second, surprised he'd gone to that much trouble. "Thanks for checking that out. Sure, I'd like to talk to her. Bri and I had a chat with Paige Irving yesterday, and that was illuminating, so maybe speaking to Miranda Barth will also shed some light on things."

"Illuminating? How so?" Zach asked.

"I'll tell you when we meet up. What works for you? I could do Wednesday after work."

"Good, so can I. My last appointment should be over in plenty of time. Around five-thirty, then? We can meet at Miranda's showroom. My friend said it's open until seven during the week."

"Sure." I made a mental note to look up the address.

"Then we can grab dinner after," Zach said. "Do you like Thai food?"

"I love all Asian cuisines, but dinner isn't really necessary."

"We both have to eat. Besides, it gives us time to compare notes."

"Okay," I said. "But we're splitting the check."

"That's fine. I wasn't going to ask you to pay for us both." There was a definite tinge of amusement in Zach's tone.

"I should hope not. Why would you assume I would, anyway?"

"Well, I *am* doing you a favor."

"Now, wait a minute—"

"Anyway, take care," Zach said, cutting me off. "See you Wednesday, Ms. Dalton."

"If I must, Dr. Flynn," I replied, earning a chuckle before his goodbye.

Chapter Twenty-One

Monday lived up to its bad press when I opened my work email and read a notice from the human resources department.

It was a reminder for a mandatory training session that I'd effectively blocked from my memory. There was nothing I hated more than presentations meant to teach me things I already knew. This particular session covered copyright, which I was certain I'd studied more comprehensively than anyone in human resources ever had. But I also knew I had to attend. HR had assigned each faculty and staff member to a particular day and time in order to verify that everyone had received the training. They'd also warned us that unless we had a true excuse, like severe illness or injury, we'd better show up.

I groaned and sent a text to Erin, reminding her that I'd be out of the writing center from two to three. Fortunately, HR had been sensible enough to schedule the staff in each department for different sessions so our areas could retain some coverage.

Poor you, she texted back. *I've already endured that one. Dry as unbuttered toast.*

This didn't surprise me. I'd experienced enough presentations from various departments to know that they were sometimes informative but rarely scintillating.

I made sure to arrive early enough at the small auditorium hosting the training session so I could choose a seat at the back. Firing up my laptop, I opened a few tabs. I wanted to be able to toggle between web pages while taking notes or at least *appearing* to take notes. That way I could conduct a few clandestine Internet searches. Fortunately, no one sat directly on either side of me, which lowered my chances of getting caught slacking off.

Not that I was surfing the net for purely personal reasons—my goal was to search for any information on Mia Jackson. I'd held off doing a deep dive into her digital footprint until now, but facing the faint possibility that she *had* been my stalker and attacker, I felt I needed to know as much as possible about any red flags in her background.

The speaker from HR fiddled with their own laptop for a good five minutes before a young woman from information technology jumped up and helped them start the session. As I suspected, it was a PowerPoint presentation, and the trainer simply read the text off each slide.

"Could've just posted this on the website and asked us to read it," mumbled a faculty member sitting in front of me.

She was right, of course, but I figured HR felt most employees would ignore such a request. At least if they had us all corralled in front of them, they could tell the upper administration that the entire campus had received the information, even if not everyone absorbed it.

Although a few staff members in the back row were obviously sleeping, I made sure to glance up from my laptop frequently so it wouldn't look like I wasn't paying attention. But my focus was on my computer screen as I honed my search results to uncover any information on Mia.

At first all I found were mentions of Mia's accomplishments, including the awards she'd won in various youth writing contests.

She'd also played basketball for her high school. As a senior she'd even been a member of their state championship team.

It was only after sifting through several of these laudatory posts that I came across one that was not so positive. I glanced up to make eye contact with the presenter for a second, then dove into the article.

Apparently, Mia had been involved in a protest the summer after her high school graduation. She'd joined a group picketing her county's school administrative offices. The school board had sent out a list of banned books they'd ordered withdrawn from all school libraries. According to the article, Mia and the other protestors were loud but peaceful, until one member of a small group of counterprotesters had attacked a school librarian as she was leaving the administrative building. Mia had struck back, knocking the attacker to the ground. The police had arrived, and Mia and a few of the other protesters were taken into custody.

The article went on to state that Mia, who was determined to have been protecting the librarian, had not been charged. But I couldn't help considering that her reaction to violence had been more violence. Looking up and staring at the projection screen, I contemplated this volatile side of Mia's personality.

Did Doug Barth put his hands on her, causing her to shove him away? Mia is tall and athletic. She could've easily pushed him hard enough to cause him to fall, especially if he was leaning against the mezzanine railing at the time.

I mulled over this possibility as the presenter concluded speaking and switched off their laptop. All around me, the attendees quickly got to their feet and fled the auditorium. I followed the mass exodus, still thinking about Mia.

It could be considered accidental, or even self-defense, but the longer Mia stays hidden, the more likely people, including the investigators, will suspect her of a deliberate attack on Doug. I shook my head, wishing I'd known about Mia's involvement in that protest when I'd spoken to her.

I still didn't see her as someone who'd commit first-degree murder, but the fact that she was hiding from the police was not a point in her favor. Of course, if she was telling the truth, and the actual killer had threatened her, her disappearance made more sense. But I only had her word for that, and as much as I liked the girl, I obviously didn't know everything about her.

When I got back to the writing center, Erin was assisting two students at one of the computer workstations. I gave her a wave and headed into my office. I was putting the finishing touches on a talk about aspects of technical writing when someone tapped on my door.

"Come in," I called out.

Erin walked into my office, her eyes shadowed beneath her lowered lashes. "I just heard some not-so-great news," she said as she crossed to the desk.

"Oh, what's that?" I asked.

"Those students I was just helping were talking about Doug Barth's death, and it seems the general consensus is that Mia Jackson killed him." Erin twisted her clasped hands in front of her. "I know you don't want to believe that, Jenn, but those girls said they'd been in other classes with Mia and she definitely had a temper. One of them witnessed her throwing a plastic water bottle against the wall when she received a bad grade on a biology project."

I drummed my fingers against the laminated surface of my desk. "I discovered something similar when checking into her background. It surprised me, because I've never seen Mia lose her temper when I was working with her."

"Because she was doing what she loves, and you always give her encouragement along with any criticism. Let's face it, we don't see all sides of the students. I think most of them are on their best behavior when they're in the writing center." Erin shrugged. "I mean, we don't give them grades, for one thing. We're just helping them do better in their courses."

"That's true." I sighed deeply. "I assumed I knew Mia well, not simply because of my personal interactions with her but also through her writing. A window on the soul, as we say."

"Sometimes. But there are great authors who write gorgeous, deeply thoughtful poetry or prose who are absolute jerks in real life. Talent and kindness don't always corollate."

"Oh, I'm aware." I pushed off with one foot, rolling my task chair away from the desk. "On another note, why don't you take a break? I can assist any students who come in before you get back."

"I haven't really been here that long," Erin said. "I got here right before you left for your training session, remember? You had to cover for me earlier."

I stood up and waved this aside. "Doesn't matter. I've been sitting too long. I'll go out and check the computers for any issues and help anyone who shows up. Take a half hour to get some air. This basement can get a little stifling."

The truth was, I was feeling suffocated by Erin's chatter about Mia and the campus's presumption of her guilt. Even though I planned to keep Mia on my list of suspects, I knew there were others who had equally viable motives.

After Erin left, I did a quick check of our desktop computers, removing the games and chatrooms that students liked to download when no one was looking. I'd just finished cleaning the last hard drive when Officer Greene entered the writing center.

"Ms. Dalton," she called out as she approached me. "I thought you should be told this information before you hear it from others on campus." She adjusted the collar of her white shirt. "We found Mia Jackson and took her in for questioning."

I stared at the officer, whose expression betrayed her satisfaction with this turn of events.

"Did you?" I managed to squeak out. I cleared my throat. "Okay, I guess that's good. She should be able to clear up all the confusion now."

"We'll see," Rebecca Greene said. "She's likely to be detained, regardless, since she's still the prime suspect. Of course, she's in the custody of the town police, since they have jurisdiction over such serious cases. They'll decide whether she'll be officially charged."

"Right," I said, my mind racing with thoughts of Mia stuck in the county jail for an indeterminate period of time. I forced a smile. "Thanks for letting me know."

"No problem." Officer Greene nodded and left the center as swiftly as she'd entered.

I slumped down in one of the workstation chairs. *Surely the police will be checking into other possible suspects, like Paige Irving or Miranda Barth.* I gazed up at the acoustic tiles of the dropped ceiling. A dried water stain darkened a section of the tiles, connecting the tiny holes in the tiles into the image of a constellation.

Orion the Hunter. A sign for me and my companions to keep sleuthing, no matter what.

Chapter Twenty-Two

I purposefully avoided walking around campus later that day, as well as Tuesday. I didn't want to get caught up in the torrent of gossip and rumors that had undoubtedly flooded every corner of Clarion.

It was still impossible to escape hearing about Mia's arrest, since that seemed to be the only topic the students using the writing center wanted to talk about. I heard Mia had been officially charged on Tuesday and sent to the county jail the same day.

The one positive tidbit to emerge from this constant flow of information was the name of Mia's lawyer, Heidi Farmer. I texted Bri and Christine, suggesting that we share anything we discovered with Ms. Farmer, as an aid in Mia's defense.

Christine called me in response. "I know Heidi," she said. "She used to date my older son, Adam. We got along quite well, despite Adam acting like an idiot most of the time, so I think I can get in touch with her easily enough."

"That's great, but wait until after Wednesday. Zach and I are going to try to speak with Miranda Barth at her design studio that evening."

"Will do," Christine said. "By the way, did you know that another professor in the English department, Andrea Karmen, had it in for Barth too?"

"I'm aware she wasn't fond of him."

Christine snorted. "I think that's putting it mildly. Anyway, when I talk to Heidi, I'll also mention Professor Karmen as a possible suspect."

Although I hated the idea of Andrea being investigated, I had to agree with Christine's suggestion. "I know Andrea. I'll try to speak with her soon, and if I pick up anything useful, I'll let you know."

On Wednesday I dressed more formally than usual, in a light gray wool suit and a turquoise silk blouse. This outfit drew a comment from Erin, but I brushed this off by saying I had a meeting with my financial advisor after work.

Of course, I didn't make enough money to consider such a thing, but Erin and I hadn't shared that many confidences, so she wouldn't know I was fibbing. *No, lying*, my conscience scolded. But while I accepted my culpability in this regard, I decided my good cause overrode any scruples.

Miranda Barth's interior design studio was located downtown, on the main floor of a former department store. I had to circle the block twice to find a spot to park, which meant when I walked into the studio Zach was already there, chatting with Miranda.

I took a look around the space as I crossed to them. Large framed photos of what I assumed were Miranda's designs were interspersed with racks and display tables holding samples of flooring, countertops, and similar items. A quick survey of the photographs confirmed Miranda's talent, although her designs were too glamorous for my taste.

"Ah, here she is," Zach said as I joined them. "My friend, Jennifer Dalton." He gestured toward the woman standing in front of him. "Jenn, this is Miranda Barth. I told her you were coming to help me make some design decisions."

I moved to Zach's side, elbowing him in the process. "Hello, Ms. Barth. So nice to meet you. I've heard you own one of the best interior design firms in the area, so I suggested that Dr. Flynn consult you before anyone else."

"How flattering." Although of average height, Miranda Barth was so slender that it looked like a strong wind could blow her off her stiletto-clad feet. Her collarbones protruded from the top edge of her boat-necked dress—a sheath of cranberry linen that skimmed her slight figure. Her dark-brown hair was pulled back into a sleek chignon, and her elegant makeup enhanced her green eyes and sharp cheekbones. She presented the perfect image of a high-end designer.

Zach side-eyed me. "We've just been discussing the basic layout of the house."

Since I'd never been inside Zach's home, I simply nodded my head. "Good place to start."

"It sounds like an interesting project. I've always enjoyed working on vintage properties," Miranda said.

I studied Miranda's composed expression, detecting no glimmers of sorrow or anxiety. "Before I forget, I want to express my condolences, Ms. Barth. I'm sure your husband's death was devastating."

Miranda arched her perfectly sculpted eyebrows. "Thank you, but there's no need to be too sorry for my situation. Doug and I were separated and engaged in obtaining a divorce, so while it was sad, his death wasn't quite as traumatic as you might assume."

"Oh, well . . ." I twitched my lips into a tight smile. "Still, I'm sure it was a shock."

Miranda flicked her fingers through the air in a dismissive gesture. "Of course, but I don't want to exaggerate my sorrow. That seems in rather poor taste, don't you think?"

"You have a very healthy attitude," Zach said. "Rejecting society's demand for fake emotion shows great mental fortitude."

A burst of bell-like laughter escaped Miranda's tinted lips. "Now I really believe you're a psychiatrist, Dr. Flynn."

"It's Zach, and actually, I'm a psychologist." Zach offered Miranda a warm smile. "I don't prescribe drugs, although I do recommend some of my patients obtain them from one of my colleagues."

"I see." Miranda looked him over, focused as a judge at a prestigious dog show. "At any rate, it is a pleasure to meet such a young and handsome therapist. All of mine have been old men with hair in their ears."

A swift glance at Zach silenced my laughter. He was blushing, which surprised me. I would've thought, given his profession, that he'd had heard much more uncomfortable comments before. I turned my gaze back on Miranda. "I'm glad you're doing well, Ms. Barth, and hope the detectives on the case won't be too much of a bother."

"Thank you for your concern." Miranda clasped her hands against her chest. "Unfortunately, they've already questioned me a couple of times, and I'm sure that's not the end of it. The spouse angle, you know." She shrugged. "Doug didn't have any life insurance, which turns out to be a good thing, since the police can't assume he was killed for money."

"Which lets you off the hook, doesn't it? I mean, in terms of the investigators hounding you." I hoped I sounded sympathetic rather than inquisitive, but when the edge of Zach's shoe bumped mine, I wasn't sure I'd succeeded.

Miranda's eyes narrowed. "You'd think so, but the detectives still said they'd be back. Such an annoyance when one has a business to run."

At that point, Zach took over the conversation, steering it back into a discussion of furniture and finishes. He exchanged ideas with Miranda for another fifteen minutes, before glancing at his watch and claiming they'd have to continue the consultation another day. "I'm supposed to meet up with someone soon," he said, with an apologetic smile. "You've given me a lot to think about, Ms. Barth. I'd like to mull over a few of the concepts you presented and then return, if that's alright with you."

"Of course." As Miranda extended her slender hand, her stack of gold bracelets tinkled. "You have my card. Call anytime to set up another meeting."

Zach clasped her fingers for a moment longer than I felt was strictly necessary. "Thanks, I'll do that."

As we hurried out of the studio, I felt Miranda Barth's stare tracking us.

"I'm not sure she bought it," I said, when we were safely outside.

Zach shook his head. "It is questionable whether she entirely believed my story about redoing the house, but one thing I'm sure about is that she isn't in the least upset over her husband's death."

"Yes, she's obviously already moved on," I said, shooting him an amused glance. "The way she was eyeing you . . ."

"That was rather unexpected," he replied, with a grimace.

"Oh, come now. Weren't you the least bit flattered? An attractive, wealthy woman ogling you isn't a bad thing."

"Right, she's wealthy." Zach paused when we turned the corner to reach the street where we'd parked our cars. "And it's her own money, isn't it?"

"Primarily. I guess Doug made a decent salary, but Miranda inherited a lot from her family, and her business has done extremely well."

Zach shoved his glasses back up to the arch of his nose. "Which means, unless they had a prenup, Doug Barth would've gotten a good chunk of *her* assets in a divorce. So even without life insurance, Miranda had a financial motive to murder Doug."

"That thought has crossed my mind," I said. "Especially since I've heard there wasn't any prenup."

"Interesting. She was being a bit disingenuous about the money—talking about the nonexistent life insurance while omitting any mention of the distribution of property when they divorced."

"Exactly." I pulled my keys out of my purse. "With Doug dead, she gets to keep everything."

Zach tapped his foot against the sidewalk. "A definite motive."

"Something to share with Mia's lawyer, for sure. I suppose the investigators will look into this issue as well, but they might not have the same inclination to dig deeper." I rattled my keys. "By the way, I bet you could get some more info out of Miranda if you took her out to dinner. I'm sure she'd say yes if you asked." Of course, I was the one who was supposed to have dinner with Zach, but I was happy to beg off. I really wasn't in the mood to banter with anyone, particularly not someone who always made me feel slightly off balance. "You could easily go back and ask her. I don't mind if you have dinner with her tonight instead of me, especially since that could help the investigation."

Zach shook his own keys at me. "Sorry, my help with your little sleuthing endeavor doesn't extend that far. I have no desire to go out to dinner with Ms. Barth, now or ever."

"Pity, you might've been able to obtain some valuable info." I wrinkled my nose at him. "Just one dinner?"

Zach laid one hand lightly on my shoulder. "Not with her. I will still consider having dinner with you tonight, if you ask nicely."

"A, I'm not a suspect, and B, I don't have any information that will help Mia's case." I stepped back, dislodging Zach's hand. "It would be a waste of time."

Zach swept his gaze over me, his expression unreadable. "Very well. Forget I said anything." He turned on his heel and strode off toward his car.

Chapter
Twenty-Three

Checking the messages on my phone and replying to a few student requests for appointments took several minutes, so I'd just started the engine in my own car when I noticed Zach jogging back.

He tapped my window. "Problem," he mouthed.

I lowered the window and stared blankly at him. "What?"

"Glad you're still here. My car won't start." He raked his hand through his hair, making one tuft stand up like rooster feathers. "I've called a tow service to haul it to the garage I use for repairs, but now I don't have a way home."

"In other words, you want a ride," I said.

He leaned in closer. "Quid pro quo."

"Ah, for you driving me back and forth when my leg was injured? I see." I tightened my grip on the steering wheel. "So that wasn't really a favor. You were just biding your time, waiting to see how I might be able to repay you."

"Whatever you say." Zach glared at me. "But I would like a ride home, if you'd deign to assist me."

I unlocked the passenger side door. "Get in."

Fastening his seatbelt, Zach cast me a sideways look. "Don't worry, I'll figure something out for tomorrow morning."

"It's alright." I pulled out onto the street. "I can pick you up."

"Thanks. By the way, your brake light is on."

"Oh, that," I said, flicking the offending light with one finger. "It goes on and off all the time. I just had the brakes checked, though, so don't worry. It's just a short somewhere."

Zach stared out the passenger side window. "As long as you know everything is fine."

We didn't talk during most of the ride. I considered turning on the radio but didn't, afraid of Zach critiquing my choice of music. As I turned onto the back road that led to Taylorsford, I looked over at him. "We seem to always end up arguing. Not sure why that is. Perhaps your psychological training can provide some insights?"

Zach turned his head to meet my inquisitive glance. "It does, but I doubt you'd like any conclusions I might draw."

"Oh, why is that? Is it something that would make me look foolish?"

"Not exactly. But I might be uncomfortable—" Zach leaned forward. "What's that?"

"Fallen branch," I said, recognizing the object blocking half the road. Unable to swerve around it in time, I slammed on the brakes.

"Did you hit it?" Zach asked.

I backed the car away from the branch. "I don't think so. At least not hard enough to do any damage."

Zach peered through the windshield. "There was a loud screeching sound, though."

"I heard it. But the car seems fine." I examined the road in front of us for oncoming traffic before slowly maneuvering around the branch. "It's driving okay."

"That's a hazard on these back roads," Zach said. "Along with the curves and hills."

"True, but it still beats the traffic on the main road." I sped up, hoping to make up lost time. I knew this road well enough to anticipate the sharp twists and other dangers. There were quite a few traps, including one tight curve that required a significant slowing down, especially since woods lined its top edge. Taking it too fast had sent many vehicles flying off the road and smashing into the unforgiving barricade of tree trunks.

"This upcoming curve is particularly notorious," Zach remarked, as if reading my mind.

I nodded and pressed the brake pedal, shocked when my foot slammed the pedal right to the floor.

"What?" I pumped the pedal again but felt no resistance. "The brakes," I said, my voice unnaturally calm.

"They aren't working?" Zach braced his hands against the dashboard.

"Nothing's happening." I couldn't see far enough around the curve to know if anyone was coming in the opposite lane but decided I had to take a chance. "Hold on, I'm going to try to swing across to the open field."

"Too fast, too fast," Zach spit out between gritted teeth.

"Can't be helped!" I shouted, as I steered the speeding vehicle across the lane and into the field.

The car sailed over a ditch and landed with a bone-jarring thump, then bounced across a washboard of dirt rows littered with shards of harvested crops and desiccated weeds. When it finally came to a stop, I was gasping for air, and Zach was swearing under his breath.

"Remind me never to ask for a ride from you again," he said.

I shot him a sharp look, but observing his pallor, I stopped myself from responding with a retort. "I don't understand it. I just had the car checked recently, and the brakes were fine."

"You must've hit that branch harder than you thought," Zach said, pulling a tissue from his pocket to wipe the sweat from his brow and upper lip.

"I didn't. I'm sure I didn't. When I drove around the branch, it was still intact. If the car had smashed into it, some twigs would've broken off, at least."

"There was that sound." Zach leaned back against the seat cushions.

"I know. But now I wonder if that was something else." I threw the lever that popped open the hood. "How much do you know about cars?"

"Very little," Zach replied. "Which is why I had my car towed to the garage."

When I opened my door and climbed out of the car, my legs were so wobbly they almost crumpled under me. I leaned against the side of the car for a moment to steady myself, then gingerly picked my way to the front. Lifting the hood, I made sure the brace was engaged and peered into the mysterious jumble of wires and tubes and metal parts. They made about as much sense to me as an Escher print.

"It's leaking." Zach leaned over my shoulder and pointed at some tubing. "See all the liquid bubbled up right there."

I squinted. "Is that the brake line?"

"Yes. I know that much, at least. And I can also tell"—Zach pointed at the line—"that it's either been tampered with or was cut by hitting that branch. It wouldn't been sliced that cleanly just from wear and tear."

"You mean it's possible someone did this? Deliberately?" I stepped back and straightened, allowing the breeze to dry the beads of sweat that had blossomed across the back of my neck.

"Quite possible. And it's both lines, actually." Zach stood back as well. "You can see that it looks like the lines were cut almost all the way through. Then there's a ragged bit where they must've torn at some point on the drive."

"The fluid leaked out over a period of time, then the brakes failed," I said, talking to myself as much as to Zach.

"Probably." Zach rubbed his hands together, as if to warm them. "Although we can't be sure it was deliberate, even if the cuts do look fairly clean. Hitting that branch is still a possibility, and definitely a less frightening one."

"Oh, I think brakes failing and the car flying off the road and bumping across a field was pretty frigging scary. Well, I suppose I need to call someone to pick us up, and a tow service. An auto mechanic should be able to determine if this was accidental or not." I reached into the car and pulled out my purse. "Know anyone in Taylorsford who'd be willing to give us a lift?"

"This time of day? I'm not sure." Zach lowered the brace and dropped the hood. "I'm afraid dinner is truly off for today, at any rate."

"We'll have to reschedule," I said, my mind occupied with thoughts of who might be able to pick us up. "I guess I could try Emily." As I slipped my phone from the purse, I noticed a text notification. I swiped that first. Casually glancing at the screen, I read the text, then yelped and dropped my phone.

"What is it?" Zach bent down to retrieve the device. "Bad news?"

"A threat," I said, when he handed me the phone. "Anonymous, of course." I turned the phone so he could see the screen.

"*Enough with the Nancy Drew act*," Zach said, reading the text aloud. "*Stop your investigating or you'd better go ahead and write your own obituary.*"

Zach met my gaze and held it. "Don't call Emily Moore," he said. "Call the police."

Chapter Twenty-Four

When the police arrived, along with a few deputies from the county sheriff's department, Zach and I answered their questions while other officers examined my car. I was told that my car would be towed to a garage associated with the sheriff's department, and I would be informed when I could retrieve it.

"In the meantime," said one of the deputies, whose nameplate identified him as Officer Coleman, "I'll give you a ride to Taylorsford."

"Thanks so much," I said. My words were echoed by Zach.

But soon, neither of us was inclined to be so gracious. A captive audience, we had to listen while Officer Coleman berated us for "sticking our noses where they don't belong."

"Civilians have no business investigating crimes," he repeated for the umpteenth time. "It just leads to trouble. Now my boss, Sheriff Tucker, he does sometimes ask this librarian lady to do some research for our department, but that's on him. Personally, I don't think it's ever a good idea to allow regular folks to mess around during an ongoing investigation. You end up with all these theories floating around on those podcasts or whatever." He snorted. "True-crime fans and such like. What a pain that is for us professionals."

Sitting in the back seat of the deputy's cruiser, neither Zach nor I responded to this barrage of opinions and criticism. We did, however, share a few eyebrow lifts, grimaces, and eye rolls.

Emily threw open her back door when the cruiser pulled into her parking area but didn't step outside. As I unbuckled my seatbelt, mentally practicing the information I should share with her, Zach laid his hand over mine.

"Are you going to the provost's party on Friday evening?" he asked.

"I hadn't decided," I said, gathering up my purse and opening the car door.

"Well, decide. I should have my car back by then, so I can take you."

Climbing out of the cruiser, I waved at Emily before turning back to meet Zach's gaze. "Like I said, I'm not even sure I'm going."

Zach leaned across the back seat. "I'll pick you up at six-thirty."

Before I could respond, he'd grabbed the handle and pulled the door shut. The deputy immediately backed up and drove off, gravel spitting out from the tires.

Emily clattered down the steps to meet me. "What happened, dear? Not an accident, I hope."

"Sort of, but no one was hurt," I said, shouldering my purse strap. "I was giving Dr. Flynn a ride home and my brakes went out. Fortunately, there were no other vehicles around, and I was able to steer the car into a field."

"My goodness, that must've given you quite a fright." Emily's dark eyes examined me with interest. "Is your car alright, other than the brakes?"

"I think so. Anyway, it was towed to a garage."

"By the sheriff's department?" Emily's eyes widened behind the lenses of her round glasses.

Naturally, she knew something else had happened. Whatever else Emily Moore was, she wasn't stupid. *And*, I thought, with a brief twitch of my lips, *she's probably had a few dealings with the law in the past.*

"They came to help, along with some police officers from Harburg," I said. "I called 911 and that's who showed up."

"I see. But it was just an unfortunate accident, right?" Emily's suspicious expression told me she wasn't fooled by my nonchalant attitude.

"Uh-huh," I muttered, not wanting to share any details. I trusted Emily, but there was no point in involving anyone else in the mess I'd made. *Don't drag her into this trouble,* I told myself. *Bri and Christine and even Zach may already be in danger. Emily doesn't need to be added to the list.*

"Would you like to come in for a drink?" Emily asked. "Sometimes it helps to settle your nerves."

"Thanks so much, but I think I just want to collapse on my sofa and watch bad TV. I would love a ride to Clarion tomorrow, though. If you're going in, that is."

Emily reached out and clasped my hand. "I can do that regardless. Let's just plan on me taking you to work and bringing you home until you get your car back."

I squeezed her fingers and pulled my hand away. "No, no, that's asking too much. You don't need to go into work every day."

"There's always something I can do in the office." Emily smiled. "Write, if nothing else. Maybe it will get me started on some new poems. I get lazy sitting at home."

"Alright then, I'll take you up on your very generous offer." I arranged the time to meet in the morning, then thanked her again.

She headed back inside her house as I entered the guest house. Although I was always careful to lock the door behind me, I checked it twice that evening. The text message I'd received had frightened me more than I'd initially realized.

The Harburg police had taken charge of the text, cloning the message from my phone so they could attempt to discover who'd sent it. But they'd also warned me that they might not be able to track down the sender. "It was probably a burner," the officer in charge had told me.

I greeted Ash, who spent several minutes complaining about my tardiness, even after I'd checked that she had plenty of water and kibble and had given her a special treat. She only calmed down when I slumped onto the sofa with a glass of wine. Jumping up to snuggle next to me, her meows finally morphed into a rumbling purr.

"Girl, you have no idea what kind of day I had," I told the cat. "It made me wonder if maybe I have nine lives, like you. Which wouldn't be bad, the way things are going right now."

Ash responded with a louder purr. I absently stroked her silky fur while I sipped my wine and contemplated calling Bri and Christine. I needed to do that as soon as possible, I realized, since they might also be targeted by whoever sent the text message.

I finished off my wine and set down the glass, then called Bri, who was horrified to hear about the failure of my brakes.

"But it does prove that there was likely someone else involved in Doug Barth's murder," she said, her tone turning more cheerful. "Mia Jackson is in custody. There's no way she could've tampered with your brakes."

"Unless she has an accomplice," I said, thinking of Francesca.

"That seems unlikely." Bri cleared her throat. "By the way, Christine has an appointment with Mia's lawyer tomorrow. She said you mentioned your plan to visit Miranda Barth today."

"Oh, right. Wow, so much has happened, I almost forgot about that." I said, before sharing my impression of Miranda and the information on her financial situation.

"She did have a motive to get rid of hubby," Bri said when I'd finished talking. "That's definitely something the lawyer should know."

"I agree, but listen—I'm so tired right now, I don't feel like having another conversation. Do you mind calling Christine and filling her in on everything?"

"Not at all. I'll give her a ring as soon as we hang up. Besides the info you gathered, we definitely need to warn her to be careful." There was a slight pause before Bri added, "I guess Zach is already aware, since he was with you today."

"Yes, he's in the loop." Bri's mention of Zach reminded me of his determination to escort me to the provost's Friday evening party. "I do trust the guy, but I'm really not sure what to make of him sometimes. He seems to blow hot and cold."

"And you don't?"

"Wait a minute, what's that supposed to mean?"

Bri didn't reply, but I definitely heard a chuckle before she hung up.

Chapter Twenty-Five

My debate about what to wear to the provost's party Friday night hadn't been resolved until fifteen minutes before Zach had said he'd pick me up. On the one hand, I didn't want to stand out too much—difficult for someone as tall as me—and on the other hand, I knew Hilda Lange wasn't a fan of casual attire at university functions.

I finally decided on a sleek black dress worn under a black velvet jacket. I chose cute black flats, of course. Already towering over most of the boys in high school, and many in college, I'd never gotten used to heels.

The doorbell rang as I was brushing cat hair off my dress with a sticky roller. I gave one final swipe, then opened the door.

Zach, looking more like an accountant than a psychologist in his severe navy suit and white shirt and striped tie, looked me over. "Missed a spot," he said, pointing at a couple of gray hairs still clinging to the hem of my dress.

I swept away the hairs in one swift motion, then dropped the roller on the console table next to the door. Lifting my long gray wool coat off its hook, I slung it over my arm.

"The forecast said it might get cold later," I said as I grabbed my clutch purse.

Zach held the door open until I walked past him. "Fortunately, my car has a heater."

"We might have to park some distance from the house, though," I said, locking my deadbolt. "Have you been to the provost's home before?"

"No, this is the first time the health clinic staff has been invited." Zach opened the passenger side door, a gesture that made me raise my eyebrows.

Slipping into the passenger seat, I gave a little bob of my head. "Why, thank you, sir."

"Don't look so surprised," Zach said as he closed the door.

When we were on the road, he asked if I'd heard anything about my own car.

"I'm supposed to be able to pick it up tomorrow," I said. "Emily has already promised to drive me to the garage."

"That's good." Zach stared straight ahead, allowing me a clear look at his rather rugged profile.

Not bad, I thought. *No wonder Miranda Barth was sending out signals.* I turned my head to stare out the window. "You obviously got your car fixed pretty quickly."

Zach tapped the steering wheel. "It was just the battery. Nothing major, which my wallet appreciates as much as I do."

"You left the lights on or something?" I asked, looking back at him. "I've done that more than once."

"Not really sure what happened. My car was parked on campus during the day, and I didn't pay any attention to whether the lights were on when I got back to the lot. The sun was still shining brightly then anyway, so it would've been difficult to tell." Zach frowned. "I did notice that the lights had been turned to *on* rather than automatic, which is where I usually leave them, but thought I'd simply made a mistake."

"Wasn't your car locked during the day?"

"No. There wasn't anything in it, so I didn't bother."

"Well, that was stupid," I said without thinking.

Zach cast me a raised-eyebrow look. "Blunt, as always."

I felt heat rise in my cheeks. "Sorry. I guess I've been so trained to always lock my doors—car, house, or whatever—that I can't imagine not doing so. But maybe that's a female thing."

"Not a bad habit." Zach glanced at his GPS. "It seems Dr. Lange lives closer to Taylorsford than Harburg. We're almost there."

"It's a mountain cabin. Well, not exactly a cabin, although it is built of logs. It's more like a lodge, I suppose." I tucked my hair behind my ears, exposing my dangling gold earrings. "I've only been there once, but it was pretty memorable. You'll see what I mean."

Zach turned on a paved driveway that meandered through a thick grove of pines and hardwood trees. The house came into view after a final curve—a magnificent two-story structure with covered timber porches wrapping both levels. Built of chinked logs, it matched its wooded lot perfectly, although it did look more like a mountain lodge than a single-family home.

"I had no idea being a provost paid so well," Zach said dryly as he parked at the far end of the expansive circular drive in front of the main entrance.

"It doesn't. Lange inherited a good chunk of change from her late husband, or so I hear." I unbuckled my seat belt and leaned over to pluck my coat from the back seat. Not waiting for Zach, I opened my door and got out, the coat draped over one arm. I didn't need it yet, but the bite of the wind told me I'd be glad to have it to slip on when we left. "Lock the doors," I told Zach.

"I already did," he replied, holding up his key fob when he joined me on the pathway that lined the perimeter of the parking circle.

As we set off toward the brightly illuminated front doors, another uneasy thought wafted through my mind. "What are people going to think, us coming to the party together?"

"Whatever they please. Why would you care?"

"I wouldn't want anyone to get the wrong idea." I paused for a second.

Zach stopped short "Which is what?" Turning to me, he tapped my pursed lips with his forefinger. "Aren't we friends, or is that too embarrassing for you to admit?"

"It's not embarrassing," I replied, taking a step back while keeping my gaze locked with his. "But when a man and woman claim to be friends, especially if they're both unattached, rumors start to fly."

"Do you really care about such childish behavior?" Zach's expression betrayed an amusement I found more infuriating than any of his criticisms.

"Not everyone has reached your state of zen. I just don't want gossip to link us together romantically, for your sake as well as mine." I started walking again, "It won't help your dating prospects if the entire campus thinks we're an item."

Striding briskly beside me, Zach let out a bark of laughter. "That's the least of my concerns," he said, turning to face me as we stepped onto the front porch. "Seriously, Jenn, it seems we've tumbled into some sort of criminal conspiracy and have even been targeted by a murderer. Random opinions on our relationship are a fairly minor concern considering all that, don't you think?"

I met his bright gaze with a wry smile. "I suppose."

At that moment one of the double front doors swung open, revealing a young woman who I assumed was a student drafted to help with the event. Zach and I strolled into the wide, two-story foyer.

"At least there aren't any animal heads," Zach said, sotto voce, as the student directed us toward an alcove holding a coat rack.

I hung up my coat while Zach continued to gaze around the space, obviously bemused by the timber columns and the rough-hewn branches that created the railings for the second-floor balconies. "Shall we split up now?" I asked. "To tell you the truth, I primarily came to see if I could glean any information that might help Mia's case. That's probably easier to do by myself."

Zach's expression grew stony. "You're still going to pursue that, despite the threats?"

I looked him in the eyes and smiled. "Of course. Why else would I be here?"

Chapter Twenty-Six

I made my way into the great room, a space that lived up to its name. A gigantic stone fireplace covered the center of the far wall, flanked by floor to ceiling windows that looked out onto the forest. Tonight, the windows were shadowed, their expanse of glass acting as dark mirrors, reflecting the flicker of the tabletop candles in their glass globes and the balletic movement of the party guests.

As usual, the party had split up into groups that reflected fields of study. Not strictly, but broadly—the scientists and engineers huddled in one corner, comparing notes, the foreign language instructors hovering near the buffet table, and the professors from the fine and performing arts disciplines claiming the bright center of the room, where the wooden plank floor was dappled with light from the wrought-iron chandeliers.

The English department faculty and staff were clustered in their typical spot, closest to the bar. I crossed to join them, almost bumping into dance instructor Richard Muir, who was standing beside a short, plump, dark-haired woman who exuded intelligence and vivaciousness. *Must be his wife*, I thought, as I excused myself. *She isn't what I expected, but I can tell by the look he gave her that he's madly in love with her.* I smiled. *Lucky her.*

"Jenn, you made it after all." Andrea Karmen met me at the edge of the English department group, brandishing an empty wineglass. "Come along, I was about to grab another drink. You should join me so I don't feel like such a lush."

I followed her to the bar. "I won't say no to that, but I doubt you're tonight's top imbiber."

"No, that would be Gary. He's already three sheets to the wind. So much for representing the department with decorum. Right now he has Miranda cornered over by the entrance to the study."

I gazed in the direction she indicated and noticed a tall, bony, older man with steel-gray hair pulled back into a short ponytail in deep conversation with Miranda Barth. At first I was surprised to see her at this event, but then reminded myself that she'd probably been invited as a tribute to Doug. Which, considering her lack of sorrow over his passing, did make me wonder why she'd shown up. *Perhaps to maintain a façade as the grieving widow*, I thought. *That would be particularly important if she was somehow involved in his death.*

"He's probably trying to weasel money out of her for one of his pet projects." Andrea flung her floral chiffon scarf over one shoulder. After we put in our drink requests, she looked me over. "That's a lovely outfit. I don't think I've seen you quite so dressed up before. Who are you trying to impress?"

"No one," I took a sip of my wine. "It was a whim. This house is so grand, I thought I should pull out all the stops."

"Nothing wrong with that," Andrea said, finishing off her wine in one long swallow.

I eyed her with concern, especially when she asked the bartender for another drink. Never having seen Andrea throwing back wine with such abandon, I wondered why she was acting so recklessly.

Because she's trying to drown pangs of guilt? I shook my head to dislodge this thought. Despite her dislike of Doug Barth, I currently had no evidence to indicate that Andrea had been involved in his death. *Except for the fact that she's the lone witness to the altercation between Mia and Doug, which means she could've fabricated that event . . .*

"Hello, boss," said a soft woman's voice behind me.

I turned and looked down into Erin's wide eyes. She was looking particularly girlish tonight, in a flounced skirt covered in a tiny floral pattern and a lacy white blouse.

"Hi, Erin, how are you this evening?" I asked.

"I'm fine. More importantly, how are you? I heard something about a car accident?" Erin's lashes fluttered and she pressed her palm to her breast. "You weren't injured, I hope?"

I couldn't help but notice Andrea's gaze snap back onto me. "You were in an accident, Jenn? How come I never heard about this?"

"It happened Wednesday evening, and with everything else going on . . ." I forced a wide smile. "Not to worry. My car needed some repairs, but I wasn't hurt."

"Nor was I, thankfully." Zach's voice sailed over my shoulder.

I shot a glare at him as he stepped up next to me. He smiled back, then took a sip from his martini glass.

"You were together?" I didn't think Erin's eyes could get any bigger, but she proved me wrong.

I swallowed a little wine. "I was giving Dr. Flynn a ride home because his car wouldn't start, that's all. We both live in Taylorsford, so it wasn't out of my way."

"Didn't realize you two were so well acquainted." Andrea swayed slightly as she examined us. Hectic splotches darkened her olive skin, and her deep brown eyes were watery. *She's definitely had too much to drink,* I thought with concern. "But, come to think of it, you do make a good couple. Similar ages and height and all that."

"Yes, but just to clarify . . ." I hadn't finished my sentence when another voice jumped into the conversation.

"What have we here?" said a booming female voice. "I didn't expect a romantic connection to arise from me simply sending you to counsel Ms. Dalton after her terrible experience in the library, Dr. Flynn. What an interesting turn of events."

We all turned to face provost Hilda Lange, a formidable-looking woman with curly white hair and piercing blue eyes. When I'd first met her, I'd amused myself imagining her as the perfect Mrs. Claus. Tonight, resplendent in a crimson velvet pantsuit, with her mouth painted red as a holly berry, her resemblance to that character made me swallow back a giggle.

"I'm afraid you didn't quite achieve that effect, Dr. Lange," Zach said, his tone smooth as cream. "We're friendly, but . . ."

Hilda Lange quirked one wild eyebrow. "No romance? What a shame. Especially since you're one of the few men on campus who's a good match for her, in height anyway."

Gary Alexander slipped into the small circle our group had formed. "I had no idea you were such a matchmaker, Provost Lange." He lifted his pointed chin and looked down his nose at me. "As for height, I believe I would qualify, but alas, I'm far too old for our young mystery author."

"Since you're older than I am, I must concur," Hilda said, the sparkle in her eyes fading. She tightened her lips as Gary took a long swallow from his tumbler.

The clear liquid could've been water, but I was certain it was more likely vodka. "Hello, Professor," I said. "I assure you that I'm not hung up about height, or age, but I do draw the line at dating my colleagues."

"As you should, as you should." Gary was already slurring his words, which didn't bode well for the rest of the evening. He held out his glass, pointing at the provost. "I need to talk with you at some point. Clarify a few things."

"Perhaps we should do that now," Hilda said. "Let's find a quiet corner, shall we?" Her smile broadened until she resembled a slightly frightening clown. "Excuse us." She swept off, with a rolling-gaited Gary Alexander trailing in her wake.

"I think I'll follow them," Andrea said. "If they're going to talk department business, someone needs to keep Gary in check."

After she disappeared into the crowd, Erin shook her head. "I'm not sure Andrea's in the best shape either, so I'm going to steer clear of that convo and join a more cheerful discussion." She wandered off.

"Looks like it's just you and me, kid," Zach said, affecting a surprisingly decent Humphrey Bogart accent. "Two little people in this crazy world."

"Whose problems don't amount to a hill of beans?" I asked with a lift of my eyebrows. "Is that what you think this is—my little group's attempts to ensure justice, and any help I've asked of you? Simply a lost cause, a flattened and scattered hill of beans?"

He clinked his glass against mine. "No, I think it's the beginning of a beautiful friendship."

Chapter
Twenty-Seven

I was sure skepticism was written all over my face, but I took a drink anyway. Being friends was fine with me, if that was all Zach was looking for.

"Just the person I was hoping to find," said a familiar voice.

I turned to face Christine, who was wearing a white chef's jacket and holding a tray of hors d'oeuvres. "How did you get roped into working this party?"

"I volunteered," Christine said. "It's great money for very little work."

Zach said hello and wandered off, obviously sensing that Christine wanted to talk with me privately.

"Want to join me over near the kitchen?" Christine placed the tray on an empty café table. "There's a little convo going on in the hallway that you might find interesting."

"That sounds intriguing." I set down my empty wineglass and followed her. "I guess Bri shared our latest findings with you?"

Christine nodded. "She did, and then I passed all that along to Heidi, who was very grateful. She's going to have her legal team look into Paige and Miranda, as well as a few others." Christine threw out her arm as we approached a hallway near the kitchen. "Stop here for a minute," she added, in a low voice. "The *few others* are huddled at the end of the hall."

I peered over her shoulder, observing a trio of people clustered in the shadowy recesses of the wide hallway. Andrea Karmen, Gary Alexander, and Hilda Lange were engaged in what looked to be a heated conversation.

Hilda threw up her hands. "It's impossible to have a civil conversation with the two of you tonight. Logic has been drowned by your drinking, so I'll leave you to fight among yourselves. We'll discuss structural changes to the department another day." She stalked off around a corner that obviously led to a connecting hallway.

"This is what all your complaints lead to," Gary said, his words as acidic as the lime floating in his drink. "Structural changes. You know what that means. Both of us could be out of a job."

Andrea took a swig of her drink before replying. "Changes are needed. You want to keep everything the same as it was when you were in college, back when dinosaurs roamed the earth." She spat out this insult with an accompanying swing of her wineglass, scattering droplets of wine across the wall behind her.

"No class, no talent, no art," Gary said. "That's what it all comes down to. You'd teach courses on creating text for comic books if you had your way."

Andrea squared her shoulders and stared up into his furious face. "And why not? It's a perfectly legitimate form of writing, in my opinion."

I leaned over to whisper to Christine. "I'm going to jump in. You might want to sneak away to avoid the shrapnel."

She grinned and hurried off toward the kitchen.

I walked up to Andrea and Gary, trying to act oblivious to their mutual fury. "Oh, hello. Hope I'm not interrupting anything."

"Nothing important." Andrea curled her lips as she continued to stare at Gary. "We were simply discussing some new ideas. Oh, wait, that isn't quite right. It's more like I was proposing new ideas and Professor Alexander was shooting them down." She pantomimed a gun with her free hand. "Bang, bang, bang."

Gary snorted. "No use wasting breath on such foolishness. Doug Barth had it right—you're nothing but trouble for our department, Ms. Karmen."

"Dr. Karmen," she said coldly.

"Well, PhD or not, I should've followed Doug's advice and gotten rid of you long before you started your tenure process." Gary fixed Andrea with an icy glare. "But you know, one of the last things Doug told me was that it wasn't too late. Said he had the goods on you at last, *Doctor* Karmen." Gary wheeled around, bumping my shoulder as he strode back to the great room.

Andrea and I stood in silence for a moment before she broke into laughter.

"Good heavens, what a desiccated dinosaur he is." Andrea pulled a linen handkerchief from the pocket of her emerald-green dress and dabbed at her watery eyes. "Such a display. Forgive us, Jenn."

I smiled wanly in response, my mind still processing Gary's claim that Doug had some dirt on Andrea. *Enough to get her fired, even though she's almost achieved tenure?* I bit my lower lip. If there was any truth in Gary's words, had it also been enough to compel Andrea to silence Doug permanently?

"Don't worry about it," I said. "I know you two don't see eye-to-eye."

"Understatement of the year." Andrea rolled the stem of her wineglass between her fingers.

"I heard something about Doug Barth, and that reminded me of a question I had," I said, deciding to jump in feet first. "Has anyone said anything about filling Doug's position? I'm sure it's too early, but . . ."

"We're all covering his courses right now. Not sure when anything will be posted, or if it will be, honestly." Andrea stepped closer to me and looked up, her slightly unfocused eyes searching my face. "Are you asking for Erin? I know she's wanted to join the department full-time for a while now. Unfortunately"—Andrea punctuated this by patting my forearm—"she may still be out of luck. The provost was just talking to us about restructuring the department. Not sure what that means, but she mentioned something about streamlining."

"Really? Something major, like eliminating positions?"

"That's what it sounded like to me." Andea swayed slightly. "Oops, I think I'd better go sit down for a while. Excuse me, would you, Jenn?"

"Of course." I moved aside to allow her to stagger past me.

I waited until Andrea disappeared into the crowd before I walked down the hall and peered into the kitchen. Spying Christine instructing a student waiter on the finer points of serving hors d'oeuvres, I waved.

"Find out anything interesting?" she asked when she joined me in the hall.

I told her about Gary and Andrea's conversation. She immediately jumped to the same conclusion I had—whatever information Doug had supposedly collected to use against Andrea could have driven her to kill him.

"I'll share this with Heidi tomorrow," she said, straightening the lapels of her jacket. "For now, I'd better go back out on the floor and check on the condition of the buffet."

I thanked her and accompanied her back into the thick of the party. Seeing Zach talking with a young female instructor from the chemistry department, I marched up to him and linked my arm with his. "Hey there," I said, adopting a cheery tone. "How about you accompany me to talk to the provost? I want to thank her for such a lovely event before heading home."

"Are we heading home?" Zach asked with a lift of his eyebrows.

It was a comment that sent the woman he'd been chatting with scurrying off, while earning an elbow in the ribs from me. "You could've phrased that better," I said when he shot me an aggrieved look.

"I think I need to counsel you about your tendency to resort to physical violence," he replied, dropping my arm to rub his side.

I pursed my lips. "Sorry, but you deserved that. Rumors are going to be spreading like kudzu after that little comment. Anyway"—I tossed my head—"I do want to talk to Hilda Lange. I just heard a tidbit about her plans to restructure the English department and I want to know more."

"And you need me there as what? A witness?"

"Something like that. I already had Christine act as backup on the other conversation, so it's your turn."

Zach slipped off his glasses and stared at them for a moment before putting them back on. "For a minute there, I thought I was seeing things, like some general magically appearing before me," he said. "But I guess it's really Jennifer Dalton, telling me what to do in no uncertain terms."

I stepped closer to him, until we were almost nose to nose. "Are you going to assist me or not?"

"You're not exactly helping quell those rumors," Zach said, with a smile. He tapped my nose with one finger. "Alright, let's go interrogate your boss. What could possibly go wrong with that plan?"

Chapter Twenty-Eight

We found Hilda sitting at a small table in one corner of the great room. I was surprised to see that she was alone, but not wanting to argue with my good fortune, I immediately sat down in the chair across from her.

"It's a great party," I said when Hilda turned her piercing gaze on me. "Thanks so much for hosting us in your home."

Hilda leaned back, lifting the front legs of her chair off the floor. "I'm delighted to do so. A house this large should be filled with people from time to time, don't you think?"

"It does provide the perfect layout for social functions," Zach said, as he settled in the chair next to mine. "Although I think I might feel a little lost living here when all the guests have gone home."

Hilda dropped down the chair legs and cast him a sardonic smile. "Ah, Dr. Flynn. Analyzing me now? Truth is, I do feel like a pebble rolling around in the Grand Canyon sometimes." Her smile faded. "My husband chose this house. He was a high-level executive with a pharmaceutical company in Maryland."

"So you lived here before you took the job at Clarion?" Zach asked.

"Not full-time. When Jasper was alive, we both worked near D.C., so we owned a townhouse in Alexandria and only came out here on weekends or holidays." A shadow flitted over Hilda's face.

She's still mourning her husband, I realized. Glancing at Zach, I could tell he was thinking the same thing. "This was primarily a vacation home, then," I said.

"That's right. But after Jasper passed, I started looking for a job in this area and was fortunate enough to end up at Clarion." The wisp of a smile twitched Hilda's lips. "I sold the townhouse and moved out here. It's a better place to host the kids and grandkids, and it does work well for events like this one."

I leaned forward, resting my arms on the table. "It must feel like a big change. But I guess you aren't averse to that."

"Change? Not at all." Hilda's smile broadened. "I actually revel in it. Which is why I'm committed to achieving some restructuring of our academic departments. I suppose you've already heard rumors about that, Ms. Dalton."

I returned her smile. "I have. Gossip and some grumbling, I'm afraid."

"Many people are resistant to change," Zach said. "It's a problem I deal with quite often."

"I'm sure. It's always easier to continue to do the same thing over and over, even if it isn't allowing individuals, or institutions, to reach their true potential." Hilda rested her elbows on the table and cradled her chin in her clasped hands. "I'm making plans that may shake things up at Clarion, but it's all for the good, I hope. At least in terms of benefiting the students, which should be our top priority, don't you think?"

Zach nodded. "Absolutely."

"Well, you see, that involves streamlining some reporting structures and shifting money from bloated administrative salaries to services that actually assist the students. Things like the writing center," she added, giving me a wink as she sat back in her chair.

"How about that, now the truth comes out," said Gary Alexander as he strode up to the table.

"Professor, this probably isn't the time and place." Hovering behind Gary, Erin appeared distraught.

I briefly wondered why Erin was trailing Gary, but chalked it up to her ongoing efforts to ingratiate herself with the department chair. "Erin's right. This is a social occasion, after all."

Gary slammed his fist on the table, causing all of us to jump. "Time and place have nothing to do with it. I overheard your talk about restructuring and streamlining and whatnot, Madame Provost. I know that's just code for eliminating those of us who've been at Clarion the longest, the very people who built the university into what it is today."

"I have no intention of eliminating anyone," Hilda said, both her tone and expression mild as a late spring day. "I simply think we need more professors back in the classroom rather than sitting on their duffs in administrative offices."

Gary wiped a bit of spittle from the corner of his mouth. "You're probably glad that poor Doug Barth is dead, aren't you?"

Hilda reared back and fixed him with a disdainful glare. "Why would you say that?"

"Because he supported me, and others, who don't approve of your drastic plans for change." Gary crossed his arms over his chest. "He was popular and had the ear of the students, so his opposition might've dashed your dreams."

Zach rose to his feet and faced off with Gary. "Listen, Professor Alexander, I think you should reconsider your words and actions tonight. It seems that you may not be in the best mindset to discuss such important matters."

"Who are you?" Gary looked down his nose at Zach.

"Dr. Zachary Flynn, psychologist." Zach extended his hand.

Gary batted it aside. "Never heard of you."

"Nevertheless, I believe you've been drinking too much to talk about anything substantive with the provost, or anyone else for that matter," Zach said equably.

"I agree." Hilda stood up and examined Gary with a critical eye. "We should not discuss such matters now. Although I will take this opportunity to correct you on one point, Professor Alexander. I'm afraid Doug Barth, rest his soul, would not have been a champion for your cause. As a matter of fact, he came to me not long before he died to let me know that he'd changed his mind. He was going to back my restructuring plan." She flashed a bright smile. "I thought you should know that."

A gasp hung in the air. I glanced over at Erin, who'd grabbed the back of a nearby chair.

"Sorry," she said, waving away any assistance. "I just had a twinge of pain. Sciatica," she added, with an apologetic smile. "As Jenn knows, I suffer with that from time to time."

This was true—I'd noticed her flinching and grimacing in the writing center when the condition flared up. I offered her a smile. "Sorry you're dealing with that again."

Gary, who was still glaring at Zach, turned his attention to Hilda. "I seriously doubt Doug ever changed his mind or told you he'd support your plans, but carry on with your little charade if you wish." He turned on his heel and stormed off.

"I should probably reconsider serving alcohol at these events." The twinkle was back in Hilda's eyes. "Nice speaking with you, Ms. Dalton and Dr. Flynn, and . . ." She looked expectantly at Erin.

"I'm Erin McHenry, the assistant director of the writing center," Erin replied stiffly.

"Ah, yes. We've spoken a few times." Hilda bent her head to acknowledge all three of us. "I'd better get back to circulating among my guests. Enjoy the rest of the evening."

As Hilda walked away, I glanced at Erin, noting her peeved expression. *She's probably upset that the provost didn't know her by sight*, I thought, with a shake of my head.

"I suppose I should mingle as well," Erin said. "That's what these parties are for, after all." She flounced off without saying goodbye.

Zach pushed his glasses back up his nose. "I sense anger and resentment emanating from your assistant."

I met his gaze and smiled. "How perceptive. Perhaps you should consider a career in psychology."

"I'll take that under consideration," he said, with an answering smile.

Chapter Twenty-Nine

O n the ride home, I shared the information I'd gathered at the party and elaborated on my thoughts concerning Andrea Karmen's possible involvement in Doug Barth's death.

"Then there's Gary Alexander. I didn't think he had any plausible motive, but now we know Doug was going to support the provost's plans. Considering his anger over such a betrayal, I think Gary should be considered a suspect as well."

"Alexander didn't know about that, though," Zach said, his gaze focused on the shadowed road ahead.

"Or did he?" I leaned my temple against the cool glass of the passenger side window. "If he discovered Doug was a traitor, he may have confronted him in the library and then . . ." I thrust my arms out as if pushing someone away.

"It's possible, especially considering his volatile personality, but if Barth really did have some information that could force Andrea Karmen to give up her professorship . . ." Zach lifted his right hand off the steering wheel. "I believe that's the stronger motive."

"You're right, of course," I said glumly. Slumping in my seat, I absently drummed the fingers of my left hand against the center console.

"I know you don't want to contemplate a friend being a killer"— Zach laid his hand over my restless fingers—"but if you're going to play amateur detective, you have to play fair. Anyone with a motive must be considered a suspect."

I froze, trying to decide whether to whip my hand away. In the end I let it be. "I realize that. Even Mia, as much as I'm fighting to clear her, could still be at fault, if only by accident."

Zach sent me a sideways glance. "Glad to hear you're not letting your emotions totally cloud your judgment." He lifted his hand and placed it back on the steering wheel. "I know it's hard to keep an open mind when personal feelings are involved."

"Are you always so pragmatic?" I asked. The darkened passenger side window reflected both of us, which was, I realized, a useful way to watch Zach's expressions without looking at him.

"Hardly. I have plenty of my own foibles." A little smile played over his lips. "Like being intrigued by certain individuals, even if they don't seem inclined to get to know me better."

"Intrigued? In what way? As a psychological study or experiment?"

Zach's smile fell away. "No. I try to keep my personal and professional life separate. Despite what people might think, I'm not constantly analyzing everyone I meet."

"You aren't trying to figure me out right now?" I asked, keeping my tone light.

"Actually, I'm trying not to." Zach glanced over at me. "You're watching me in the glass, aren't you?"

I shifted in my seat and looked straight ahead. "You caught me. Sorry."

"It's fine. I suppose you're trying to figure me out as well. But I must warn you I've been told it's a very difficult thing to do."

I shot him a questioning glance. "By whom? Your former girlfriends?"

"Among others," he said, meeting my gaze for a second.

"Ah, a man of mystery." I scrunched up my face at him.

"Not quite that glamorous," he replied, looking back at the road. "But I've done enough self-reflection to know I can be challenging."

I toyed with my dangling earring. "You don't say."

This earned me a chuckle. Zach only spoke again after a short stretch of silence. "To be honest, I don't always think it's a bad thing, being difficult to understand. It means there's always more to learn about the person. And, to be fair, I prefer the company of people who challenge me."

We'd reached Taylorsford's main street. I buttoned up my coat and closed my fingers over my clutch purse. "You appreciate a battle of wits. I think I've learned that much," I said, keeping my gaze lowered.

"It's true. Which is one reason I like you, Jenn."

I glanced over at him from under my lowered lashes. "Are there more?"

Zach pulled into Emily's driveway and parked the car before replying. "Of course. Let me count the ways." He unbuckled his seatbelt and turned to me.

"Hah—that old line. I need to introduce you to some new material," I said, right before he leaned in and kissed me.

* * *

"I have to tell you, Ash, I think I'm in trouble," I told the cat, who simply blinked her golden eyes as she stared up at me from her position on my lap. "I really don't have time to deal with any sort of relationship right now, especially not one that demands a lot of attention."

I frowned and leaned back against the sofa cushions, staring up at the ceiling. The kiss had taken me by surprise, not only because I wasn't expecting it but also because of how I'd responded to it. I'd meant to remain cool and collected, but . . .

"That didn't happen," I told Ash, not bothering to elaborate on what had transpired. A deep sigh rattled my chest. "Then afterwards I just said 'thanks' and jumped out of the car. Classy, huh?"

Ash nudged my hand with her head. "Alright, I'll pet you some more. Then I need to go to bed and get some sleep. Or *try* to get some sleep," I added, aware that I'd probably be agonizing over my schoolgirl behavior all night. "I just ran away, like a fifteen-year-old on her first date," I said, shaking my head.

My phone, set on vibrate, skittered across the side table. Ash meowed and leapt off my lap as I reached to grab it. There were two text messages. One was from Bri and only said, *call me*. The other was from Zach. It said, *you're welcome.*

"That man," I said, one hand fanning my face as I called Bri.

As soon as she answered, Bri told me to sit down.

"I'm already seated," I said.

"Good, because what I'm about to tell you will be a shock." Bri cleared her throat. "I just got off the phone with Christine and she said something major happened at the provost's party after you left."

"Skinny-dipping in the fountain out back?" I asked, remembering that a few students had engaged in that activity at a welcome party in August.

"Nothing so innocent, I'm afraid. This is something else entirely."

"Okay, you have me hooked. What's this all about?"

"Someone died," Bri said flatly.

"What?" I jumped to my feet, sending Ash dashing across the room to a protected spot under the kitchen chairs. "Who? And how?"

"The how is falling off the top balcony at the back of the house. The who"—Bri exhaled a gusty breath—"is Professor Gary Alexander."

Chapter Thirty

M y shriek sent Ash scurrying from the kitchen into my bedroom. "An accident, I presume?" I asked once I could speak.

"That's the assumption," Bri said. "No one actually saw him fall,
but everyone agrees he was drunk enough to tumble over a balus-
trade if he wasn't careful."

"That's terrible. I mean, he wasn't my favorite person, but
still . . ." I tightened my grip on the phone. "They're sure it's an accident? Two men in the same department falling to their deaths is a
little suspicious." *Especially since both had ongoing conflicts with others
at the university, like Andrea Karmen and the provost,* I thought. *Also,
who's to say Doug hadn't confided in Gary about his marriage? Miranda
was at the party last night, and Gary spoke with her in private. If she
threatened Doug to his face, and he told Gary about that, maybe Gary
planned to reveal that secret unless Miranda did cough up some money
for his "pet projects." That certainly could've provided enough motiva-
tion for her to want to give him a good shove.*

"I suppose the authorities will investigate just in case, but everyone's saying it's an accident at this point. Apparently, no one saw
anything, though, so who knows?"

"There were so many people at the party, it'll be difficult to get a clear picture," I said, frowning. "It must've happened later in the evening, though, when many of the guests had already left. That may narrow down the investigation a bit."

"Yeah, I heard the crowd had thinned out. I guess knowing who was still there might tell us more, like whether there was any chance that it was *not* an accident. If some of our top suspects in Doug's death were around when Gary died, that would raise my suspicions."

"I'm not sure how we can find out—" I snapped my fingers. "Christine was still there when the accident occurred. She was the one who called you about Professor Alexander's fall, after all."

"Right, so she should also know who was still at the house. I'll call her back. But tomorrow, better be tomorrow. It's far too late now, especially since she had to work all evening. Speaking of which, I should let you go too. I'm sure you're ready to get some rest." Bri promised to text me with any additional information and wished me a good night.

I sat, staring at my dark phone screen for several minutes. My brain felt like it had been put in a blender. "Too much happening," I muttered. "Way too much all at once."

Dragging myself off the sofa I headed into my bedroom. I got ready for bed, thankful I could do so by habit, since my mind was definitely elsewhere. Crawling under the covers, I prepared myself for a long night, but surprisingly, it only took Ash leaping up onto the bed and settling in next to me, her loud purr rumbling like a steady storm, for me to fall asleep.

* * *

Except for Emily taking me to pick up my car, I spent most of Saturday at my desk, distracting my mind from real-world problems by finally diving into serious planning for my next book. After everything that had happened, it was actually refreshing to immerse myself in the fictional adventures of my two amateur sleuths.

"The nice thing is, whatever dangers you get into, I can get you out," I told Annabelle and Olivia. "Wish I could do that as easily in my own life." Sometimes my characters talked back to me, but not in this case. They obviously recognized the wisdom of my words.

Checking my phone during one of my breaks, I noticed a text from Christine. She'd sent Bri and me a list of names—the party guests who'd still been at the provost's house when Gary fell to his death. I wasn't actually surprised that the names correlated with our suspect list. This simply reinforced my suspicion that Gary Alexander, like Doug Barth, could've been murdered.

"So Miranda Barth, Andrea Karmen, and even Paige Irving, who I never saw, were still at the house when Gary died," I said, in a conference call with Christine and Bri.

"Paige was there as the date of one of the business school professors," Christine said. "I recognized her from the photo on her website."

"Could it have been suicide?" Bri asked. "If Gary murdered Doug, maybe his guilt, fueled by too much alcohol, got the better of him."

"I doubt it. When I encountered him at the party, he was fired up, ready to take on the provost and derail her plans. He was already pretty tipsy by then but not morose. I can't imagine any amount of alcohol would've turned him suicidal."

"Of course, Dr. Lange was there the whole time." Christine blew her nose. "Sorry, leaf mold allergy. Drives me nuts this time of year."

"The situation does eliminate Mia, at least," I said.

"Not really," Bri said. "You may not have heard, but she's out on bail. Of course, she wasn't invited to the party, but it wouldn't have been difficult to park among all those other cars and sneak into the house. She could've heard about the party from Francesca or some other students, and she'd likely assume Gary would be there."

"But why would Mia want to harm Professor Alexander?" Christine asked. "I know she had issues with Barth, but not the department chair."

"Yeah, I guess you're right. Still, it isn't impossible for her to have been at Hilda Lange's house last night. Or Francesca, if it came to that," Bri said. "I don't think either girl had anything to do with Gary's death, but we have to consider all the angles. Law enforcement is so focused on Mia, they might jump down that rabbit hole."

"Good point," I said. "We do need to anticipate such things."

Christine expressed her agreement with this mindset. "I'll talk to Heidi again as soon as possible. She says our info has been extremely helpful for her team's independent investigation and has encouraged me to continue to share any of our thoughts and findings with her."

We agreed to meet in the writing center early on Monday morning, before any of us had to start work. "Well, technically, I should be at the cafeteria at that time, but I can have one of my assistants cover for me," Christine said.

Bri asked me to stay on the phone when Christine signed off. "This is totally unconnected with the Mia Jackson case," she told me. "I just keep forgetting that I want to invite you to an exhibit opening at the art department gallery next Friday evening."

"Okay," I said dubiously. "But why do you need a date? Isn't Rachel coming home on Tuesday?"

"Yes, and she will be my date, but this is a special exhibit." Bri's voice quivered. She sounded nervous, which caught my attention.

Bri feeling anxious was highly unusual. "I didn't tell you before, because I wasn't sure how it would go, but I used my staff tuition credit to take an art course this semester."

I sat up in my desk chair. "Wait—do you have artwork being displayed in this exhibit?"

"I do." There was no mistaking the pride in Bri's tone. "Two paintings, to be exact."

"Congratulations, and of course I'll attend the opening. Text me the details and I'll be there," I said, before offering her a goodbye and hanging up.

There was another text on my phone. Noticing who'd sent it. I took a moment to collect my thoughts before opening it up.

We never had that dinner, Zach's text said. *How about this evening?*

I glanced at my office clock. The message had been sent at two, and it was five. Responding now felt awkward. But I realized things would get more awkward if I ignored it.

I texted back: *Sorry, I was working and didn't check my phone*—a slight exaggeration, although not entirely untrue. *It's probably too late to make plans now, but thanks for the invite.*

Too late for what? I'm not making reservations at a four-star restaurant. There are plenty of places one can go to whenever.

I tapped my phone against my palm. It would be easy to claim I had a headache, or that I needed to work on my book, or any number of other excuses. But despite the twinge of anxiety tightening my shoulders, I decided to take a page from my own books and plunge bravely into the unknown.

Alright, as long as it's casual dress and we split the bill. What time?

I'll pick you up at six-thirty.

There was a slight pause, then another message came through:

We are not splitting the bill. I'm paying.
Then I pay next time, I texted back.
Next time? Making assumptions, Ms. Dalton?
My fingers were poised to type a retort when Zach sent a final text and signed off:
Good. Keep making them.

Chapter Thirty-One

When Zach showed up at my door, I was glad to see that he'd accepted my suggestion to keep things casual. His well-worn jeans, long-sleeved henley and windbreaker definitely presented a different look from his typical work attire. *Not a bad look*, I thought, tugging the bottom of my turquoise sweater down over the waist of my jeans. *In fact, he's more attractive in this outfit than he was in the suit, which is a little . . . disconcerting.*

"You said you like Thai, so I thought we'd give that a try," he said, as I slipped on my denim jacket and slung my purse strap over my shoulder. "The restaurant's on this side of Harburg, so not too far."

"Sounds good." After locking my front door, I walked over to the car and climbed in.

"I would've opened the door for you," Zach said, as he slid into the driver's seat.

I fastened my seatbelt and clutched my purse to my chest. "It's not really necessary. I mean, this isn't some formal date or anything."

Zach's eyebrows shot up. "Maybe we're not being overly formal, but I think it *is* a date."

"Really? That seems a bit old-fashioned. Most people don't label relationships these days," I said as Zach drove onto the main road. "You know, it's more like friends get together, hang out, or whatever. No big deal."

"Hmm. I think we're a little old for that sort of relationship, don't you?" Zach cast me a wry smile. "I used to 'hang out' in college, and 'get together' in grad school. Now I prefer to date."

I sank back in my seat. "Call it what you want. I was simply trying to lighten the mood and keep things fun."

Zach side-eyed me. "I assume you've had relationships in the past. Is that what you've always done—kept things light and fun?"

"Well . . ." I squirmed in my seat. Of course, I'd had relationships in the past, some of which had lasted for a decent amount of time. Were they all as superficial as Zach seemed to be implying? I gnawed on the inside of my cheek. Maybe. "Is there anything wrong with that?"

"No. I'm simply curious." Zach shrugged. "I was just wondering if you'd ever had what you'd call a serious relationship."

"Have you?" I shot back.

"Once," he said.

"Obviously it didn't work out," I said, then slapped my hand over my mouth.

Zach appeared unfazed by my rude comment. "It did not. The truth is, she was entirely too sweet."

"You mean she didn't enjoy going toe-to-toe with you."

"Exactly. I often upset her without meaning to," Zach said.

"Hardly surprising," I muttered.

From the grin Zach cast my way, I could tell he'd heard me. I sat up and swiveled to view his profile. "So let me get this straight—you like me partially because I'm *not* sweet?"

"That's right. You're nice but not sweet. There's a difference."
Zach pulled into the parking lot of an unassuming restaurant. "As
you can see, it's nothing fancy, but the food is good."

"Hold on, I want some clarification on this conversation," I said,
as Zach exited the car.

He circled around to open my door. "We can talk inside," he
said, leaning on the top of the door frame. "Or would you rather get
takeout and eat in the car?"

"Of course not," I said, pushing the door, and him, back a few
inches. I climbed out, trying to be graceful and failing spectacularly
by stumbling over the curb.

Zach grabbed my arm and steadied me. "Let's not have another
fall," he said.

I shook off his hand and marched into the restaurant ahead
of him.

We were seated in a booth in a shadowy corner. "Speaking
of falls, I suppose you heard about Dr. Alexander?"

"Hard to miss that." Zach lowered his menu and gazed specula-
tively at me. "Don't tell me you and your merry band of sleuthers
have decided Alexander was murdered as well."

"Okay, I won't tell you," I said, keeping my eyes glued to the
menu.

"Hello, I'm Kim. I'll be your server tonight. What would you
like to drink?" asked the young woman who'd appeared at our table
with two water glasses.

She looked vaguely familiar. I knew a lot of students from Clarion worked in area restaurants, so I supposed that wasn't too
surprising.

"I'll have a gin and tonic," Zach said, as Kim set down the water
tumblers.

Kim nodded and turned to me. "Ms. Dalton," she said, her eyes brightening, "how are you? I never did thank you, but that assistance you gave me on my history paper was really great. I was totally lost until you showed me how to cite facts and quotes and all that."

"I'm glad I was able to help," I said. "I'll have a house Chardonnay, please."

"You know," Kim said, leaning in as if sharing a secret, "I always made sure you were in the writing center whenever I came in. No offense to the student assistants or whoever, but I knew you were the one who could really help me. If you weren't there, I'd just walk out again.

I frowned. It always upset me to hear that students were dissatisfied with the center. "Did you have a problem with how anyone treated you? You should've let me know."

Kim shrugged. "It wasn't a big deal. I also wanted to avoid Ms. McHenry, to be honest. I mean, it wasn't her fault. It's just that I took her poetry class and totally tanked it. So I felt kinda embarrassed to ask her for help."

Leaning against the wooden back of the booth, Zach crossed his arms over his chest. "You think she would've held that against you?"

"Not really. It's just that I felt so stupid in her class. She used all these allusions and metaphors or whatever right away. I was confused from the start and never really caught up."

"Sorry to hear that," I said.

Kim tossed her long dark braid behind one shoulder. "Anyway, let me put in your drink orders, and I'll be right back to get your food order."

As she walked away, I noticed Zach seemed lost in thought. "What is it?"

He met my gaze with a smile. "Nothing really. Wondering how well you know Erin McHenry, that's all."

"We've worked together for four years." I ran my finger around the rim of my water glass. "But honestly, I don't think I know her very well. She's very self-contained."

"She doesn't talk about personal matters?" Zach paused to thank Kim when she set down our drinks. He waited to speak again until after we put in our food orders and Kim left the table. "As I mentioned the other evening, Ms. McHenry projects a lot of anger and resentment. Do you know why?"

"I think it's because she's frustrated with her career." I took a sip of wine as I organized my thoughts. "The thing is, she's always wanted to be a full-time instructor. Tenure track, preferably. That's her dream. Right now she only teaches one course. She's been waiting and hoping that a position would open up in the English department, but it hasn't."

Zach rattled the ice cubes in his drink. "Interestingly, it will now."

I stared at him, opening my mouth and snapping it shut again without saying anything.

"Has your Scooby gang looked into her, by any chance?" Zach asked.

"No, but come to think of it, she was still at the party when Gary fell. She was one of the names on Christine's list." I took a long swallow of wine.

Zach leaned forward. "Did she have a problem with Doug Barth?'

"She didn't like him, I know that. She thought he and Gary were old fogies who didn't want her to have any say in the department, even if she was teaching a class."

"Might be worth looking into her, then." Zach sipped his drink. "I wouldn't dare diagnose someone I've only met in passing, but I will say that Ms. McHenry presents with several indicators of a problematic personality."

"In other words, she's a little off the rails?" I asked, sitting back as Kim placed our meals on the table.

Zach again waited until Kim disappeared before answering me. "That's not a very scientific way of phrasing it, but . . . it's possible."

As we dug into our food, Zach suggested that we change topics.

"This pad Thai is delicious," I said, afraid he was steering the conversation back to more personal matters.

"So's my red curry." Zach laid down his fork and studied me for a moment. "I was actually thinking of continuing our conversation from the car."

"As in, why you think I'm nice but not sweet?"

"As in, why would that bother you?"

I speared a piece of pickled cabbage with my fork and lifted it over my plate. "The opposite of sweet is sour. Are you saying I'm sour?"

Zach laughed. "I should've known a writer would get caught up in the words. No, I'm not implying that you are mean, sour, or anything like that. I'm saying you're someone who'll stand up for herself and give as good as she gets. And I like that, okay?"

"A tough girl," I said, stabbing a noodle with my fork.

"Not at all. An independent woman. Someone who knows her own mind. A self-assured individual who won't let me get away with any nonsense." Zach grinned and waved a forkful of shrimp at me. "You won't, will you?"

"Absolutely not," I said, digging back into my food.

"And, in return, I will also call you on your crap."

I looked up to meet his wicked grin. "Really? Is that part of your oh-so-romantic offer?"

"Absolutely. It's the only way people like you and me can get along. Besides, I believe in equality."

"You believe in getting the last word," I said, earning another laugh.

Chapter Thirty-Two

On Monday I got to work early to meet with Bri and Christine before the writing center opened.

"It seems we really have four major suspects, excluding Mia," Bri said. "Andrea Karmen, Miranda Barth, Paige Irving, and Hilda Lange. Interestingly, all women."

I settled back in my office chair. "I don't know about including the provost on that list. She has enough power to override the objections of professors and even department chairs. I can't see her murdering either Doug or Gary simply because they opposed her plans."

"Yes, but if we assume that Doug's death happened in the heat of an argument, that could've involved her." Bri paced around my office. "That death would be manslaughter or second-degree murder since it wasn't planned. But then, think about it—what if Gary saw something or somehow put two and two together from things Doug told him? Hilda would've had a reason to get him out of the way too."

Christine, who was sitting in the office guest chair, primly crossed her legs at her ankles. "I dunno. That sounds pretty far-fetched to me too. I kinda think Miranda Barth should be at the top of the list. She had the most to lose, and since Jenn saw Gary having a heated conversation with her at the party, it's possible he was blackmailing her. That's motive enough, in my mind."

"Then there's Paige Irving." I drummed my fingers against the arm of my chair. "She certainly may have been furious with Doug for taking all the credit for their shared book. When Bri and I spoke with her, she acted like she didn't know anything about Doug's deceit, but she could've been acting to protect herself."

"Yeah, but why would she then murder Gary?" Bri halted her pacing and faced us. "Unless he did witness Doug's death, I can't see any connection."

"That's assuming it was the same killer both times," Christine said thoughtfully.

I switched my focus to her. "You're right. We don't know that for certain, either. Good point."

"Great point, actually. What if Gary and Doug argued over Doug's betrayal? I mean, Doug siding with the provost's ideas about restructuring the department." Bri clapped her hands. "If Gary shoved Doug off the library mezzanine in the heat of the moment, who's to say someone didn't see him? Maybe even Paige. Suppose she wasn't acting when we spoke with her, and she didn't know anything about Doug stealing all the credit for their book. She could've wanted revenge on Gary for killing her lover and coauthor."

"I hadn't thought of a scenario like that, but it's as likely as anything else, I guess." I rolled my chair up to my desk and grabbed a pen and notepad. "I'll write down these new theories so you can share them with Heidi Farmer, Christine."

"Okay, but I'll be busy with work all day," she replied, rising to her feet. "I probably can't send anything until this evening."

"That's fine. As long as she gets it. You said her team was already investigating these people anyway," I said.

"Is there anything we're missing?" Bri ran her fingers through her blue-tipped hair. "I know we have to leave Mia, or even Francesca Silva, on the suspect list, but is there anyone else who had a beef with both Doug and Gary?"

Zach's comments about Erin flitted through my mind. "There could be, of course. They both made enemies of people with opposing views, like Andrea Karmen. Perhaps I can dig a little deeper into that possibility. I haven't accused Andrea of anything at this point, so she'd probably be willing to talk to me about anyone else who supported her opinions." I almost brought up Erin's name but decided I needed to speak with her first. I didn't want to implicate her simply based on her attitude toward the two victims.

"Sounds like a plan." Bri glanced at her watch. "But I'd better run. I have an early shift on the reference desk today."

"I need to get going too," Christine said. "Biscuits don't make themselves, more's the pity." She crossed to my desk and took the notes I'd jotted down from my outstretched hand. "Thanks, I'll share these with Heidi as soon as I can."

After they both left my office, I sat and doodled on the notepad, my thoughts circling around the possibility of Erin being involved in the murders. It seemed unlikely, given the fact that she'd been at a planned appointment off campus around the time Doug had been killed. Of course, I supposed that could've been a ruse. She had been at the provost's party when Gary fell. But would someone who appeared so meek and unassuming have the inclination to murder anyone?

I tapped the pen against my desktop. Zach said he'd picked up signs of repressed anger from his encounters with Erin, which was something I had to consider. But it was strange—in all the time I'd worked with her, I'd never seen her lose her temper.

Thinking about Zach brought up memories of the end of our dinner date on Saturday night. Zach had walked me to my door, hovering as if hoping I'd invite him in. I hadn't, of course. It was too soon for that.

But not too soon for another round of kissing that had turned more passionate than I'd anticipated. Recalling this, heat rose up the back of my neck. I had to do some careful analysis before seeing Zach again. The one thing I knew for certain was that while a relationship with him might sometimes be fun, it would never be the light and breezy kind I'd always preferred.

By the time Erin arrived for her shift, I'd already dealt with several students who were more interested in talking about Gary Alexander's unfortunate death than any form of writing.

"You're going to have to manage the fallout too, I'm afraid," I told her. "Be prepared to hear about Alexander's accident ad nauseam."

Erin shrugged. "I don't mind. It's simply normal curiosity."

"Following that topic, and not to bring up bad memories, but were you still at the party Friday night when the accident occurred? I'd left by then, thank goodness."

Erin turned away, leaning over to reset one of the computers. "Unfortunately, I was. I didn't see anything, though."

"That's a blessing." I studied her for a moment, noting the tension lifting her narrow shoulders closer to her ears. "I guess you still had to deal with questioning from the police."

"Yes, but I didn't mind. They were just doing their job." Thinking of Zach's comments about looking more closely into Erin, I decided to try a new tactic. "Oh, one more thing. I know you had an appointment the day Doug Barth died. Was that with your dentist?"

"Yes," Erin said, shooting me a puzzled expression.

"I thought so. Anyway, the reason I asked was because I'm thinking of changing to a new dental practice. Mine's gotten so busy, it's hard to even schedule annual exams. Do you mind sharing who you see?"

"No problem." Erin hurried into her office and immediately returned, holding out a business card. "It's this practice. They're good and take most insurance."

I thanked her and pocketed the card. "Well, I have some work to do in my office if you're okay out here."

Erin raised one hand to wave me off. "Sure thing."

I returned to my office, closing the door for more privacy. Pulling the business card from my pocket I examined it for a moment, then placed a call.

The receptionist greeted me cheerfully, but sounded befuddled when I mentioned that Erin McHenry had recommended their practice.

"Really? We've been trying to get in touch with her but can't seem to get any response. If you know her, could you ask her to contact us? We need to schedule an appointment. It's been over a year since she's come in for a check-up."

I stared at the phone, speechless.

"Hello, hello, are you still there?" the receptionist asked.

Hanging up without replying, I gazed through the open blinds that covered the windows separating my office from the main portion of the writing center. I could see Erin moving around, assisting a small group of students.

There was no appointment, I thought. *Or, at least, not the one you used as an excuse to leave work early. So where were you, Erin?*

Chapter Thirty-Three

L ater in the day, I caught up with Erin again when we were both grabbing a snack in the break room.

"I'll keep a lookout," I told her, remaining on my feet while she sat at the table. "You've been doing most of the work with the students today, so I'll assist the next batch to give you a breather."

"Thanks." Erin looked up from her diet soda and bag of chips. "Actually, I'm glad we have a minute to talk, Jenn. I've been wanting to give you a heads-up about my future plans."

Her eyes shone brighter than I'd seen them for some time. "You're thinking about leaving the writing center, I assume?"

"Yes." Erin fiddled with the pop top on her drink can. "I know it may sound heartless, and I don't mean it that way, but I have to be practical—there will be some open positions I can apply for in the English department soon."

I tossed my own soda can in the recycling bin. "I suppose. But I also heard the provost say something about restructuring that department, so we can't be sure what it will end up looking like."

"Oh, I know. I've already had a conversation with the provost about her ideas, and her plans actually might make it easier for me to get a full-time teaching position." Bent back and forth by Erin's restless fingers, the pop top broke off and sailed across the table.

I leaned down to pick up the circle of metal from the floor. "Because she's hoping to add a greater variety of literature and writing courses?" I straightened and met Erin's cheerful gaze.

"That's right. I could keep teaching my poetry class, but there will also be other courses suited to my background. I studied graphic arts too, you know, and have done some research on graphic novels and serial web novels." Erin balled up the empty chips bag in her fist. "I could easily teach those classes. I don't think anyone else currently in the department could."

"Well, there's Andrea Karmen," I said, discarding the pop top in the trash.

"Sure, but she's likely to be tapped to be department chair. She could only teach a limited number of courses if that happened." Erin smiled. "I wouldn't mind that. I think Andrea and I would get along quite well. We could work together to make some substantive changes in the curriculum."

"I see," I said, my mind racing to process these comments. This information revealed a motive for Erin to eliminate Doug and Gary but could also further implicate Andrea. *If both of them knew this—if they'd had serious conversations with the provost before the deaths—maybe they even colluded to murder the two men who stood in their way.*

"I thought you should know, even though it may seem a little too soon to discuss such things," Erin said. "I didn't want you to feel blindsided later."

"I appreciate that," I replied automatically. "Okay, speaking of Andrea, I'd better get back to work on that presentation for her mystery and thriller writing course. You take your time, though. I can keep an eye out for any students from my office."

"Thanks. In that case, I think I'll take a short walk outside. Get a little air and sunshine while I can." Erin pushed back her chair and stood, stretching her arms over her head.

She's small, but wiry, I realized. There's definitely some muscle in her arms. Enough to shove someone off a balcony? Maybe.

Back in my office, I waited until Erin left the center, then called Andrea.

"Hey there, I hear you may get some good news soon," I told her after our hellos.

"What do you mean?" Andrea's voice expressed confusion.

"Erin McHenry just told me about the provost's plan to restructure the English department, making you chair," I said.

"Say what? I don't know anything about that," Andrea replied.

"Really? Erin implied that you'd both spoken with the provost concerning some major changes in the department."

Andrea huffed. "Maybe she did, but I wasn't involved. Of course, there will be changes, but nothing has been decided. Certainly not anything concerning the position of chair, at any rate."

"I see. Interesting. She seemed so sure."

"In her own head, maybe. She's a bit . . . imaginative, I guess you could say. She seems to think she's guaranteed a teaching position in the department now that we've tragically lost two faculty members, but that may not be the case." Andrea audibly exhaled. "It's a little creepy, if you ask me. I even saw her cozying up to Miranda Barth at Doug's funeral. I can't imagine why, unless they were commiserating about how badly Doug treated them both."

"Treated them badly?" I asked, trying not to sound too excited. "I know about Miranda's situation, but I wasn't aware that Doug had specifically done anything to Erin. Other than look down on her and ignore her, I mean."

"Oh, it was more than that. He did everything in his power to keep her from getting a tenured position in the department. He actively blackballed her. Apparently, it was based on some old feud between them," Andrea said.

"You mean, before Erin ever came to work at Clarion?"

"Yes. The story I heard was that Erin was doing book reviews for one of the trades when Doug brought out his book about the works of Henry James. Erin trashed him in her review, even claiming that he'd plagiarized some sections. Well, you can imagine how Doug felt about her after that."

"There was bad blood between them, then," I said, my thoughts spinning.

"Definitely. Doug hated Erin and shot her down every chance he could. To tell you the truth, I think it was the reason he supported Gary's opposition to the provost's plans. Gary was totally resistant to change, but Doug was actually more open-minded. If he hadn't wanted to stick it to Erin, who thought she'd have a chance at a full-time position if the department was restructured, he'd probably have been on the provost's side."

According to Hilda Lange, Doug had changed sides right before he died, I recalled. *No one but Hilda seems to have known that, though. Not until Hilda mentioned it at her party.*

"That does explain some things," I said. "Sorry I was misinformed about the chair position, but I bet you will be up for it, eventually." I wished her a good afternoon and hung up.

I wanted to immediately pursue this new line of inquiry, but I did have to complete prepping for the presentation to Andrea's class on Wednesday. My questions about Erin, and the rest of the suspects on my list, would have to wait.

When I got home Monday evening, I was still filled with nervous energy. "I think I'll take a walk," I told Ash as I changed into sweatpants and a T-shirt.

Ash, who was content now that I'd fed her and given her some attention, opened one eye, then went back to sleep on my bed.

It was a reasonably warm fall day, so I simply threw on a hooded sweatshirt and headed out. I strode down the sidewalk, brick-paved in keeping with Taylorsford's historic status. The red and gold leaves of the trees shading the sidewalk rustled overhead, and the sky was threaded with scarlet ribbons that announced the impending sunset.

Keeping up a brisk pace, I walked to the edge of the historic portion of town, where an old mill had been converted into a rather overpriced restaurant and inn. On the way back, I paused in front of the public library. It was a lovely stone building, with a small front lawn shaded by maple trees.

"I really need to stop in and visit someday," I said, talking to myself.

"Yes, you should," said a familiar voice.

I spun around and came face-to-face with Zach. "Oh, hello. What are you doing here?"

"Did you forget? I live nearby." Zach's smile took the edge off his words. Like me, he was wearing sweatpants and a sweatshirt.

"Are you out for a walk or jog too?" I asked.

"Just finished. I'm heading back home now." His eyes were shadowed behind the dark transition lenses of his glasses. "Would you like to tag along? I can offer you a glass of wine and show off the house."

"Well . . ." I couldn't think of a good reason to refuse and besides, I was curious about his home. "Alright."

Zach led the way down the lane that ran between the library and some residential buildings. "There's the archives I mentioned," he said, pointing out a small stone building sitting at the edge of the library's gravel parking lot.

The lane connected to a narrow road that paralleled Main Street. We turned right and walked a block, stopping in front of a one-story home with a small front yard dotted with flowerbeds and enclosed by a white picket fence.

Like Emily's, the house was a bungalow, although it was clad in stucco instead of brick. An arched enclosure over the front door and the rustic-style brown shingles gave it a storybook air.

"Charming," I said, as Zach opened the gate and escorted me into the front yard.

"Not what you expected, I bet," he said, unlocking the bright-blue front door.

I glanced at the window boxes filled with vibrant orange and yellow chrysanthemums. "Not exactly, no. It's a little more whimsical than I would've predicted."

Zach held open the door for me to enter. Inside, the aura of a storybook cottage continued, although one without any homey clutter. The foyer table held a single glazed porcelain bowl, while the only other decorations were a braided rug and an abstract painting.

"It reminded me of houses in books I read as a child," Zach said, closing the door behind us. "Which I suppose does show my more whimsical side." He gestured toward the living room, which lay beyond an arched opening off the foyer. "Please, have a seat. I'll go grab a couple of glasses of wine." He strode off toward another arched opening that revealed a small portion of the kitchen.

I wandered into the living room and chose a sofa set at right angles to the stucco fireplace. Sinking into the soft pale-green cushions, I allowed my gaze to sweep over the combination living and dining rooms.

There wasn't a lot of furniture, and most of it was either constructed of plain wood or upholstered in muted earth tones. A large bookcase filled the wall across from the fireplace, extending from the living room into the open dining room. A couple of vibrant paintings hung on the walls, but there were very few other decorative items, lending the space a rather spartan look.

No nonsense, like its owner, I thought, my lips twitching into a smile.

"So you approve?" Zach returned and handed me a glass of white wine.

"It's very nice. How many rooms?"

Zach settled into a chair that faced the sofa. "Three bedrooms and two baths." Obviously noticing my surprise, he nodded. "It's bigger than it looks from the front. The house extends pretty far back into the lot. Fortunately, there are only trees, not houses, behind the back yard."

"So rather private," I said, taking a sip of my wine.

"That's the idea." Zach stretched his long legs out across the hardwood floor in front of his chair. "I deal with people and their problems all day, so . . ."

"You just want to be alone when you're at home," I said, with a nod.

"Well"—Zach cast me a seductive look from under his thick lashes—"not all the time."

Chapter Thirty-Four

I took a long swallow of my wine before I replied. "I should tell you about some new info I've discovered that may have a bearing on the deaths of Doug Barth and Gary Alexander."

"Must you?" Zach rose to his feet and crossed to the sofa. Sitting next to me, he clinked his glass against mine. "Alright, go ahead. I know you won't be satisfied until you spill all your new clues."

I stared straight ahead, acutely aware of his proximity, and launched into a description of what Christine and Bri and I had discussed earlier in the day, along with the revelations about Erin. "The thing is, she could've been in the library that day," I said. "She certainly didn't go to the appointment she used as an excuse to leave work early."

"Agreed. But so could Andrea Karmen, or Paige Irving, or Miranda Barth, or even Gary Alexander. Not to mention, we know Mia Jackson was there." Zach leaned over me to set his empty wineglass on a side table. "You haven't really uncovered hard evidence against any of them. Except perhaps Mia, unfortunately, since she was seen in the area by Andrea."

"I know," I said, setting my empty glass next to Zach's. "But according to Mia's lawyer, what we've discovered has been helpful in building her defense. So I call that a win."

"Looking at it that way, you're right." Zach leaned forward, gripping his knees with his hands. "But there's still that threat you received via text. Have the authorities told you anything about who might've sent it?"

"No. They claim it was probably a burner, discarded or even smashed after it was used." I leaned forward and turned my head to meet his concerned gaze. "Nothing else has happened, so I'm not terribly worried."

"Nothing's happened *yet*. Unless you count Gary Alexander plunging to his death at a party we both attended." Zach placed one hand on my knee. "You should still be cautious, Jenn. Don't go out at night by yourself, at least until we identify the real culprit or culprits."

"Speaking of that," I said, thinking of my conversation with Bri, "I wonder if you're free Friday evening."

"I can be. What's happening on Friday?"

"It's the opening of a campus art exhibit. Normally I wouldn't bother; I'd just go check it out during the day. But Bri asked me to come on opening night because she took an art course and has two paintings in the exhibition."

"Okay, just let me know what time to pick you up."

"I'll text you." I sat back. "I could drive this time, you know."

Zach gave a fake shudder. "Not after the last experience I had in your vehicle. No, I'll drive."

"Very funny." I gazed around the living and dining room again. "You have a good sense of what works in a house like this."

Zach sat back as well. "Thanks. It wasn't that hard. I lived in a similar style home as a child and teen."

"Did you grow up around here?" I asked.

"No, a couple of hours south, in Charlottesville. My parents still live there."

"Really? Do they work for the University of Virginia?"

"As a matter of fact, they do." Zach shifted his position on the sofa. "They're both professors at the Darden School of Business."

"Impressive," I said. "What field?"

"International economics." He shot me an amused look. "Not my thing, which disappointed them a little, I think."

"Hey, you have a doctorate in psychology. Surely that's good enough."

"You'd think." Zach laid a hand on my shoulder. "What about you? Does your family live around here?"

I shook my head. "My mom has a home near Frederick, Maryland, which is where I grew up. But she's hardly ever there. She's a travel photographer. All those beautiful resort pictures on brochures and the web? She took a lot of those."

"So she's a globe trotter," Zach said.

"Most definitely. Especially since my dad passed away. That happened when I was in college." I turned my head so Zach couldn't see my eyes clearly. This wasn't a subject I liked to dwell on. "Then there's my older sister, April, who's an art restorer. She's in Italy right now, working in a church in Verona. My younger brother, Josh, is a naval officer. He's out to sea on one of those enormous aircraft carriers for months at a time. I don't get to see any of them that often, although we try to stay in touch with video chats and things like that." I turned back to meet his interested gaze. "Are you an only child?"

Zach pressed his hand to his chest. "Do I act like one? No, I actually have a twin sister. Her name's Claudia, but she goes by Dee. She lives in Charlottesville with my parents."

"A twin?" I arched my eyebrows. "That's intriguing. What does she do?"

"Well . . ." It was Zach's turn to look away. "She's an artist, when she can work. She has challenges, you see."

"I'm sorry," I said.

"Nothing to be sorry about. She's bipolar, which is no one's fault, least of all hers. She does pretty well on medication, but it has to be adjusted or changed quite often and the side effects . . ." Zach cleared his throat. "Now—how about that house tour I promised you?" He stood up and took hold of my hands to pull me to my feet. "I'm rather proud of the kitchen and my study."

"What about your bedroom?" I asked, without thinking.

Zach shot me a sly glance. "What about it?"

"Aren't you proud of that too?" I walked a few steps ahead of him, entering the kitchen before he did. "Oh, this is nice," I added, as I gazed around the space.

The kitchen had obviously been renovated but still felt appropriate to the house. Shaker cabinets in a light wood were paired with black hardware and simple white quartz countertops. The backsplash was a mosaic of glass tiles in various shades of green. A small café table and two chairs filled the corner of the room that included large windows opening onto the side and back yard.

"The bedrooms and baths are this way," Zach said, striding off down a hallway on the opposite end of the kitchen.

I followed him, glancing briefly into the guest bathroom and one guest bedroom before Zach opened the door on a room he called the study. Obviously intended to be a bedroom, it had been converted into a comfortable office, with bookshelves covering three walls and a sleek wood and metal desk that looked out a large window onto the backyard.

"Very nice," I said. "I could see reading or writing in here."

"It works well," Zach said. "Now, for the final room, which is across the hall."

Of course that's the main bedroom, I thought, as Zach swung open the door.

It was even more sparsely furnished than the rest of the house. There was a bed and nightstands and that was all. I noticed two doors leading off the room. "Closet and bathroom, I guess?"

"Exactly. I did a more extensive renovation so they'd connect directly to this room. I think the closet was originally a small nursery."

"I guess you needed to keep things simple with that big bed," I said.

Zach, who was standing behind me, tapped my shoulder. "Tall people need big beds."

"Hmm, right." As I turned to leave, I realized that Zach had stepped to the side so that I walked right into him. "Sorry."

"No need to apologize." He slipped his arms around me.

"You did that on purpose," I said.

"Yes, I did. I'm going to kiss you on purpose too."

"So you think," I said, stepping back and breaking his loose embrace. I dashed out of the bedroom, down the hall, and through the kitchen. Zach followed slowly enough that I was already standing in the living room when he caught up with me.

"Did I offend you?" he asked, facing off with me in front of the fireplace.

"No, but I'm not ready to kiss you anywhere near a bed," I said, staring him directly in the eyes.

"Because you're worried about me getting carried away, or you?" Zach asked with a lift of his eyebrows.

"Both." I laid a hand on his shoulder. "If you want to kiss me, do it here."

I soon knew I'd made the right decision. The fire that kisses lit between us was far too combustible to ignite in a bedroom.

Of course, at one point, Zach made some smart remark about the sofa. "Or the floor," he whispered in my ear.

"You wish," I said.

* * *

By the time I left Zach's house, it was dark enough that he insisted on escorting me home.

"Only to the door. No farther," I said.

"Alright, message received," he replied with a chuckle.

"It's not that I'm a prude," I said, as we walked side by side. "I simply like to take things slow."

"So do I, usually," Zach replied. "Not this time, though, which is a little unnerving, to tell you the truth."

"I make you nervous?" A smile twitched my lips.

Zach threw his arm around my waist. "You do. You definitely do."

"Wow, and here I thought you were totally self-assured."

"I typically am. Which should tell you something." Zach dropped his arm as we approached my front door.

"Such as what?" I slipped my keys from my pocket.

"How attracted I am to you." Zach placed his hands on my shoulders and leaned in to press a gentle kiss on my lips. "How much I like you."

"I've sort of figured that out," I said, fixing him with a stern gaze. "Unless you're playing me, of course."

"I'm not. Scout's honor." Zach raised his right hand, palm out.

"You were never a scout," I said, unable to resist smiling.

"You got me," he replied. He waited until I unlocked my door, and added, "And like it or not, Jenn, you absolutely do."

Chapter Thirty-Five

Tuesday thankfully passed without incident. I kept a close eye on Erin, looking for any opportunity to pose questions that might reveal her role, if any, in the murders. Unfortunately, even when I relayed the dental office's request that she contact them, she didn't give anything away, maintaining her pretense that she'd been off campus.

"Oh, that," she said, with a flick of her wrist. "The truth is, I double-booked appointments by mistake. I ended up keeping an appointment to deal with my sciatica. I completely forgot I was supposed to go to the dentist. Thanks for letting me know; I'll contact them soon."

Although I wasn't sure I believed her, there was nothing I could say to dispute this. I had to look for something else if I wanted to present Erin as a suspect to the police.

I did share Erin's suspicious appointment mix-up with Christine and Bri, and Christine passed that info, along with Andrea's comments about Erin and Doug's feud, to Heidi Farmer. According to Christine, Mia's law team was continuing to investigate anything that might link another perpetrator to Doug Barth's death. They were more than happy to add Erin to their "possible suspects" list.

Late Wednesday afternoon I was discussing a short story written by one of my mentees when the door of my office swung open and banged against the metal molding.

"Excuse me?" I said, looking up to meet the furious gaze of Miranda Barth.

"We need to talk," she said.

"As you can see, I'm working with a student," I replied.

Miranda's nostrils flared. "I don't care if you are working with the next Pulitzer Prize winner, tell them to come back later."

"It's okay, we have another meeting scheduled on Friday," my mentee said, jumping up and scurrying out of the office. He carefully pulled the door closed behind him.

Miranda stalked over to the guest chair and sat down. "You need to stop," she said.

"Stop what?" I pressed my palms against the top of my desk to still my trembling fingers.

"Spreading rumors about me." Miranda toyed with the strand of pearls draped over the collar of her sleek navy dress. "Not only have I had to return to the police station to answer additional questions, but I've also been interrogated by some junior lawyer on Mia Jackson's defense team."

"They're simply trying to do the best for their client."

"By implicating me, I suppose." Miranda lifted her pointed chin and swept an imperious gaze over me. "I know you and some of your friends have been digging for dirt on me, as well as a few others, then sharing that with Heidi Farmer and her team. I'm telling you now, you need to cease and desist or I will sic the law on *you*."

"Who told you we were doing that?" I asked, convinced it wouldn't have been Heidi or her team.

Miranda smoothed her dress over her knees. "A reputable source. Someone who's observed what you've been up to."

It couldn't be Bri or Christine, I thought, *and surely Zach wouldn't say anything either.* I puzzled over this while Miranda continued to berate me.

"You don't have a scrap of evidence to link me to any crime," she said. "Yet you suggest that Farmer's team treat me as a suspect. In my own husband's murder, no less."

I studied her indignant expression. *Was she truly angry because she was innocent, or because she might get caught?* "To be fair, you admitted to me and Dr. Flynn that you weren't too broken up about Doug's death."

"That has nothing to do with it. No, I didn't love the man anymore and wanted out of the marriage. But I was going about that legally. At this point, everyone knows I'd filed for a divorce."

I rolled my chair away from the desk and swiveled to face her directly. "Really? Someone told me that Doug was the one who initiated divorce proceedings."

Miranda released a trill of laughter. "Doug? Want the split? Of course he didn't. He knew which side his bread was buttered on."

"But the rumor is that you didn't have a prenup, so he'd get half of your joint assets."

"Not exactly." Miranda examined her perfectly manicured fingernails. "The bulk of my wealth was inherited. It was put in trusts long before I married Doug. He had no claim to any of that money."

"Which is why you didn't bother with a prenup," I said thoughtfully.

"Exactly. Although I was also madly in love with Doug back then, fool that I was." For the first time since she entered the office, sorrow flitted over Miranda's face.

I leaned forward, my hands on my knees. "I'm sorry for any inconvenience you've been caused, Ms. Barth, but my friends and I . . . Well, our true goal was simply to encourage the authorities to consider suspects other than Mia Jackson. They zeroed in on her right away, and we were afraid they wouldn't consider any other angle. We aren't trying to prove that you're guilty, we just don't want Mia to be treated unfairly."

Miranda sniffed. "To be honest, I don't believe the girl did it, either. My bet is on either Andrea Karmen or that Paige creature."

"Why them?" I asked, sitting back in my chair.

"Because Doug spoke endlessly about the animosity between him and Professor Karmen. It was a subject I was heartily sick of. He swore she was out to get him somehow, and he was always trying to find something in her background he could use as leverage against her."

"Did he?"

Miranda shrugged. "I'm not sure. He made some vague comments about taking evidence to Gary Alexander, but I don't know if that referred to Professor Karmen or someone else."

I looked her over. Now that her anger had dissipated, she appeared perfectly calm. "Were you aware that Doug was planning to cheat Paige Irving over some book they'd coauthored?"

"I wasn't. I didn't even know he'd written a novel. Not until that woman accused me of forcing him to cut her out of the book deal." Miranda flicked an invisible piece of lint from her sleeve.

"Paige Irving came to you? Was that before or after Doug died?"

"Before. Not long before, come to think of it." Miranda tapped her chin with one finger. "Apparently, she'd just found out. I find that coincidence rather interesting."

I rubbed my temples with my fingers. *So Paige was lying when she spoke to me and Bri. She knew about Doug's betrayal but obviously didn't want us to realize that she knew. Perhaps because it was a good motive for murder?*

"At any rate, I've instructed the police and Farmer's team that they should be looking at Paige Irving, not me," Miranda said as she gracefully rose to her feet. "Or perhaps Andrea Karmen, although I believe my husband's mistress had the stronger motive." She strolled across the room, pausing after opening the door. "Doug stole all the credit for that book and lied to her about leaving me and wanting to marry her. I'd have wanted to shove him off a balcony too."

I remained seated for several minutes after Miranda left. Her revelations, if true, definitely painted Paige Irving in a different light. But then again, perhaps it was Miranda who was lying.

Shaking my head, I stood up and grabbed my coat and tote bag. As I locked my office, I noticed Erin, her purse strap slung over one shoulder, watching me. "I'm leaving now," I said. "Jim's here, though, so you can still take a dinner break if you want."

"Good, because I made plans to meet someone. I'll be back in an hour," she told Jim as she draped her jacket over one shoulder and sauntered out the main doors.

I cast a smile at Jim. "I hope it doesn't get too busy. If you run up against anything difficult, tell the student to come back later, or tomorrow."

"Will do," he said, with an answering smile.

I hurried out of the center before anyone could stop me with a question or request for help. After the encounter with Miranda, I was yearning to get home and enjoy a glass of wine and Ash's feline company. I rushed to my car, glad I'd been able to park closer to the library than usual. As I pulled out of the lot and onto one of the campus roadways, an older model sedan pulled out behind me. It was a ubiquitous white compact car, so at first I paid it no attention. But as I drove off campus and headed for the back roads I preferred, I grew a little uneasy. The white car continued to follow me, making every turn I did, but staying far enough behind my vehicle that I couldn't identify the driver.

I sped up on the straightaways, but no matter how far ahead I pulled, the white car caught up with me, especially when I had to slow down on the curves. I told myself I was being foolish but couldn't shake the feeling I was being deliberately followed.

I'd almost reached the turn leading into Taylorsford when the white car accelerated and passed me on a double line. Swearing, I tried to catch a glimpse of the driver, but all I could determine was it was a woman in a voluminous hat and sunglasses. I couldn't identify hair color or any other distinguishing features.

A few seconds later, the white car slammed on the brakes, forcing me to do the same. This sent my car into a skid. Trying to avoid hitting anything, I steered into the spin.

My car ended up in the proper lane but facing the wrong direction. Gripping the steering wheel like a lifeline, I turned the car around and drove into town. The white car was nowhere to be seen.

Fortunately, I didn't start shaking violently until I was inside the guest house and had locked the door behind me.

I called Zach after one glass of wine.

I blurted out my question as soon as he answered. "Speaking of quid pro quo, would you like a tour of my house?"

Chapter Thirty-Six

Zach showed up in a matter of minutes. "What happened?" he asked, as soon as I let him in.

I detailed the white car incident while I carefully relocked the door.

He stood, unmoving, until I finished talking, then strode forward and pulled me into a close embrace. "What about calling the police?" he asked, after a minute or so.

I shook my head. "I don't think it will do any good. I didn't get a good look at the person or their license plate, and the car was indistinguishable from a million others."

"Did anything happen before you headed home from work?" Keeping one arm around my shoulders, Zach guided me to the sofa.

"Miranda Barth came to see me." Leaning into the sofa cushions, I stared up at the ceiling and recounted my encounter with Miranda. "But I can't imagine her driving an older, not very expensive-looking car. It's not her style. Come to think of it, I don't believe it's Paige Irving's style, either, and I know Andrea Karmen drives an SUV."

"It could've been a rental." Zach sat down next to me. "Which is why you should inform the police. They have the tools to track such things."

I pressed my arm over my eyes. "I suppose."

"I think you're in shock right now. Allow yourself time to recover, then give the authorities a call. I can understand not wanting to go to the station, but at least report it." Zach slid his arm across the back of the sofa, his fingers brushing my right shoulder.

I lowered my arm from my face and reached for his hand. "Thanks for coming over," I said, squeezing his fingers. "It helps to talk about things like this."

"I wouldn't have a job if it didn't," Zach replied, a trace of humor creeping into his tone.

I turned my head to look at him. "Are you switching into doctor mode now?"

Zach, still holding my hand, dropped his arm onto my shoulders. "No. Friend mode." He pulled me closer to his side. "Comfort, not counseling."

"I'll accept that," I said.

We sat in silence for several minutes. Zach released his hold on my hand and rubbed my upper arm while I lowered my head to rest on his shoulder

"Ah, the cat," Zach said at last. "What's her name? She's eyeing me with ill intent. I think I should try to talk her out of slicing me to ribbons."

I sat up and looked toward the dining table chairs where Ash huddled, swishing her tail like a saber. Her eyes, wide and unblinking, were fixed on Zach. "It's Ash, and don't worry. She likes to put on a fierce show, but she's really a big cuddle bug."

Zach's chuckle made me whip around to stare into his eyes. "Don't say it."

He lifted his hands. "Who me? What do you think I was going to say?"

"Never mind," I said, slumping back into the sofa cushions. "Sometimes I want to smack you."

"I often have that effect on women." Keeping his elbow propped on the sofa arm, Zach leaned his cheek against his fist and examined me in a way I found slightly unnerving. "You look like you're feeling better now."

"I am, thanks." I glanced over at Ash, who was still watching us but appeared calm.

"So how about that house tour?"

"You've seen most of it," I said, waving my hand through the air. "Living area, dining area, kitchen, and that's the office up there." I gestured toward the loft.

"Where the magic happens," Zach said, rising to his feet.

I stood up as well. "I don't know about that. It's where I write, but creating a book is hardly ever magical. It's a lot of sitting at a desk when you'd rather be somewhere else and pounding words into a shape that sort of makes sense."

"So it's like regular work? How disappointing." Zach flashed a grin. "Okay, I've seen most of the house, and I assume there's a bathroom behind one of those doors in the back, but where's the bedroom?"

"Back there, under the loft," I said, indicating the direction with a tilt of my head.

Zach crossed his arms over his chest. "I don't get to see it? I showed you mine."

Resisting an urge to make a slightly off-color joke, I squared my shoulders and met Zach's gaze without faltering. "It's a bedroom. It has a bed. It even has a dresser and a nightstand and an attached bath and closet. End of story."

"I see. You're saving that part of the tour for another day." Zach slipped off his glasses and tucked them into the pocket of the flannel shirt he was wearing over a faded T-shirt.

"Perhaps," I said, my lips unconsciously curling upward. "Why did you take off your glasses? Don't you need them for your drive home?"

"I didn't drive, I ran," Zach said, moving closer to me. "And I wasn't planning to go home quite yet."

"Well, as you said, I'm feeling better. I think I'll be alright on my own now."

Zach plopped back down on the sofa. "Come sit down," he said, patting the sofa cushion beside him.

"Alright, but hand me my phone off the end table. I'll make that call to the police now." I settled next to Zach and took the phone from him. "No, wait—it isn't the Harburg police, is it? I think the sheriff's department has jurisdiction around here." I searched for the appropriate number while Zach asked why I didn't simply call 911. "Because this isn't really an emergency. Not at this point. I'm just making a report."

"Hmm, okay. Let's see what they say." Zach slipped his arm around my shoulders again. "Don't be surprised if they ask you to go to the department tomorrow to file an official report."

Which was exactly what the deputy I spoke to wanted me to do. Since I hadn't been harmed, and my car hadn't been damaged, she said she would make a preliminary report, but that I should stop by the next day to provide more details and talk to the sheriff.

"You were right, they want me to come in," I told Zach when I completed the call. "Which is going to be inconvenient, since I have to be on campus all day tomorrow."

He set my phone back on the end table. "They probably have someone in the office twenty-four-seven. You can stop by after work. You might not get to speak with the sheriff, but you can complete the report."

"You're right, I wasn't thinking." I leaned into him. "This is nice. Your shirt is very soft and cozy."

Zach pulled me closer. "At least my shirt gets some compliments."

"Hey now," I said, without lifting my head off his shoulder. "I thought you were too self-assured to require tons of praise."

"No one is that self-assured." Zach kissed the top of my head. "If I promise to behave, may I stay a while longer?"

I glanced up at him. "Can you behave?"

Zach smiled. "Of course. Besides being wonderfully self-assured, I also possess great self-control."

"Really?" I sat up and shifted position so I could place my hand behind his head and pull him in for a kiss.

"I call foul," Zach said, when I sat back. "That's taking advantage."

"And you mind?" I asked..

Zach didn't reply. At least, not with words.

Chapter Thirty-Seven

I was planning to leave work a little early on Friday, so I could get home and get ready for the art show opening at seven. I mentioned this to Erin earlier in the day and thought everything was set, but then around four Erin asked to leave, claiming she had a severe headache. Fortunately, the writing center closed at five on Fridays, so I let her go. Even though Zach planned to pick me up at six-thirty, I figured I'd still have sufficient time to change my clothes and touch up my hair and makeup. If necessary, I could always send a text and tell him we needed to meet a little later.

About fifteen minutes before I needed to close the writing center, I noticed that Erin's office door was slightly ajar. *She must've rushed out without checking it*, I thought, standing with my hand on the doorknob.

I knew I should simply pull the door shut, but my curiosity got the better of me. There was probably nothing in Erin's office that would provide clues about her connection to any crime, but it wouldn't hurt to take a quick peek.

Erin's office was messier than mine. I didn't like to leave a lot of things out on my desk, but she had no such scruples. Her desk was piled with books, reports, notepads, and various printouts. Sticky

notes decorated some of these items as well as the frame of her laptop, which she'd left turned off but open. I gingerly poked through
the papers, shifting a stack of books to reveal her blotter-style desk
calendar. It was covered with notes, but when my gaze flew to the
day Doug Barth died, the calendar square was blank.

No appointments marked on here. I looked over the rest of the
month, noticing other meetings and appointments jotted down on
other dates. Not all were professional, which confirmed that Erin
used this calendar to keep track of her personal appointments along
with work presentations and meetings.

I slid the books and a few loose papers back, covering the suspicious date. Stepping away from the desk, I considered the implica-
tions of this discovery.

Erin had requested time off for her supposed appointment at
least a week before Doug's death. I clutched my upper arms and
hugged myself as the full import of this fact hit me.

If Erin did have anything to do with Doug Barth falling off the
mezzanine, it wouldn't have been a spur-of-the-moment decision.
She would have arranged to meet him in the library that day ahead
of time.

Maybe she hadn't planned to kill him, but she definitely could've
argued with him. Which meant Erin was certainly another person
who might have shoved Doug in the heat of anger.

And another prime suspect to add to the list.

* * *

My inclination was to immediately call Bri and Christine, but I
decided to hold off. Since Christine had texted Bri and me earlier
and mentioned working the event, I'd see both of them at the art
show opening. *It would be better,* I decided, *to speak to them in person
about this new development.*

Glancing at the clock on Erin's office wall, I realized it was almost time to lock down the center. I crossed to the door of her office and switched off the lights. Stepping out into the main room of the center, I caught a glimpse of movement out of the corner of my eye, right before the main doors slammed.

I mentally kicked myself. There'd been someone in the writing center while I was in Erin's office. This was a serious error on my part. If a student had arrived, looking for help, they'd have felt ignored, something I'd promised never to do.

The truth was, I'd been so mesmerized by what I'd discovered on Erin's calendar that several people could've come and gone without my notice. I closed and locked Erin's office door, then checked all the open areas of the center before retrieving my tote bag and coat from my own office. After a final check of the desk computers, I turned off the lights and slipped out of the center, locking the doors behind me.

Walking to the elevator, I searched both hallways, hoping to see the student or other individual who'd been in the writing center while I was preoccupied. I saw no one, but noticed the elevator was coming down from the first floor. Whoever had entered the center could've easily exited the library by the front or back doors on the main level.

Still feeling uneasy, I decided to use the main road to drive home to Taylorsford, not just because it was a variation of my usual route but also because there were many more vehicles, and thus more witnesses, on that road.

At home I greeted Emily, who was pruning the shrubs that lined the back of her house. "Are you going to the art show opening at Clarion tonight?" I asked.

She looked up from under the brim of her straw garden hat. "I hadn't planned on it. I think I'd rather wait and check out the exhibit during the week, when it isn't so crowded."

"That's what I'd normally do too, but my friend Brianna Rowley wanted me to come tonight. She has a couple of paintings in the show."

"I'm sure that's a thrill for her." Emily straightened and looked me over. "Are you going by yourself?"

"No." I bounced my keys against my palm. "Dr. Flynn is going to be my escort this evening."

"That's not surprising," Emily said, her dark eyes sparkling. "I've noticed that he's been around quite a bit lately. Which is perfectly fine, of course."

I was thirty-two, and no innocent miss, so why was I blushing? "We're friends," I said.

"Nice to have friends like that." Emily sent me a knowing look. "Have fun, dear. And give your painter friend my congratulations." She turned back to her pruning.

Heading inside the guest house, I completed my petting and treat ritual with Ash, then looked through my closet to decide what to wear. I finally settled on jeans and a black jacket over a colorful Cubist-inspired print sweater.

"Nice," Zach said, when he arrived to pick me up. "We match."

It was true. Zach was also wearing indigo jeans with a brightly patterned knit sweater. Fortunately, his jacket, while also dark, was charcoal rather than black, but the fact that we looked like we'd coordinated outfits made me want to go and change. I resisted this urge, knowing it would probably elicit some psychological analysis I didn't want to hear.

By the time we arrived on campus, Zach and I had dissected the new mystery series we were both streaming. Zach was particularly interested in my take on the plot.

"You're the mystery writer. Can you see where things are heading when you watch a show like this one?" he asked.

"Usually," I said. "There are certain clues. Like when the camera lingers on an object or image that doesn't seem to be that important."

"Yet," Zach said, as he parked the car.

"Right. When you see where the director places the emphasis, you know that object or image has, or will have, significance."

"Interesting." Zach waited for me in front of the car, then offered his arm. "Might as well make an entrance," he said when I cast him a quizzical look.

"Okay, but you should know that doing so will blast any hopes you have of dating anyone else on campus." I took his arm to stroll down the brick path that led to the fine arts building.

"That's fine." Zach pulled me closer. "I'm always willing to sacrifice quantity for quality."

Chapter Thirty-Eight

I tried to ignore the stares we got when we walked into the gallery, focusing instead on locating Bri and her partner, Rachel.

I noticed Rachel first, which wasn't surprising. Tall and slender, she looked like a model instead of what she was—a nonprofit economist who assisted small woman-owned businesses around the world. Tonight, she was wearing a sleek red dress that offered a perfect contrast to her dark skin and eyes. Ever since I'd been introduced to Rachel, I couldn't help but admire her for her beauty as well as her intelligence. She was one of the few people I knew who could crop their hair close to their scalp and still look feminine and glamorous.

Beside her, Bri looked like a young, chestnut-haired Stevie Nicks in a black lace top and flounced peasant skirt, her neck and arms dripping with unique, handcrafted jewelry. Although she only came up to Rachel's shoulder, her vibrant presence made her just as memorable.

"Hi there!" Bri said, rushing to greet Zach and me. "Look at you two. Did you get together to color coordinate?"

"No," I said, while Zach tossed off a smart remark about great minds thinking alike.

"Hi, Rachel, glad to see you're back," I said, giving her a hug. I turned to Zach. "This is Bri's partner, Rachel Morton."

Zach extended his hand. "Nice to meet you. My official title is Dr. Zachary Flynn, but please call me Zach."

Rachel clasped his hand and flashed one of her brilliant smiles. "Oh, you're the psychologist. Bri's told me a good deal about you."

Zach quirked one eyebrow. "Has she?"

"All good things," Rachel said, releasing his hand.

"Putting a gloss on it then, huh, Bri?" I said archly.

Bri rolled her eyes. "Honestly, Zach, I don't know how you put up with her."

"I give as good as I get." Zach slipped his arm around my waist and gave me a little squeeze. "That's how you deal with this one."

I elbowed him. "Stop it."

Rachel smiled "I see what you mean about a perfect match, Bri."

"I knew you had good observational skills," Zach told Bri, who grinned.

Pretending to fuss with my hair, I took the opportunity to fan my heated cheeks. "Okay, why don't we go take a look at some art?"

The four of us toured the gallery, entertained by Bri's insight into the art pieces she'd seen worked on in the studio. When we reached Bri's two paintings, she turned away, shuffling her feet.

"They're amazing!" Rachel grabbed Bri by the shoulders and spun her around to face the artworks. "I had no idea that you were hiding such talent, love."

The two paintings were both still-life studies of the same flowers, but one was the bouquet in full bloom, its colors lush and vibrant, dewdrops beading on vibrant green leaves. The other painting displayed the same arrangement of flowers after they'd faded. Fallen petals littered the tabletop, and the colors of the remaining blossoms were muted and shaded with the brown and black of rot.

"Interesting," Zach said, moving closer to the paintings.

"I'm sure they reveal some weird psychological quirks," Bri said, with a tenuous smile for Rachel.

"Not at all," Zach said, stepping back to stand next to me. "This is the work of someone with a very healthy mind." He cast a warm smile at Bri. "You see the beauty of life and death, and how they are both part of a whole."

Bri blushed. "Yeah, that kind of captures what I was going for."

I gave Zach a sideways look. "Not bad," I told him under my breath.

"I have my moments," he replied.

"A few. Here and there," I said, distracted by Bri and Rachel walking off to view the next part of the exhibit.

Zach turned me to face him. "Quite right." He pressed two fingers to my collarbone, "Here," he said, then shifting the fingers to my lips, "And there."

I stared at him for a second before bursting into laughter.

The eyes of all the people in our section of the gallery focused on us. I put my hand over my mouth but couldn't stop giggling. Zach looped my arm in his and pulled me away, toward a pair of doors that opened onto an outdoor sculpture garden.

"I think you need some air," he said. "I know I do."

The night was cool, but at the moment, with the heat that had flooded my body from my bout of laughing, it felt refreshing. I leaned against one of the pillars supporting the decorative roof over a flagstone patio and took several deep breaths.

Zach stood near me but kept his hands in his pockets. "If I'd known how that would set you off, I wouldn't have done it," he said.

I waved this aside. "No, it's alright. It was just funny, that's all."

"Sadly, it seems my efforts at seduction are a bit ridiculous," Zach said, the amusement edging his voice reassuring me that he wasn't being entirely serious.

"Don't worry, you aren't that far off the mark." I rested my back against the pillar while I looked at him. "It's just that with everything that's been happening, I guess I've been more anxious than I realized, and then what you said struck me as funny and I couldn't hold back."

"A healthy response," Zach said, stepping closer. He cupped the side of my face with his hand. "Do you mind if we head inside? I noticed a few colleagues I should say hello to, just to be polite. If you want to stay outside for a few more minutes, that's fine."

"I'd prefer spending a little more time out here," I said, glancing at one of the larger sculptures that had been set up on the patio. "I'll come find you once I'm back inside."

"That works." Zach leaned in and kissed my cheek before walking back into the gallery.

I inhaled a deep breath, enjoying the faint aroma of smoke that drifted on the breeze. *Somewhere, someone has built a fire*, I thought. There was also an acrid scent rising from the tall boxwoods that created backdrops for many of the larger sculptures in the garden.

Raised voices broke through the peaceful evening air. I turned and peeked around the column.

"It was you, wasn't it?" Miranda Barth, wearing an ankle-length gray wool coat and black leather gloves, faced off with another woman in front of a polished marble sculpture.

"Don't be ridiculous," Paige Irving said, her voice shaking. I questioned whether this was from anger or the cold. Her short, sleeveless purple dress, while flattering to her lovely figure, wasn't suitable for an autumn evening. She clutched the front edges of her lilac cashmere shrug together with one hand. "Why would I want to murder Doug? How would that benefit me?"

"You could claim the book for yourself," Miranda said. "Besides, I doubt you planned to kill him. I imagine you shoved him in the heat of an argument."

Paige tossed her blonde hair. "I was nowhere near that library the day Doug died. Can you say the same?"

"Of course." Miranda clasped her gloved hands together "I've given the police a full accounting of my movements that day. As soon as they confirm my statement, no one will be able to accuse me of such nonsense again."

"They can prove I was elsewhere too," Paige said. "So where does that leave us?"

Miranda looked her up and down. "Anyone can say that. I haven't heard that the investigators have come to any conclusions, so I'm not convinced. After all, you were able to conduct a clandestine affair with my husband, so why should I ever believe you're telling the truth?"

"I don't have to listen to this." Paige turned and stalked off, heading deeper into the shadows of the sculpture garden.

"Wait a minute, we're not done here," Miranda said, hurrying after her. "There's still the matter of who gets what from the book deal . . ."

I curled my fingers into my palms in frustration. Zach would be expecting me to show up soon, but I wanted to listen in on more of the conversation between Paige and Miranda. It might be my only chance to either eliminate them as suspects or find proof that one of them was the culprit.

I decided to follow the two women. This was my opportunity to prove that I could reveal important clues in a real-life mystery as well as in my books, and I wasn't about to miss out.

Chapter Thirty-Nine

I'd walked through the art department's sculpture garden before but always in the daytime. At night it became a different place—the various sculptures and manicured shrubs taking on a fantastical appearance. There were a few scattered solar-powered lights, but most of the garden remained in shadow.

Paige and Miranda's voices rose and fell like the tide. I couldn't understand what they were saying, but the prospect of hearing more of their conversation drove me on. Walking deeper into the garden, I remained focused on my sense of hearing, passing various large-scale sculptures without giving them a second glance.

Following their voices to track the women, I soon discovered that the interference of oversized metal or stone objects made this almost impossible. Sound bounced off the surfaces of the sculptures and was absorbed by the dense leaves and limbs of the boxwoods, to the point where I couldn't tell if Paige and Miranda were in front of me or behind me.

Pausing beside a sleek metal sculpture shaped like two radio telescopes set back-to-back, I zipped up my jacket as I strained to hear any voices. But it seemed the two women had fallen silent. *Or perhaps*, I thought, *they've already circled around and gone back inside.* The garden was also only a few buildings away from the main parking lot. Either woman, or both, could've decided to call it a day and already headed home.

As I moved forward, hoping to reach one of the garden's boundaries, the irregular placement of the boxwoods and sculptures made me question whether I was walking in circles. The garden had been designed to function somewhat like a maze, so it was difficult to determine where I was headed and where I'd already been. *Should've paid attention to those sculptures earlier,* I thought. The garden was not laid out on a grid, so I'd had to follow grass paths that twisted and turned. Since I hadn't marked the way by memorizing the specific sculptures I'd passed, it would be difficult to find my way back.

Clouds obscured the moon and deepened the shadows. I slid my cell phone from my pocket and turned on its built-in light. The sudden flare of light threw the face of a sculpted bear into high relief, startling me. Stumbling backward, I tripped over an exposed boxwood root and fell, my cell phone flying from my hand.

The short grass covering the well-trod path didn't provide much padding. I hit the ground with a thud, landing on my left hip, then banging my elbow as I attempted to brace myself.

I swore under my breath, angry that I'd probably ruined my jacket along with my pants. I was also concerned that my phone, which had hit the nose of the bear with a crack, was broken beyond repair.

Then there was the pain. The shock of the fall had insulated me for a moment, but as I struggled to sit up, the pain blossomed, spreading down my left leg and arm in electric waves.

I knew I had to get back on my feet but wasn't sure of the best maneuver to make that possible. Finally, after attempting to rise up using my right arm as a brace. I dropped forward on my knees and used my hands to push myself into a squat. Sharp zings of pain screamed at me to stop, but I simply gritted my teeth and forced my body up to a standing position. Wavering slightly, I staggered forward. Pressing my right hand against the cool stone of the bear sculpture, I stared down at my phone.

It was shattered, the screen crazed with jagged lines and one side of the case splintered. I sincerely doubted it would function but felt I had to give it a try. I wasn't sure I could hobble back to the art gallery without falling again. I needed to call for help.

I kept my right palm braced against the bear as I bent down, sliding my hand down the polished curves to keep my balance. As I grabbed the battered phone and rose back up with it in my hand, the entire back panel fell off.

"That's not good," I said, noticing that the on button was part of the splintered side of the phone. I tried to start the phone anyway, but it was completely dead.

Shoving it into the pocket of my jacket, I encircled the sculpted bear's neck with my right arm and leaned against its bulky shoulder, breathing heavily. I had no idea whether anyone would come looking for me. I hadn't said anything to Zach about wandering into the sculpture garden, so he might look for me inside the gallery for quite a while before even considering that option.

I had to make it back to the gallery. I simply had to. Straightening, I slid forward a few steps. It was slow going, but keeping my feet on the ground and shuffling them seemed to work. Pain throbbed in my left hip and elbow, slowing my progress. I had to fight through it. If I could just get close enough to the building to yell for help . . .

The problem was trying to figure out which direction would lead me closer to the gallery. I'd gotten so turned around, I couldn't be sure. I also no longer had any light to help guide me.

Silly, aim for one of the lampposts. That will provide some illumination and also give you something to act as a marker. If you move from post to post, you might be able to determine whether you're walking in the right direction. I kept shuffling, my focus fixed on the closest light.

When I reached it, I slumped against the lamppost, clutching the slick metal pole with my right hand. Although the light spilled around me like a protective circle, it didn't extend very far into other areas of the garden.

A shadow fell across the circle. A human-shaped shadow.

"Oh, thank goodness," I said, lifting my head. "You found me."

"Yes, I did. How fortunate," said Erin McHenry.

Chapter Forty

I forced a smile, certain it came across as a grimace. "I'm glad to see you," I told Erin. "I tripped and fell and broke my cell phone, so couldn't call for help. If you'd simply phone my friend, Zach, that would be great."

The lamplight, spilling over Erin, tinted her face an eerie green. "I'm afraid I don't know your friend Zach's number."

I stared at her with bemusement. She hadn't bothered to step forward to take my arm or otherwise support me, despite the fact that I was obviously in pain. *She's a suspect*, I reminded myself. It seemed impossible to connect this rather petite woman with two murders, but still, I had to remain on high alert. "I can give you his number. I know it would be hard for you to help me back to the gallery, given our height difference, but he can do it easily enough."

Erin shoved her hands into the pockets of her black knit cardigan and surveyed me with an odd, detached expression.

A black cardigan with a hood, I realized. *Like the one my attacker on the campus path was wearing.* I straightened and considered my options. I certainly couldn't outrun Erin at this point. I needed to play it cool and hope she didn't see me as a threat. "Really, it's fine.

Zach and I came to the event together. He won't be bothered a bit if you call."

"I saw you the other day," Erin said in a conversational tone. "When you were snooping through my office. Did you find what you were looking for?"

I blinked rapidly. The figure I'd seen fleeing the writing center had been Erin. She'd come back, for whatever reason, and seen me digging through the materials on her desk. "No. The thing is, I'd misplaced the notes from our last meeting with the English department and thought you might've left a copy on your desk—"

"You expect me to believe that?" Erin took a step closer." I think you were searching for something else. You see, I haven't forgotten about you asking questions about my dentist appointment. After noticing all your previous fumbling around, playing at being a detective, that further raised my suspicions, and then when I caught you sneaking around in my office, I figured you were looking for some sort of proof that I'd lied to you." She took another step. "Did you find it?"

"Not really," I said. "Except I did notice you hadn't marked down any appointment on your calendar for that day, even though you'd asked for leave ahead of time. There were all sorts of other appointments noted on the calendar, for many other days. But not that one."

Erin's smile did nothing to relieve my anxiety. "Oh, here we go. You and your little band of amateur sleuths, dashing around like madcap Nancy Drews. Coming up with all kinds of crazy notions. I thought it was terribly reckless, and yes, I warned a few people about your activities, including Miranda Barth."

"So you were the one who told her about Christine and Bri and me helping Mia's lawyer with her investigation," I said.

Erin shrugged. "I thought she should know. If only to protect herself."

If only to muddy the waters and make sure no one was looking at you, I thought, biting my lower lip. "How much do you know about cars, Erin?"

She narrowed her eyes. "A little more than most. My stepfather owns a rental car company, and I used to help him when he was doing repairs on the fleet."

"Sorry, I know that sounded like a non sequitur, but I was curious for . . . reasons." I was treading on thin ice, but as long as we were playing the game where Erin pretended not to know what I was getting at, and I pretended not to notice her pretending . . .

"You need an opinion on a mechanical problem related to your car?" Erin asked with a sneer.

"No. It's just that I've had some bad experiences involving vehicles lately. Someone chasing me down in an old white car, and brake lines being tampered with, and things like that. I mean, the brakes thing—well, someone would have to know something about mechanical systems to pull off something like that, don't you think?"

Erin stared at me, a little smile playing over her lips. "Oh, Jenn. You've always thought you were so smart, haven't you? So proud of the skills learned from writing those murder mystery books. As if writing about investigations qualified you to embark on one. The truth is, you simply wanted to pin Doug Barth's death on anyone but the person who was obviously the culprit."

"You mean Mia Jackson." Slipping one hand into my jacket pocket, my fingers grazed the sharp edges of my broken phone. "It seems, like the authorities, you're determined to pin Professor Barth's death on her."

"She's the one with the strongest motive." Erin pulled her hands free of the cardigan's pockets, revealing a short piece of metal pipe clutched in her fist. "Doug humiliated her, more than once. They were even seen arguing in the library before he died. And then he'd given her a C minus on one of her short stories, the one found by his body. I'm sure that must've been the final straw. No writer likes to be told their work is crap."

I swallowed back a yelp. *I never mentioned the exact grade on that paper*, I thought, fear washing over me like a rouge wave. While I'd seen the papers by Doug's body, no one else but the police had, and they'd immediately collected that story as evidence. The only people who could've known that Doug had scrawled a C minus on the title page of Mia's story were Doug, Mia, and me.

And the person who'd stood facing Doug on that mezzanine. Who'd been there when Doug had picked up the story Mia must've thrown at him and held it, dangling from his fingers.

The person who had killed him.

Chapter Forty-One

Erin had murdered Doug. She'd decided ahead of time that an accident could easily be arranged if she met with him on the library mezzanine. She must've set up that fake dentist appointment as an alibi, then asked him to meet her on the top floor of the library. Perhaps she'd even told him she wanted to discuss their old feud and make things right by publicly retracting her original claims about plagiarism. And Doug might've desperately desired that vindication, especially before the publication of his novel.

And that was probably why Doug had suggested that he and Mia take their discussion up to the mezzanine. He was already planning to meet Erin there and wanted to be in the right place. I could only imagine that he'd intended to finish his talk with Mia and send her on her way before Erin appeared.

Which was exactly what happened, I realized. *Mia exited using the stairwell, but then decided to return to take back her story. In the interim, Erin arrived. Perhaps she'd even been waiting in the shadowy stacks on the mezzanine until Mia left. She must've shoved Doug over the railing almost immediately. Again, it didn't happen accidentally, during an argument. It was planned.*

Erin had killed Doug, and she probably wouldn't hesitate to murder me, but had she shoved Gary Alexander off the provost's balcony? On that point, I couldn't be sure. But there was no time to try to determine her guilt in Gary's death. Erin was obviously aware that I knew her secret and was planning to silence me, one way or another. After all, she'd already tried by tampering with my brakes. I had no doubt she was also the driver of the white car. Although she may have hoped for more, those events had only ended up being warnings. But she'd even taken advantage of that, as evidenced by the text she'd sent after the brakes incident.

I gritted my teeth. She had to have been following us at a distance then, or how would she know when it happened and that we'd survived?

"You are pretty cool and inventive under pressure," I told her. "Surprisingly so."

"Because you've always seen me as weak and ineffectual?" Erin gently tapped the metal pipe against her opposite palm. "Admit it—ever since you were awarded the director position over me, you've felt you were my superior in all ways. Better than me as a writer too, simply because you wrote some silly books that've sold enough to make your publisher happy."

I swallowed. There it was—the animosity Erin had been bottling up for years. "I never looked down on you. That was all in your imagination."

"Whatever you say." Erin thumped the pipe harder.

I had to get away. Shifting my weight, I tested my ability to move. My hip and arm still ached, but I could move them, which meant nothing was broken. If I could fight beyond the pain, I had a chance to escape.

You have to, I told myself. *This is life or death.*

Erin eyed me, obviously cataloging my injuries. "It's nice of you to do some of my work for me. You're already in bad shape. One good hit"—she held up the pipe—"and your little Miss Marple act will be over."

"This isn't very clever," I said. "I can see how you'll probably get away with murdering Doug, and even shoving Gary off that balcony, but no one will buy that it's an accident if I'm walloped with a pipe."

"First of all, I never touched Gary Alexander. But more importantly, all evidence of the blows from my little pipe will be obliterated if I tip one of these marble sculptures over on you. They aren't all fastened to their platforms, you know. Everyone thinks they're too big to move, so they'll never fall." Erin lifted her chin and fixed me with a haughty glare. "But I have a crowbar hidden nearby, and I know how to use it to topple heavy objects. It's a matter of leverage, you see."

Keep her talking, the logical part of my brain told me. *Keep her from taking any action.* "So somehow, out of the blue, one of the statues is supposed to jump out and smash me flat? That doesn't seem too likely."

"Oh, I don't know. It's happened before, in graveyards and other places with large monuments. Anyway, there's nothing to link me to your death. I came into the garden from the parking lot, so no one at the art show has seen me. I used a rental car to drive here, so I can prove my own car never left my house. Which means I'll easily be able to claim I was home, nursing my headache, all evening." Erin moved forward until she was only an arm's length from me.

"I'll scream," I said, shoving my hand back into the pocket holding the broken phone. A shard of glass nicked my thumb. I tightened my lips to prevent any expression of pain.

"Go ahead. I doubt anyone will hear you," Erin said. "Besides, we're on a university campus, on a Friday night. They'll just think it's kids out partying."

Sadly, she had a point. I whipped the broken phone from my pocket and hurled it right at her face.

Erin's shriek might be heard by someone, I thought hopefully, as I stumbled away from the light and slipped behind the nearest boxwood. I knew I'd only bought myself a little time, but if I stuck to the darker paths and kept moving, I might be able to hold out until someone came to my rescue.

Come look for me, I told Zach in my head. *Use that big brain of yours and figure out where I must be.*

I crept from boxwood to boxwood, ignoring my injuries, even though they were screaming at me. I couldn't give in to the pain. I had to send my mind to a place where it was irrelevant. To distract my thoughts, I puzzled over why Erin refused to accept any involvement in Gary's death. She'd basically admitted to killing Doug, so why claim she hadn't touched Gary? Was his death truly an accident, or was there yet another killer in the area, looking to get away with murder?

Or is she lying? asked my logical brain, while I scrambled over a plinth holding up a whimsical assemblage of old machine parts that had been worked into something resembling two figures locked in an embrace.

"There you are."

Light flooded my vision. I blinked, trying to adjust my eyes to the glare of a cell phone flashlight. Looking up, I saw Erin looming over me. Blood dripped from a gash on her cheek and one of her eyes was swollen almost shut. *The phone did some damage, at least,* I thought with a flicker of satisfaction.

"You really thought you could get away, stumbling around like a drunken camel?" Erin reached down and grabbed a hank of my hair.

That was a mistake, on her part. When she yanked my head up, the new jolt of pain sent my adrenaline into overdrive. No longer caring about anything except striking back, I slammed my right fist into her throat.

Gasping, Erin released me and fell backward, the iron pipe rolling from her hand and clanging against the metal plinth. The sound resounded like a bell, reverberating throughout the garden.

I scooted over and plopped down on the pipe, wincing when my left hip landed on the ground. But it didn't matter. Sitting tight, I was too big for Erin to move, and while she could attempt to retrieve her crowbar from wherever she'd stashed it, I thankfully realized she wouldn't have time to return and harm me.

Voices filled the air, shouting, "Over there, over there!" as the beams of flashlights flitted through the darkness like a contingent of gigantic fireflies.

I'd been found.

Chapter Forty-Two

B ri was the first person to reach me. Squatting down, she looked me in the eyes and said I was safe now.

Standing behind her, Rachel gazed down at me with concern. "We need an ambulance," she said.

"Already called 911. That'll come along with the police." Christine took off her chef's jacket and draped it around my shoulders. "You're trembling like a leaf," she said, when I protested. "Hardly surprising, what with all you've been through."

I sat up straighter and peered around the three women. "Where's Zach?"

"Taking out the trash," Christine said, with a jerk of her thumb toward the closest lamppost.

Illuminated by the lamp, Zach stood as still as one of the garden's statures, holding Erin's arms behind her back. She writhed in his grip but couldn't break free. A torrent of obscenities flew from her lips.

Sirens pierced the air, wailing louder as they drew closer. From the back of the garden, a contingent of police officers and EMTs stormed forward. One group split off to deal with Erin, while the other headed in my direction.

233

Zach, relieved of duty as the police took charge of Erin, rushed over to me. "Are you alright?" he asked, his eyes shining with concern.

Or tears, I thought. *How odd. I know he cares, but that much?*

"Not totally, but it's nothing that won't heal," I told him, as one of the EMTs shooed Bri, Rachel, and Zach aside.

"Give us room to work," the EMT said, gesturing for his partner to bring a stretcher.

I sat quietly while he checked me over, only yelping when he manipulated my left leg and arm.

"Nothing seems broken, but we should still take you in for X-rays," the EMT said.

Glancing over at the cluster of police surrounding Erin, Zach frowned. "Why are they bringing a stretcher for her as well?"

"She apparently took a pretty good hit to the face." Officer Rebecca Greene moved closer and looked me over. "From some type of sharp object."

"Broken cell phone," I said, earning a thumb's up from the second EMT.

Zach grinned. "That's my girl."

"Woman," I said, grimacing as I was shifted onto the rolling stretcher.

"I see your smart mouth is intact," Zach said, leaning over to steal a kiss. "Thankfully."

"I almost died," I said, as he walked beside the stretcher. "I mean, I'll probably have PTSD after this."

"Fortunately, you have a handy psychologist to help you deal with such things," Zach said with a wry smile.

"Handy indeed. Way too handy sometimes," I muttered, which made Zach laugh and the EMTs share amused looks.

When we reached the ambulance, Zach grasped my fingers and told me he was going to drive to the hospital in his car. "So I can take you home if they don't keep you overnight," he said.

As the stretcher was loaded, Christine called out, saying she, Bri, and Rachel would also drive to the hospital.

"You don't all have to come," I said.

"Yes, we do," shouted Bri. "We're a team, remember?"

The rest of the night was a blur of waiting to be checked out in the emergency room, waiting for a room, and waiting after being wheeled to other rooms for X-rays, MRIs, and CT scans. I was given pain medication that provided some relief but also made everything seem a little fuzzy.

A police officer stopped by to speak with me but didn't stay long. He said he'd just get the basics and would come back the next day for a more thorough interview.

"Probably a good idea," I told him. "I'm not quite all here right now."

The officer smiled. "That's fine. You were banged up pretty bad. Get some rest. We'll talk when you feel better."

Zach appeared not long after I was taken to a regular hospital room. "They wanted your family instead, but I told them they were all too far away, and anyway, I'm a doctor."

"A doctor of the mind, not the body," I said, waving my arm, complete with intravenous line, at him. "Didn't they ask?"

Zach pulled up a chair next to my bed. "Nope. I can be quite authoritative when I want to be."

"Is that so?" I leaned back against the pillows propping me into a semireclined position. "I'd never have guessed."

He just grinned and took hold of my right hand. "I told Bri, Rachel, and Christine to go on home once we knew you were going stay the night. They plan to come back to see you tomorrow."

"I hope I won't be here tomorrow. Not for long, anyway." I cast him a look from under my lowered lashes. "You really don't have to stay here all night."

Zach pressed his free hand over his heart. "What? Miss a chance to say I spent the night with you? Not on your life."

I squeezed his fingers. "Thanks for coming to find me, by the way."

"I was terribly worried," Zach said, his expression sobering. "As were Bri and Rachel. We couldn't imagine where you'd gone. I searched all over the gallery, then Christine came out of the kitchen and said something about the gardens outside. She'd seen Miranda Barth head that way. That clicked with all of us. We figured you were probably following her."

"It was actually Miranda and Paige Irving," I said, launching into a description of the conversation between the two women. "But I lost them in the garden. I don't know where they went."

"Probably home, as you guessed." Zach laid my hand on the blankets and sat back in his chair. "Now explain what happened with Erin. I know you already had her on the suspect list, but what convinced you that she'd killed Doug Barth, and what made her see you as a threat?"

I explained how I'd added up all the clues, with Erin's mention of the C minus grade on Mia's story being the final piece of the puzzle. "I don't know when she started suspecting that I knew too much. She must've hated the fact that Bri and Christine and I were conducting our own amateur investigation, and saw me as the instigator of that, so I think she wanted me out of the way from the get-go. That's why she tampered with my brakes and pulled that stunt with the white car."

"She admitted knowing enough about cars to cut the brake lines," Zach said.

"Yes, and I bet she borrowed that white car from her stepfather's rental fleet. The only thing is"—I pulled the blankets up to my chin—"Erin was adamant about not having anything to do with Gary Alexander's death."

"So it was accidental, as the authorities initially said."

I cast him a conspiratorial glance. "Or someone else killed him."

"No, no, no. We're not falling down that rabbit hole again," Zach said, waving his hands through the air. "Just keep repeating: it was an accident, it was an accident."

"But what if it wasn't?" I shifted my position, trying to sit up straighter, but groaned as the pain in my hip and leg flared again.

"Whatever it was, we won't solve it tonight." Zach stood up and leaned over the bed. "You should get some rest. I'm going to go sit in that decidedly uncomfortable-looking recliner and see if I can get any sleep."

I reached up and took hold of the lapel of his jacket. Pulling his face closer to mine, I planted a kiss on his lips. "Good night," I said, as I released my hold.

He straightened and shook his finger at me. "There you go again, taking advantage."

"Okay, to be fair, I'll let you take advantage of me next time."

Mischief glinted in his eyes. "A dangerous promise, Jenn. Are you sure you want to stand by that?"

I leaned back against the pillows. "I can't stand by anything right now. But I'm willing to make that deal, as long as you promise not to take things too far."

Zach's smile broadened. "Hmm, I'm sure I can manage to remain a gentleman."

"I didn't ask you to do that," I said, eliciting another warning shake of his finger and a laugh.

Chapter Forty-Three

Although I was told I could leave the hospital the next day, the discharge process took hours, which allowed plenty of time for Bri and Christine to stop by for a visit.

"Rachel sends her best wishes," Bri said. "She had a meeting at the main office in D.C. today, so she had to leave home early."

Propped up to a sitting position, I rolled my eyes. "On a Saturday? That's devotion."

"Yeah, and the MARC trains don't run on the weekends, so she had to take the car." Bri sighed. "I hate it when she has to drive into the city. It always makes me nervous."

Christine settled in the recliner. "She travels all around the globe and driving into D.C. makes you nervous?"

"Have you tried it recently?" Bri pulled a comical face. "Seriously, those drivers are nuts."

"Heck no. If I'm going into the city, I drive to the nearest metro station," Christine replied.

"I suppose Rachel could've done that, but she said she had too many sample items to transport." Bri, sitting on the chair next to my bed, met Christine's inquiring gaze. "She always brings back samples of new goods made by the businesses she mentors when she returns from a specific region or country."

"That sounds like an interesting and important job," Christine said.

"It is, but she has to travel so much . . ." Bri shook her head. "I shouldn't complain. I'm lucky to have her in my life at all. If I have to share her with the world, oh, well."

"That's the right attitude," I said, sipping orange juice through a straw.

Bri cast Christine a sly look before focusing on me. "Speaking of having someone in your life, where's the handsome and charming Dr. Flynn this morning?"

"I don't know where that person is, but Zach went to grab some breakfast," I said, setting my glass on the tray swung over my bed.

"Hey, I'm right here," Zach said from the doorway.

"I know." I wrinkled my nose at him. "I saw you."

He entered the room, waving Bri back down when she stood up to offer him the chair. "I've been sitting for too long. I'll just stand here near the bed, nursing my pride."

Bri chuckled. "Sometimes I can't tell if you two are friends or foes."

"The jury is still out," Zach said, before leaning over to kiss my temple.

"Speaking of juries, I'm happy to report that Mia won't be facing one," Christine said. "I heard from Heidi that all charges have been dropped against her as of this morning."

"Excellent," I said. "What about Erin? I know she's in custody, but has anyone heard any more about her? I wonder if she's confessed or still stubbornly maintaining her innocence."

"Heidi didn't know about that." Christine grimaced. "Erin should be glad she's in custody. If I got close to her . . ." She made a twisting motion with her hands.

"Come now, we don't need another murder," Zach said with a smile.

"Another murder." I glanced over at Bri. "That's something I've been thinking about while lying here, you know."

"You mean Gary Alexander. The authorities have declared that an accident, Jenn. I don't believe we need to look into that any further. If, despite her disclaimers, Erin was involved in Gary's death, I'm sure the investigators will figure that out."

"What if it wasn't Erin?" I asked.

"Two killers in our little community?" Christine frowned. "That's hard to believe."

I crossed my arms over my chest. "I still think we have to consider it."

A knock on the half-open door silenced any response to my statement. A nurse holding a clipboard marched into the room and announced that my paperwork was finally ready.

"The doctor will still need to stop by and check you over before she signs off," he said. "But you can go ahead and initial all the required paperwork."

"We should leave you to that," Bri said, standing up as the nurse handed me the clipboard and a pen. She turned to Zach. "I assume you're driving her home?"

"Yes, and I'll make sure she settles in to rest too," he replied.

"Good job," Christine told him, as she joined Bri. "See you soon, Jenn. Get some rest, and don't worry about anything."

"Yeah, I heard the provost sent a message out to the students to let them know the writing center will be short-staffed for a while.

The student assistants are apparently going to fill in some hours, though," Bri said.

I handed the clipboard to the nurse. "Glad to hear it, but I should be able to go back to work by Monday."

He shook his head. "Not sure the doctor's going to recommend that, Ms. Dalton."

"We'll see," I said, waving as Bri and Christine followed the nurse out the door. "I mean, a recommendation is just a recommendation," I added, looking up at Zach. "If I feel well enough . . ."

"We'll see," he said.

* * *

As Zach left my house on Saturday evening, he opened the door on Emily.

"Good, you can come in and keep an eye on her," he said. "Make sure she rests."

Emily offered him a warm smile. "I'll do that."

"And I'll be back with breakfast tomorrow morning," Zach called out as he exited.

"He seems quite devoted," Emily said, sitting down at the other end of my sofa.

Ash, who was curled up next to me, lifted her head and stared at the older woman for a second, then lowered her head between her paws and started purring again.

"It's that therapist instinct," I said. "He has a need to take care of people."

"I think it's a little more than that." Emily gazed at me, a smile tugging at the corners of her mouth. "At any rate, I stopped by not simply to see how you were doing, but also because I heard some news I was sure would interest you."

"Oh, what's that?"

"According to my source, Erin McHenry has confessed to murdering Doug Barth. She even told the authorities what drove her to do so—apparently, she believed Doug was the one standing between her and the tenured position she wanted in the English department. She was convinced Doug was aligned with Gary to maintain a firm resistance to any of the provost's plans to restructure the department."

"Erin told me that she'd spoken to Hilda Lange, who'd promised to update the English curriculum, which would've then included new courses Erin was qualified to teach," I said thoughtfully. "I guess she felt Doug, who had always fought against her getting a full-time position, was supporting Gary primarily for that reason." I absently stroked Ash's back. "The irony is that Doug did change his mind, or at least that's what Hilda told us at her party."

"Too late to stop Erin from shoving him off the mezzanine." Emily crossed her hands, one over the other, in her lap. "It's like some Greek tragedy. Doug Barth changes his mind at the last minute, which would've benefited Erin in the long run. But she didn't know he'd done so, and murdered him, destroying her life along with his."

"It is sad." I cast Emily a speculative look. "What about Gary's death? It seems Erin found out about Doug's reversal of opinion at the provost's party. Gary mentioned it in front of a group that included her, and she appeared startled. After some thought, she must've been furious with him for keeping quiet about that detail until after Doug's death."

"Perhaps, but Erin McHenry didn't kill Gary Alexander." Emily met my quizzical gaze and held it. "My source told me that the investigators found an eye witness who places Erin in an entirely different location at the exact time Gary fell off that balcony. She couldn't have pushed him."

I lifted my hand off Ash's back. "Your source seems awfully knowledgeable. Who is this person?"

"A gentleman who always seems to know everything going on in and around this area, especially when accidents or crimes are involved. I must say I trust his information. He rarely gets the facts wrong." Emily smiled. "I'll have to introduce you someday. He's quite a character."

"I look forward to that," I said, dubiously. It sounded like Emily's source might not always be playing on the right side of the law. "So Erin didn't murder Gary, even though she had a motive to do so. Which means it was an accident, or . . ."

Emily took off her glasses and held them up to the light. "Or someone else was involved in Gary's death? Darn, these things are always getting smudged." She pulled a handkerchief from her pocket and rubbed the lenses.

"What does your source say about that?" I asked, not bothering to temper my curiosity.

"Just that the investigators are looking into the situation, even if they're keeping their inquiries on the down low, so as not to alert any suspects." Emily popped her glasses back on and turned to me. "My source was also aware that you and a few friends were looking into both cases and wanted me to let you know that there might be more to Gary's death. He was concerned that the culprit might be aware of your activities too and wanted to warn you all to stay on guard."

"Thanks," I said. "I'll share that with the others."

"Good. Now—is there anything I can get you while I'm here?" Emily rose to her feet. "Water or juice or coffee or something else? I would say wine, but I'm sure you're on painkillers and that's not a good combination."

"Just some more water." I picked up my refillable bottle from the end table and handed it to her. "And maybe some snacks? There's a bag of pretzels in the cabinet above the fridge."

Emily headed toward the kitchen, turning back to add, "Seriously, Jenn, you should be careful. I've dealt with some scary people in the past, and they don't all appear dangerous at first glance."

"Trust me, I'm aware of that," I said, thinking of Erin. Of all the people I'd met in my life, she was one of the last I'd have pegged as a murderer.

Which meant I had to stay alert. A second killer could be just as difficult to identify.

And, I thought, *just as dangerous.*

Chapter Forty-Four

I didn't end up going back to work until the following Thursday, primarily because I didn't feel comfortable driving myself until then, and both Zach and Emily refused to chauffeur me.

"The provost has given you the time off," Zach said, when I protested on Monday, Tuesday, and Wednesday. "You might as well make the most of it."

By the time I returned to the writing center, our student assistants looked tired and harried. "Now you guys need a break," I told Jim and the others. "Dr. Lange has agreed to shorten our hours this week and next, so it won't be that difficult for me to keep the place up and running."

I was alone then when Mia and Francesca appeared, both clutching large bouquets.

"We wanted to thank you for everything you did to help Mia," Francesca said, as she offered me her flowers. "And really, me too, since for the longest time the police thought I was helping her cover up Professor Barth's murder."

"You're quite welcome," I said, taking the bouquet Mia offered as well. "I'm just glad the truth came out."

"I swear, I'm going to dedicate my first book to you, Ms. Dalton," Mia said, perching on the edge of my desk. "You saved me and my career."

"It wasn't only me. Ms. Kubiak and Ms. Rowley helped a lot as well."

"I know. I plan to thank them too." Mia swung her feet, creating a tattoo beat as her heels hit the front panel of the desk. "I guess it was Ms. McHenry who threatened me when I came back up to the sixth floor and saw Professor Barth's body."

"Yes. She must've fled the scene immediately after that, while you were still hiding in the stacks," I said.

"I wish I'd run after her immediately. I mean, right when I heard someone head down the stairs." Mia glanced over at me. "If I could've identified her, maybe at least Professor Alexander would still be alive."

I shook my head. "Erin McHenry didn't push him off the balcony. She has an alibi for that incident. And as for you chasing after her, I'm glad you didn't. If Ms. McHenry realized you had the opportunity to recognize her, I have no doubt that she would've actually tried to kill you too. As it was, she left you alone because you were a good fall-girl for her crime."

Mia jumped down off the desk. "Francesca was another one of my saviors," she said, throwing her arm around the dancer's slender waist. "She helped me hide at first, even though that could've made her an accomplice."

Francesca tossed her long black hair over her shoulders. "No biggie. I knew you'd never hurt anyone, Mia. You won't even kill cockroaches in the dorm."

I looked over both girls, glad to see the happiness that lit up their young faces. "Well, look at it this way, Mia. You now have some very interesting experiences to use in your writing."

"And I plan to do that." Mia smiled. "As a matter of fact, I want to talk to you about a new story idea, Ms. Dalton. One about a young woman unjustly accused of a crime."

"You know where to find me," I told her, before thanking them again for the flowers and wishing them a great day.

After Mia and Francesca left, I sat down at my desk to answer some emails. But my mind was elsewhere. I knew I was fixating on the puzzle of Gary Alexander's death, but I couldn't help myself. Helping uncover the truth behind Doug Barth's murder had given me a rush I'd only felt before when successfully completing the final draft of a novel.

I tapped a pen against the legal pad lying on my desk. Now that Erin had been eliminated from the suspect list, there were only two other people I suspected of shoving Gary off that balcony. *No,* I thought, *perhaps three.*

I hated to include Hilda Lange in my suspect list, but the death had happened at her home, a structure she obviously knew how to move around in better than anyone else at the party. I didn't think Hilda would've *planned* to kill anyone, but she did have an embattled relationship with Gary Alexander. If they'd argued, and she'd simply shoved him in anger . . . Drunk as he'd been, he could've easily lost his balance and tumbled over the railing.

Of course, there was also Miranda Barth, who I'd seen engaged in a tense conversation with Gary earlier that evening. If Andrea was right, and Gary was trying to squeeze money out of Miranda through some form of blackmail, she certainly might have wished to silence him for good.

Which brought my thoughts back to Andrea. The truth was, she could've been the one to argue with Gary on that balcony. It wouldn't have been out of character for their acrimonious relationship. And if what Erin had shared with me was true, the provost was considering a plan to appoint Andrea as the next chair of the English department.

I realized I was grinding my teeth and relaxed my jaw. I didn't want either Hilda or Andrea to be guilty. To be honest, I wasn't even that keen on Miranda being the culprit. She'd been caught up in a bad situation during her marriage to Doug. If Doug had lied to Gary about Miranda threatening him . . . Well, I hated to think that some misunderstanding on Gary's part had driven him to blackmail and Miranda to murder.

Doodling on the legal pad, I was lost in thought for several minutes. It took three raps on my office door for me to look up and tell the visitor to come in.

"Oh, hello," I said, recognizing the woman who stood in the doorway. "What brings you here, Ms. Irving?"

"I just wanted to thank you for your help in revealing Doug's murderer," she said.

"There's a lot of that going around today," I said, before holding up my hands. "Sorry, that didn't make much sense. I'm still a little rattled, I guess, from everything that's happened recently."

"Of course you are." Paige bobbed her head in acknowledgement when I gestured toward the guest chair. "I don't want to take up a great deal of your time, but I just had a few questions." She pulled a tissue from her purse and dabbed at her carefully made-up eyes. "The police aren't sharing much, which I know is partially because I didn't have any official relationship with Doug, so I thought I'd talk to you." She met my gaze with a tentative smile. "Can you? Share more details, I mean?"

"About what, exactly?" I asked, with a quick glance at my watch. It was almost four o'clock, which was when we were supposed to close down the center during the period of shortened hours.

"Why Ms. McHenry killed Doug." Paige delicately blew her nose, then shoved the tissue back into her purse. "I think it was because he opposed the provost's plans for change in the English department, but that seems so . . . minor in the grand scheme of things. I mean, I thought there could be something more. I know Ms. McHenry once accused Doug of plagiarism and wondered if perhaps he'd stolen work from her or something."

Like he did from you? I stared at Paige, wondering what she was getting at. Was she hoping Erin could provide more evidence of Doug's treachery in terms of claiming someone else's work as his own? Was this part of a plan to wrest all revenue from their book from Miranda or any other heirs?

"I've never heard anything like that," I said, rolling back my chair and standing. "Sorry, but it's about time for me to close up. If you want to wait a minute, we can walk out together and talk a little more, but I do need to shut down the center."

"Of course," she said, rising gracefully to her feet. "Why don't I wait for you out in the hallway, so you can complete your tasks without my interference." She crossed to my office door. "I do appreciate you taking the time to speak with me," she added as she left.

I found a vase and filled it with water for the flowers, then collected my belongings, still wincing as I slipped my left arm into my coat sleeve. Locking my office, I checked the rest of the center, then headed out into the hall. "Where are you going?" I asked Paige, as I double-checked the locks on the main doors. "I'm parked in the library lot. If your car is there too, we can talk and walk."

"Sounds good," Paige said, as she followed me onto the elevator. "But listen, why don't you let me buy you a drink? There's a nice bar near my office. You know where that is," she added, with a bright smile.

"Yes, of course." I looked her up and down. I wasn't dying for a drink, and in fact didn't want one because I was just coming off of pain pills, but I thought I should take advantage of this opportunity. Perhaps Paige had some information that might shed more light on Miranda, Andrea, or Hilda and their actions at the provost's party. Although I didn't remember seeing her there, according to Christine, Paige had been at the party as the date of some business professor.

"Alright, I'm game," I said.

Paige flashed a brilliant smile. "Or, as you mystery writers would say, *the game's afoot.*"

Chapter Forty-Five

Paige's smile faltered when I didn't respond to her little joke. "Okay, if we're going to talk over drinks, why don't we each just head to our cars and meet up at your office," I said.

Agreeing to this plan, Paige took off at a faster pace than I could manage, given my still aching hip and leg.

By the time I parked and walked to the realty office, Paige was engaged in talking to a good-looking young man in a charcoal-gray suit. I hung back, not wanting to interrupt their conversation. However, they were talking loud enough for me to clearly hear what they were saying, and I took advantage of the opportunity to eavesdrop.

"I'd just like to know where you went," the young man said, raking his hand through his short auburn hair. "I know we drove separately and met up at the party, but then you went AWOL. I was worried about you."

"You needn't have been," Paige replied, with a dismissive wave of her hand. "You know it was a one-off date. You needed someone to accompany you, and I needed . . ." She shook her head, dislodging a lock of her honey-blonde hair from her sleek updo. "Never mind."

"You wanted to be at that party," the young man said flatly. "Whether it was me or someone else escorting you didn't seem to matter."

"Of course it mattered." Paige's practiced smile rang false, even from a distance. She reached out to caress the man's arm. "I enjoyed my time with you."

"Which is why you disappeared halfway through the party and never returned?" The young man shook off Paige's hand. "Forget it. As you said, it was a one-off." He strode away without a backward look.

I dawdled for a moment, hoping Paige would think I'd just arrived. I'd already surmised that the young man in the suit had been her date to the provost's party and was intrigued with his comments about her disappearing at some point in the evening.

"Hello again," I said, walking up to her. "Where is this bar you were talking about?"

"First, do you mind if we pop into my office?" Paige lowered her lashes over her bright blue eyes. "I need to check on something before tomorrow morning."

"Sure, no problem," I said, thinking that this would provide an even better atmosphere to pose some subtle questions about Miranda and the others on my suspect list.

Paige punched a series of numbers into the keypad lock and held the door open for me. "Just have a seat in the reception room for a moment," she said, hurrying off toward her office.

I sat in one of the reproduction Chippendale chairs, stretching out my left leg to ease the throbbing of my strained muscles. Musing over the conversation I'd just heard, I began to feel a little uneasy.

According to her date, Paige had disappeared at some point in the evening. Yet Christine had told me some time ago that Paige was still at the party when the police arrived, after Gary had fallen to his death.

"Something is off," I said aloud, as Paige returned to the reception room.

Holding a gun.

"Excuse me," I said, my gaze fixed on the revolver. "What's this about?"

Paige pulled up a chair and sat down, facing me. "I went to visit Erin McHenry in jail," she said, keeping the gun pointed at my chest. "I truly did want to know why she'd killed Doug. That was my intention, I swear. But she didn't want to talk about that. What she wanted to say"—the barrel of the gun rose until it was aimed at my forehead—"was how I should be wary of you. She said you were playing amateur detective a little too well, and if I had anything to hide, I should keep an eye on you."

"And you do have something to hide," I said, calculating how fast I could hit the ground if she fired.

"Unfortunately. You see, it wasn't actually Doug's idea to cut me out of receiving credit for our book or rob me of the profits. I figured that out after talking with Miranda. Someone else must've suggested it, must've convinced him."

"Gary Alexander," I said, my voice hollow as a drum.

"Yes. I suspected it as soon as Miranda told me about Doug claiming all credit for our novel. Gary was such a misogynist. He always thought female authors were lesser creatures. I knew that from the time I spent as a student in the department, but I had no idea he'd try to brainwash Doug into betraying me."

I shifted in my seat, acutely aware of the revolver and Paige's finger on the trigger. "So you attended the party, hoping to have a chance to confront Gary."

"No." Paige tilted her head, examining me like some museum specimen. "I attended the party intending to kill him. I knew he'd drink too much; he always did. All I had to do was lure him up to

that balcony. It wasn't difficult. He thought he was a ladies' man."
Paige's thin-lipped smile turned her face into a macabre mask. "He'd
tried to hit on me when I was a student, you know. Doug put a stop
to that back then. That's why I thought Gary would jump at the
chance to get me alone. And believe me, he did."

I swallowed, devastated by this story of old and new horrors.
"You met and got into an argument, and things just happened. I can
understand that."

Paige rolled her eyes. "Silly woman, there was no argument.
Gary met me and tried to put the moves on me, as I knew he would.
And I . . . Well, I maneuvered him back against the railing, as if I
was interested." Paige's smile was humorless as death. "Then I moved
closer, all cozy-like, and gave him a little push."

Picturing this scene, I shivered. "Why tell me this?'

"I've been wanting to tell someone. Every since the authorities
declared it an accidental death. Of course, that decision benefited
me, but the whole thing felt a bit hollow, you know?"

"No, I'm afraid I don't." I gestured toward the revolver. "You
could get away with Gary's death easily enough, but shooting me
will be much harder to explain."

"I was all alone, working late, when an intruder broke into my
office . . ." Paige shrugged. "I own this gun legally, for protection.
And you are known to be someone who plays amateur detective. I
can claim that you suspected me of assisting Erin McHenry in covering up Doug's death. Of course, that will be easily disproved, and
with Gary's death being ruled accidental, well—" Paige placed her
other hand on the gun grip to steady her aim. "I think everyone will
simply assume that your foolish tendency to stick your nose in where
it didn't belong turned tragic."

I wasn't in my best shape, but I definitely outweighed twiggy-little
Paige by a good number of pounds. If I could take her by surprise . . .

"I really don't have anything against you, Jenn, but I have to think of my own interests, you know?" Paige smiled again, placid as a plaster Madonna.

Leaning over and clutching my stomach as if I was going to be sick, I took a deep breath and dove forward, my body sliding across the polished wood floor, head first. A gunshot cracked above my head. As I'd suspected, Paige hadn't been able to adjust her aim fast enough to hit me. I flung my arms out and grabbed the delicate legs of her chair. Ignoring the pain in my left arm, I lifted the legs and flipped Paige's chair over backward.

Paige screamed as she hit the ground. The revolver flew from her hand, ending up halfway across the room. I didn't bother to go after the gun. I didn't even know how to use one, anyway. Instead, I crawled forward and threw my six-foot, well-endowed body over Paige's slender form.

She shrieked again, but I ignored this and slid my cell phone from my pocket, thankful I'd bought a new one earlier in the week.

"911, what's your emergency?" the dispatcher asked.

"Someone tried to kill me," I said, using my free hand to slam Paige's flailing arm back against the floor. When the dispatcher asked if I was okay, I expelled a burst of nervous laughter. "I am," I said at last. "She might not be."

Chapter Forty-Six

The Harburg police arrived within minutes, crashing through Paige Irving's real estate office door and confiscating her gun. Once a couple of officers reached me, I rose to my feet and allowed them to take charge of Paige, whose string of invectives would have shocked even my brother's navy buddies.

Of course, I had to answer questions yet again, a process made a little easier by the fact that I'd recently had lots of practice. One of the officers, who'd also been on the scene when Erin had been arrested at Clarion, made an offhand suggestion that I should consider joining the force.

"Sorry, that might cut into my writing time," I told them, earning astonished looks from the people on the scene.

"I didn't know writers could be so resourceful," one of the officers remarked.

"Oh, mystery authors plot this kind of scenario all the time," I replied. "Come to think of it, I guess it has trained me to think creatively in difficult situations."

When the police released me, with several reminders to stay in the area so I'd be available for more questioning, I simply drove home. I gave Ash some cuddles and treats, then took a long, hot shower and changed into my coziest yoga pants and a fleece sweatshirt. Only after I settled on the sofa with a large glass of white wine did I even consider calling anyone.

"Hi," I said to Zach when he picked up the phone. "Guess what?"

"Your first day at work was tough?" he asked.

"No, not really. It was after work that things got dicey." I patted the cushion next to me, encouraging Ash to jump up, but she just flicked her tail and sauntered into the kitchen. "Anyway, remember how I had this theory that there was a second killer who murdered Gary Alexander?"

"Yessss." Zach drew out the word, concern rippling through his tone.

"I was right!" I said, as cheerful as someone announcing they'd won the lottery. "In fact, funny thing—the second killer held me at gunpoint today, but don't worry, I'm okay—"

I'd barely gotten those words out when Zach yelled, "Be there in five!" and hung up.

I waited a few minutes, then stood and crossed to the front door, unlocking it. Zach showed up a moment later, clutching his chest and breathing hard.

"You ran over, I see," I said.

He grabbed me by the shoulders and pushed me into the living room, allowing the front door to slam behind him. "What the heck are you talking about? Held at gunpoint? What kind of nonsense is this?"

I laid my hands on his shoulders. "It isn't nonsense, it's what happened, and no, I didn't instigate anything. I was taken by surprise, to be honest."

Zach's eyes narrowed as he stared at me. "Who held a gun on you?"

"Come and sit down," I said, dropping my hands and pulling free of his grip.

I headed for the sofa. Following on my heels, Zach sat down the exact moment I did. "A gun? A gun, Jenn? Did this crisis arise from more of your amateur detective work?"

"Not really. I mean, I did agree to meet this person for a drink because I thought she could help me figure out who killed Gary Alexander, but it wasn't like I believed it was *her*. Well, not at first, anyway."

"Someone pulled a gun on you at a bar?" Zach's incredulous expression was almost comical.

"No. She said she had to stop by her office, so we did. That's when she pointed a gun at me. It was Paige Irving, by the way. She shoved Gary Alexander off the balcony at the provost's home." I sank back into the sofa cushions. "I mean, she had her reasons, but unfortunately, she also thought she had to kill me."

Zach buried his head in his hands. "Now I need therapy," he muttered.

I patted his back. "It's okay. I'm fine, and now another murderer is behind bars. A good day's work."

Lifting his head, Zach fixed me with a stern gaze. "You're entirely too giddy, Jenn. This is a response to trauma." He held out his arms. "Stop pretending."

I stared at him for two seconds before bursting into tears.

Zach wrapped me in a close embrace. "It's okay," he whispered in my ear. "Cry all you want. I'm here. It's okay."

* * *

Two weeks later, Zach hosted a Sunday afternoon dinner party at his house.

Bri and Rachel showed up first, followed by Christine and her husband—a jovial bald man named Ralph who I'd never heard her mention.

"Did you help cook, Jenn, or did Zach make this entire spread by himself?" Bri asked, as she took her seat at the dining room table.

"It's all Zach," I said, setting a basket of dinner rolls on the table. "I showed up about fifteen minutes before you and Rachel did."

"Really?" Bri shared a look with Rachel. "So you weren't here for breakfast?"

"What are you implying, Bri?" I asked as I sat down across from her. "You know I have a home of my own."

Bri swept her linen napkin through the air before placing in her lap. "For now. Luckily, it's a rental."

Rachel tapped the back of Bri's hand with her short but well-manicured fingernails. "Behave."

"And this is it," Zach said, striding in from the kitchen holding a large platter. "I hope everyone likes grilled salmon."

"What's not to like? It looks absolutely delicious." Christine cast a smile at her husband, who raised his wineglass in a salute. "Here's to the chef," he said, holding his glass aloft until everyone at the table joined the toast.

Zach sat down beside me, his face coloring slightly. "It's really nothing that extraordinary. But thank you all the same."

As we passed the dishes around the table, Rachel kept us entertained by talking about some of the more unique foods she'd encountered on her travels.

"I'll stick with the salmon," Ralph said when she finished speaking.

"Me too, honestly." Rachel smiled and lifted her own wineglass. "Now I'd like to make a toast to our three intrepid detectives, Jenn, Bri, and Christine, who helped to prevent a young girl's life from being ruined."

"And, in Jenn's case, exposed a second murderer," Christine said, clinking glasses with Ralph.

Zach set his glass down. "Not sure I want to drink to a celebration of such dangerous activities."

"Oh, come on. You know Jenn can take care of herself." Bri speared a forkful of marinated green beans. "She's one tough cookie."

"Only sometimes the cookie crumbles." His action hidden by the tablecloth, Zach laid his hand on my knee.

I cast him a sideways look. "Always with the last word," I said, covering his hand with mine.

Zach grinned. "That's what my profession is based on, you know. Words."

"I suppose that's right," Christine said, eyeing him with interest. "All that talk therapy and stuff."

"That's part of it. Sometimes other methods are required." Zach squeezed my fingers before placing his hand back on the table. "Anyway, I think I speak for Rachel and Ralph as well as myself when I say that perhaps Clarion's newest detective agency should be shut down. For the safety of its members, if nothing else."

"Hear, hear," Ralph said, ignoring the sharp look Christine cast him.

Rachel dabbed at her lips with her napkin. "Well, I know I can't control what Bri does, so I'll keep out of this."

"A wise woman," Bri said, nodding her head.

The rest of the dinner party was a heady mixture of thought-provoking discussions on current literature and media, world events, and, courtesy of Ralph, gardening, interspersed with bouts of laughter.

After everyone else had left, I joined Zach in the kitchen.

"You wash, I'll dry," I told him, plucking a kitchen towel off a hanging rack.

"I do have a dishwasher," he said.

"You can't put those pans in, though. There won't be enough room, for one thing."

Zach picked up a sponge. "Alright. I was just going to do the handwashing later, but if you insist on helping—"

"I insist," I said firmly.

While we did the dishes, I learned that Zach had a pretty decent singing voice, since he jumped into singing some pop songs I hadn't heard since high school.

"I wouldn't have pictured you as a boy band enthusiast," I told him while drying my hands.

Zach set the sponge back in its holder. "I wasn't. My sister was."

"Oh, right. Twins. I guess you guys were pretty close." I kept my gaze fixed on my hands as I folded the towel.

"We were. Until things changed. But we're still connected, in our own way." Zach took me into his arms. "Now, how about we spend a little quality time on the sofa, talking, or whatever."

I pressed my hand against his chest. "What makes me think you're more interested in the *whatever*?"

"Well, think about it," Zach said, taking my hand and leading me into the living room. "Talking is part of my job. *Whatever* isn't. And since this is the weekend . . ."

I laughed and sank down beside him on the sofa. "Okay, you can cash in on that promise now."

"What?" Zach slid his arm around me.

"You know, the taking advantage one," I said.

"Oh, *that* one." Zach leaned in and brushed a kiss over my lips. "I'd almost forgotten about that."

"No, you hadn't," I said with a shake of my head.

Zach grinned. "No, I hadn't."

Acknowledgments

I offer my sincere thanks and gratitude to:

My agent, Frances Black of Literary Counsel.

My editor, Faith Black Ross, and the entire team at Crooked Lane Books.

Cover designer Tim Barnes.

My author colleagues who've provided me with friendship, insight, and support.

The bloggers, podcasters, YouTubers, and reviewers who've reviewed and/or boosted my books.

All the bookstores and libraries who have acquired, stocked, and promoted my books.

My family and friends—some read my books and some don't, but they all support *me*.

And, as always, readers!